I0739518

Incident at St. Albans

Ted Tedford

The Tamarac Press
Warren, Vermont
Fall 2014

Copyright © Ted Tedford 2014
All rights reserved

No copy of this work, in full or in part, in any medium now or in
the future available, may be made without express permission
in writing from the author.

Photographs were provided by the
St. Albans Historical Society and Museum
and are used with their generous permission.

Front cover design by Jonathan Draudt, Warren, VT

ISBN-10: 0990779203
ISBN-13: 978-0-9907792-0-9

Published in Vermont by
The Tamarac Press
Warren
Fall 2014

To Marie
My loving wife of many years, whose brilliance and
persistence convinced me to do things to make this a better book.
Yours forever. Forever yours.

Incident at St. Albans

Bennett H. Young

A Word from the Author

ON a chilly October day in 1864, twenty-one Confederate soldiers shattered the peace in the bustling town of St. Albans, Vermont. Led by a twenty-one-year-old officer, Bennett H. Young, the men attacked the town in the northernmost land action of the Civil War.

After three grueling years of war the Confederacy was on the ropes, and its leaders grasped for any straw that might turn the tide. One tactic was to raid northern towns along the border with Canada and force the Union Army to pull troops from Southern battlefields to send them north.

Bennett Young, a son of Kentucky's Blue Grass country, was newly promoted to lieutenant and commissioned to lead the first raiding group. He chose St. Albans as his target.

Young had been a divinity student, but he left school to join the Confederate cavalry under famed raider John Hunt Morgan to seek revenge for what he saw as atrocities the Union forces were inflicting on the South. Young's action-filled journey from student to veteran soldier, to prisoner-of-war, and later to defendant in a trial in Canada that could cost him his life has never been fully explored. This book, in fictionalized form, brings it all together from Young's point of view.

I learned about the St. Albans Raid soon after moving to Vermont many years ago, and I wanted to know more about the people who were involved in this historic action. Who was the young man who planned and carried it out? Was it a rogue action akin to today's terrorist attacks, or was it sanctioned by the Confederate government? How did the leader bring his men together? How was it financed? What happened to Young and the others after the raid? How did it affect the people of St. Albans at the time? What happened to the stolen money? Why did the Canadian government arrest Young and his men? What happened then?

The more I read about the raid, the greater my interest was piqued until I knew I had to write about it. The journey from then to now has been a long one. After an attempt to write an historical account for young adults, I realized I had to write a novel based on fact, but embellished with some scenes and dialogue that never happened. I wanted to offer readers some insight into the events that occurred in St. Albans in context with what was happening in the North and South during the Civil War.

I also discovered that there was very little factual information about Bennett Young to go on. Young was a private before the raid, and books and articles on war are mostly written from the viewpoint of generals. Many of the sources I found were sketchy. One claimed Young joined the Confederate army near his Kentucky hometown while another claimed he went to Tennessee, a Confederate state, to join up. I fictionalized a scene in Kentucky, and to bring in some active scenes regarding Morgan's Raiders, I've had Young join up a year before he actually did so he could "ride" with Morgan on some of the raids.

I also included a scene that showed Young visiting Ann Smith, the wife of Vermont Governor J. Gregory Smith, at the Governor's home on the hill in St. Albans, but no other source could be found to verify that event.

Most of the dialogue between Young and his men while they fought with the famed Confederate raider General John Hunt Morgan is fictional, as is some dialogue between the Rebels and their lawyers in Canada, but some is taken from court records. All the liberties I have taken along with fact-based events were meant to draw readers into the story.

Books and historical accounts used in researching this book are listed in a bibliography at the end of the narrative for those who would enjoy further reading into actual events that took place in the North and South and in Canada before and after the Incident at St. Albans.

For a well-researched and highly readable account of the men who pulled off the raid in St. Albans, and thoughts about where the stolen money may have gone, read *The St. Albans Raiders* by Daniel S. Rush, MD, and E. Gale Pewitt, available from the Blue and Gray Education Society, 110 Franklin Turnpike, Danville, VA 24540.

Ted Tedford
Underhill Center, 2014

Part One

CHAPTER 1

St. Albans, Vermont
Mid-October 1864

THE young man lay on the lumpy bed in his second-floor hotel room in St. Albans, Vermont, his booted feet hanging over the end of the mattress. He glanced through the room's only window at clouds that hung low over the village. A chilling mist that had fallen the day before had stopped. Once again he mentally reviewed elements of his plan, trying to pick holes in it. Would it go off as anticipated? Would something intervene to thwart what could be one of the most audacious acts of the war raging in the South?

Unable to remain still for long, he sat up, swung his legs off the bed and went the few steps to the window to stare at the muddy Main Street. For the third time in an hour, his eyes searched for signs that the last of his men had arrived in town.

A lieutenant in the Confederate Army at twenty-one years of age, Bennett Young was in this cold railroad town far from his Kentucky home, sent by the highest officials of his government. His orders: raid the town; rob its three banks; terrorize its citizens. And with twenty men following his lead, burn as many buildings as he could.

Fear. Revenge. Terror.

Young opened the window and leaned out. Below him, farmers and their wives from outlying areas of town had set up business on the street to sell their harvest and their crafts to people in the village. The young lieutenant's eyes swept the busy street where the action would take place. He shivered as a cold Yankee wind swept into the room.

"I swear this climate will be the death of me," he muttered.

When he first arrived here nine days before, he'd discovered this village was the hub of commercial activity for the entire town, a community of small working farms, most of them situated between Lake Champlain five miles to the west and the village itself. The town boasted a population of about 4,000 residents.

Staring down at the Yankee street, Young yearned for his beloved Blue Grass country. He lowered the window and picked up the latest edition of the *St. Albans Daily Messenger* from a chair next to the bed. During the time he had spent in his room at the Tremont Hotel, he had followed events in the local newspaper. A headline on the front page blared:

Sherman Burns Atlanta, Marches Southward

He read the article a second time. Union General William T. Sherman's army had burned the city of Atlanta, destroying most of its homes and factories and wrecking its railroad facilities. Along a swath a mile wide, Yankee forces resumed their march to the south, continuing their scorched-earth policy, setting houses ablaze, flattening cornfields, and stealing everything they could get their hands on. As they swarmed over farms, they burned the buildings and crops.

The reporter conjectured that Sherman was headed for the Carolinas and the Atlantic Ocean, intending to cut the Confederacy in two. His anger at peak pitch, Young slammed the paper down and returned to the window.

His eyes wandered to the block-long Green diagonally across Main Street, partially hidden by Brainerd's general store. The last of the area's gold and red leaves fluttered slowly to the ground, signaling the approach of winter.

Winter. He remembered with a shudder how much he and his fellow raiders suffered during the Christmas Raid with General John Hunt Morgan on his ride through Kentucky two winters before...how the ice and rain had frozen his fingers to the horse's reins, how he had fumbled with the cartridges as he tried to load his carbine, how rain and sleet had found its way under his oil cloth coat and rough shirt to run down his neck and back. He thrust those thoughts away now as he scanned the sidewalk again. He didn't see any of the others.

"Where are they?" he snapped, aloud. "What's keeping them?"

He closed the window and tried to curb the tension eating at his nerves. His thoughts once more returned to his raiding days, to the debacle on that scorching hot day a year before at Buffington Island in Ohio and the hail of shot and shell that killed and wounded so many of his comrades. The battle that day had sent so many captured men to Yankee prison camps.

No. Not now. Forget that. No time to think of the past, of the men who had fought and died with him, and those who shared the dangers and the humiliation at the hands of sadistic Yankee prison guards.

He thought again of the task that lay ahead in this far northern town. Could he strike another blow against the oppressors before a bullet cut him down? Could he and his men escape after the raid? How many would he lose? He shuddered and closed his eyes.

Young knew the raid would not be easy. The Vermont Central Railroad was headquartered in St. Albans, its offices located a long block below Main Street with a busy foundry close by. Most of the men living in the village worked at the foundry or the railroad. Young assumed some of them, and others along Main Street, had guns, rifles, and pistols. This might be a pleasant town, but it could kill him and his men once its residents were aroused. He shook off that thought, too.

When he arrived in St. Albans days before, he had been pleased to see how busy the village was. Its three banks on Main Street seemed to be thriving. Busy street-level shops, many with apartments located above them, lined the dirt Main Street. He had easily spotted two hotels and another under construction. In the heart of the village, a block-wide town green sloped uphill toward Church Street.

Since his arrival, Young learned that farmers worked the land that stretched from the edge of the village west to Lake Champlain. The farmers depended on villagers to buy their produce and milk, and they in turn supported the village shopkeepers, buying their wares.

While Young pondered possibilities for the raid back in his hotel room, two men disembarked from the Montreal train at the Vermont Central Railway station a long block down Champlain Street. Alamanda Pope Bruce, medium height with a full beard and bushy mustache and wearing a rumpled black suit, looked around at the Northern town.

Beside him, his companion, James Alexander Doty, studied the street around them. He was tall and thin with a high forehead and drooping mustache. The sleeves of his dark-gray jacket were too short for his long arms but his pant legs covered expensive-looking though scuffed boots.

Hoisting haversacks up on their shoulders, the two men looked toward the busy foundry across the railroad tracks. Two rows of new machines, threshers and silage cutters, stood beside the structure.

Three shiny black train engines stood in bays in the railroad building sitting just off the main line that ran from Montreal to New York City. The sprawling headquarters of the railroad also included a freight station, offices and a roundhouse.

"Lots of men working at that railroad and the foundry," Doty said.

Bruce nodded but said nothing. They both knew this meant the town could put up a good fight when the time came for their raid. They'd just have to deal with it.

The two walked diagonally across Foundry Street to Champlain Street, their haversacks hanging from long straps on their shoulders. They shivered and pulled their jacket collars tighter around their throats as they walked up the sloping street. At Main Street, they stopped in front of the two-story American House. Bruce looked up at the second-story veranda.

"Looks like a decent place," he said. He leaned on a black iron hitching post and turned his glance to the sloping Green across the street and then up and down the busy sidewalk. Most of the buildings on their side of the street were made of red brick, a few, like the American House, of wood. Several buildings were four-stories high, housing shops at street level, offices and apartments on the upper levels. Most of the shops had large plate-glass windows on the ground floor exhibiting wares for sale.

The two men walked toward the Franklin Bank next door to the hotel. They paused in front of the bank and peered through its plate glass windows. A lone clerk waited on customers from behind a low counter. Behind the clerk, the heavy steel door of the bank vault stood open.

"This should be easy to rob," Doty said.

"Maybe," Bruce replied, closely surveying the bank's interior.

The two men walked farther along the wooden sidewalk, looking in store windows. This is a thriving town, Bruce thought, with people taking their daily business seriously. It could be harder to pull this off than we thought. They continued past a throng of people buying fruits, vegetables, and wares from the backs of wagons or makeshift booths that farmers had set up, eager to sell goods to their friends and neighbors for the coming winter.

Market Day.

A time to do business, to visit friends and catch up on the news of the war. The two men paused at a cart to look at some glass jars containing a golden liquid labeled "Maple Syrup." They overheard two women talking.

"You know Bessie Mayo got news yesterday. Her Jeremiah ...," said one, surveying a merchant's wagon loaded with vegetables.

"Oh, Lord, her youngest boy," the woman standing beside the wagon lamented. "And her first-born, too, was killed there in Virginia. God help us all."

"They said it was dysentery that killed Jeremiah. I read that our boys are being sent back home to Vermont to be cared for, now. The military hospitals are full of our soldiers. Too late for Jeremiah, though. Poor soul." The first woman shook her head.

"Yes. A pity indeed. I heard the hospitals are terrible down there in Louisianna," her friend clucked her dismay. She reshaped a small pile of butternut squash on her wagon.

"This horrible war will kill all of our young men before it is over," she said. The women grew silent for a moment as though the thought just expressed might come true. The first woman hefted a squash in her hand, set it down, and fiddled in her handbag for change.

"I'll stop by the farm later to see if Bessie needs anything," she said, tying the string on her cloth bag.

The two Rebels looked at each other and walked on.

They continued north on Main Street, pausing at the St. Albans Bank close to Kingman Street. They looked briefly through the bank window. It, too, was busy. Walking on they spied the Tremont House, a four-story brick structure identified by a sign between the second and third stories, its huge white letters stark against a black background.

At the entrance to the hotel, Doty glanced back down Main Street. He noticed a man walking toward them. Edward D. Fuller, owner of a livery stable just off Main Street, nodded at the strangers.

"I beg your pardon, sir," Doty said to Fuller, trying hard to disguise his soft Kentucky accent. "Are there any more hotels farther up this street?"

Fuller shook his head. "No, I'm sorry, there aren't, but the Tremont House here is one of the finest in town." The strangers nodded their thanks and entered the hotel lobby. In contrast to the bustle of townspeople outside, the hotel lobby was quiet. At the registration desk, they looked around for someone to help them. Doty rang a silver push bell on the counter. After a few minutes, a clerk emerged from a door behind the desk.

"I hope I haven't kept you waiting, gentlemen. May I help you?" the clerk asked, smiling his best hotel smile.

"Has a Mister Clyde registered here?" Bruce asked. Young had told the men he would use the false name as a measure of security.

"Yes, he is here," replied the clerk. "Second floor, room twenty-three. Third door on the left from the head of the stairs." The pair thanked him and climbed to Young's room.

Doty knocked on the door. Young opened it and broke into a smile.

"James, Alamanda. I'm happy to see you. Come in, come in."

When his comrades had entered his room, Young glanced up and down the hallway before closing the door. No one there.

"How was your trip?" he asked, motioning the men to set their haversacks down.

"Fine, Bennett. Fine," said Bruce, briskly shaking Young's hand. "This is a busy town. Is everything set for today?"

"No. No, I'm putting it off until tomorrow," Young said. "You saw it. It's too busy out there today." He motioned toward the street. "Tomorrow will be better."

"It is a might crowded," Bruce agreed. "I think it's prudent you decided to hold off."

He glanced at the pile of newspapers on the bureau.

"What's the latest on the war?"

Young sighed. "Things look bad. Atlanta has fallen and Sherman is moving south. The newspapers are speculating he'll march to the sea."

"Atlanta is gone? Oh, God, what next?" Bruce said.

Young picked up his copy of the *Daily Messenger* and pointed to a dispatch in which the writer had described the fall and burning of Atlanta.

"Sherman wrecked and burned everything, all the way from Chattanooga," Young said. "According to this article, the Yankee strategy is to drive a wedge between the upper and lower Southern states. It sure looks like Lincoln will be re-elected next month."

He shook his head, envisioning Atlanta consumed by fire and the farms, livestock, and crops in Virginia's Shenandoah Valley destroyed by Sheridan.

"They'll burn everything in the South, destroy our farms and starve our families," he said. "I will not rest until every last one of those plundering murderers is forced off our soil."

Doty looked at his friend. He had often heard laments like this from Young. He took the paper from Young's hand and read a passage.

"According to this," Doty noted, "that drunk, Grant, is still besieging Petersburg." He shook his head in despair. "Lee can't maneuver the way he always has."

He looked bleakly at Young, who feared his friend was right. Young was certain Lincoln had indeed appointed the right man this time, the general who could lead the Northern forces to victory over the Confederacy, General Grant. The lieutenant was lost in thought for a moment, but then his face brightened.

"But it isn't over yet," he said.

"Aye, Bennett, if we can carry this off, maybe we can give our boys some relief," Bruce agreed.

"Oh, I know we can pull it off," Young said, his face animated now. "We'll make old Abe sit up and take notice."

"I sure hope so," Bruce said. He picked up his haversack and turned to Doty. "I think we ought to get a room." Doty agreed, shouldering his own bag.

"Try the St. Albans House. I hear the rooms are better than here," Young told them. "You passed it on your way up here."

"Yes, I noticed it," said Doty. "It's just up from the railroad station."

"Yes sir, Lieutenant," Bruce jested.

He and Doty left the hotel, tracing their way through the crowd on Main Street and back down Champlain Street to register at the St. Albans House.

Young stood before the window again, his mind hundreds of miles away, recalling his service with the famed raider General John Hunt Morgan threading through the Kentucky countryside. He recalled the violence of attacks on towns along their route, some defended by state militia and others by more dangerous regular Union Army troops. Soaked from rain in the warmer months and shivering from sleet and snow in the colder months, all of the Morgan's raiders wondering when they would rest or die. He shook off the memory and once again ran over his plan of attack on St. Albans.

Meanwhile, not far away on Main Street, a tall Irishman with a shock of curly black hair stepped from a carriage. Captain Thomas Collins, Confederate States Army, had ridden from Montreal, but he'd remained on the train, debarking in Essex Junction, twenty-five miles to the south. There he hired a carriage to take him back to St. Albans. He had been concerned that too many men arriving by train would raise eyebrows, though he later learned he was the only Raider to arrive by carriage. He, too, carried a long-strapped valise over his shoulder. Now in civilian clothes, Collins inquired at a nearby shop about the location of the St. Albans House. The busy clerk stopped long enough to give him directions.

Collins walked south a block and then down Champlain Street, crossing over to the hotel. Before entering, he, too, noticed the bustling railroad and foundry buildings.

A clerk behind the hotel counter stepped up.

"I'd like a room," Collins told him, putting on an Irish brogue.

"And how many days will you be staying with us?" the clerk asked.

"Oh, just a few lovely days, I'm sure," Collins replied. The clerk handed over a key and Collins went up to his room.

That same afternoon, two more strangers carrying knapsacks swung off the train from Montreal and walked up to the St. Albans House. One of them, Charlton Hunt Higbee, registered signing his real name, listing his residence as Toronto, Canada. Balding, with a full beard, Higbee was a lawyer in civilian life. He had ridden with the infamous raider William Quantrill before fleeing to Canada with about $75,000 he had stolen from Quantrill, who had stolen thousands of dollars more from banks during a brutal attack on Lawrence, Kansas.

Originally from Syracuse, New York, Higbee had moved with his family to LaGrange, Georgia, when he was twenty-three years of age. When war broke out, he sided with the South.

Higbee's companion, William H. Huntley, a wild-eyed twenty-seven-year-old, registered without comment. Higbee asked if a man named Collins had registered, and the clerk replied that he had.

"How is the fishing in the area?" Huntley asked the desk clerk. "Are there any good streams to dip a line in?"

"Oh, you're on a fishing trip, sir?" the clerk asked. "We have some very fine fishing streams hereabouts, and of course there is Lake Champlain only about five miles to the west."

"Perhaps my colleagues and I will land a few," Huntley replied, trying hard to match the clerk's Yankee twang. "If we aren't lucky enough to catch some fish, maybe we can bag some game. Do you know of anyone who has rifles to rent?"

"I'm not really certain where you can rent rifles, sir," the clerk replied. "But there is a very good gun shop just up the street. Perhaps you will find what you need there." Huntley nodded his thanks. The two strangers picked up their room keys and climbed the stairs.

Later in the day, the last of Young's men stepped off the train from Montreal. Cabel Wallace, nephew of former United States Senator John J. Crittenden, looked skyward and cursed the cloudy day. He, too, walked up to Main Street, located the Tremont House, and reported to Young. All but two of the twenty cavalry veterans arriving in town were in their twenties. Charles Higbee and Joseph McGrorty—his companions called him "Gramps,"—were in their late thirties.

With the exception of Higbee, most of the men, including Young, had ridden with Morgan's Raiders and had at one time or other been captured and sent to Yankee prison camps.

After escaping from confinement, some of them had settled in St. Catherine's or Toronto in Upper Canada, others in Montreal. They'd heard of the movement to organize former prisoners and made contact with an officer who'd ridden with Morgan's Raiders, Captain Thomas Hines. The Captain worked closely with two Confederate commissioners who were sent to Canada to look after the interests of escapees and of Southern civilians who fled there. Now they were here.

The last of Young's men had arrived in St. Albans to set out on what one of them called "A Vairmont Yankee Scare Party."

CHAPTER 2

St. Albans, Vermont
October 18, 1864

WHILE he waited for his men to arrive, Young had familiarized himself with St. Albans and its Main Street. Every mid-morning since his arrival, he'd walked a block down the street from the Tremont House to the general store to chat with the owner over a cup of coffee and pick up a copy of The *St. Albans Messenger*.

"Coffee, Mister Clyde?" the owner, John Herkimer, asked holding up a coffee pot and a tin cup on one such morning. He always kept a full pot on the stove at the rear of his shop. Young felt guilty drinking real coffee when his fellow Southerners had only ground chicory or some other bitter concoction, but he wanted to chat with the owner without raising suspicions.

"Lucky you Canadians aren't caught up in this terrible war, Mister Clyde," Herkimer said, wiping the counter with a damp rag. Young and his men were telling folks they were Canadians visiting Vermont for some hunting and fishing.

"It's a terrible thing," said Young. He blew along the ridge of his cup and sipped the brew carefully.

"So many young men killed or dying of disease. All for what?"

"All for a cause I expect the people in the South believe in," replied Young quietly. Don't argue with anyone you meet here, Young had instructed his men. He needed to heed his own advice.

"What did those Rebels expect when they seceded?" the store owner asked. "Did they think the rest of the country would just say, 'Go ahead, we don't need you?' Well, they didn't say that. That's why we're fightin' this here war."

"I don't honestly know what your Southerners think, sir," Young said. He set the steaming cup on the counter.

Herkimer persisted. "Supposing the six New England states decided they was goin' to set up their own country. And all the other parts of the United States. We would be nothin' more than a continent of small countries like Europe. Hmmpph. You look at what has happened over there."

Young remained silent, finished his coffee and picked up the newspaper, briefly scanning the headlines. The storeowner watched him.

"You certainly take an interest in what's happening, Mister Clyde."

Young nodded.

"I like to keep current with events wherever I happen to be." He handed the man several coins for the coffee and for a copy of the newspaper.

"The New York papers say it looks like the Confederacy can't last much longer. Good thing. There has been too much killing," Herkimer commented.

Not enough killing outside the South, Young thought as he turned away.

"Good day, sir."

In his room once again, Young set the newspaper on the bed. He saw his image in the oval mirror atop the white oak bureau: six feet tall, black hair brushed straight back from his forehead, hazel eyes grown cold and hard, framed by dark brows. Face clean-shaven, Young's strong mouth turned down slightly at the corners.

Growing up among the farming gentry in the Blue Grass country of central Kentucky, he'd been conscious of girls giggling and fawning over him. He had received additional confirmation of his attractiveness to women as recently as the previous night in the hotel's dining room where he took his meals alone. Several times he saw women at various tables looking his way, barely concealing smiles of interest behind their napkins or over their husbands' shoulders. His looks served him well and people were disposed to trust him.

One chilly morning that forewarned a coming frost, Young had visited the imposing Victorian home of Vermont Governor John G. Smith, located among equally large homes situated up the hill past the St. Albans Green. This was the neighborhood where most of the town's business owners and railroad executives lived. When the Governor's wife, Anna, answered the door, Young politely explained his visit.

"I beg your indulgence, Mrs. Smith," he said. "I'm Harold Clyde. I hear the governor and you have some of the finest Morgan horses in the county. I wonder if you would allow me to see them."

"Oh, Mister Clyde. How do you do," Mrs. Smith replied, extending her hand. "I have heard from some of my friends about you visiting our town. Please, do come in." Young stepped in and closed the door.

"Just let me get my shawl and we can go out back to the stable."

On the way out, she commented, "I understand you are studying for the ministry, or at least my friends say you are."

"Yes, that's true," replied Young. "But at present, I am taking some time off from my studies in Toronto." Mrs. Smith opened the door to the stable and the two stepped inside. He welcomed the warmth emanating from the horses, and the smell of horseflesh and hay brought back visions of his family farm. With his cavalryman's eye, Young looked over the mares in their stalls. He was impressed.

"Are you an experienced rider, Mr. Clyde?" Anna Smith patted one of her husband's Morgans on the neck.

"Well, you might say that," Young replied with a smile. "My family has thoroughbreds and I have ridden since I was a mere lad." Young admired one Morgan mare. "Oh, she is a beauty, Mrs. Smith."

"Thank you. She's one of my favorites. My husband and I ride as often as we can and I usually ride her. Of course, now that he is Governor, we don't ride as much as I would like."

"That's a shame," Young sympathized. "There is something about riding that satisfies the soul."

"From such a young man, that is a lovely way to put it," Mrs. Smith said. "Are you a sportsman, Mister Clyde?"

"I can't say I'm a sportsman, but my friends and I are here for a short vacation and we hope the fishing and hunting are good."

"Most of the men in this town like both. I wish you luck whichever sport you take part in."

"Thank you, ma'am," Young said. "But I've taken enough of your time. I do appreciate you letting me see your horses."

They left the stable.

"It's too bad my husband is at the capitol today, "she said. "The Legislature is in session, you know, and that takes a good deal of his time. I am sure he would have liked to meet you. Perhaps when he is home again you two could go riding."

"Why, that's very gracious of you, ma'am."

"Thank you, Mister Clyde," she went on as though reluctant to see the young man leave. "This is a busy time. Most of the prominent men of St. Albans are either in Montpelier for the Legislature or in Burlington. The state Supreme Court is in session there, you know." Young softly breathed a sigh of relief, thankful for this talkative woman. The town was without many of its leaders, a bit of unexpected luck and a good omen.

He thanked her again, and as he walked back down the hill to his hotel, he thought: Governor Smith will have a long wait if he wants to go riding with me. Too bad those horses are so far up the hill, I'd like to ride that three-year-old.

Young did not know that only six days before, at a joint session of the House and Senate in Montpelier, the Governor had warned the Legislature about Confederate activity in Canada. He had derived his concerns from information sent to him by the War Department in Washington. Months before, Secret Service agents uncovered and prevented one attempt by expatriate Confederate soldiers to free thousands of their comrades from the federal prison at Johnston Island on Lake Erie. Young himself had been a part of that botched attempt.

"Vermont stands destitute of any arms of defense or any effective power to resist or prevent invasion," the Governor told the legislators.

"The dangers to our frontiers are by no means inconsiderable. Therefore, I have wired the War Department for five thousand rifled muskets and ample ammunition. I have also asked for authority to station troops at Burlington, Swanton, and in St.

Albans." His frustration had been evident when he reported: "So far, I have heard nothing from the War Department."

As it turned out, states along the border received authorization to station troops after Young and his men carried out their mission at St. Albans.

Before his visit to the Governor's home, Young had rented a horse from Edward Fuller's stable located behind his hotel. He had headed north out of town toward Canada to determine the best escape route for him and his men. The ride had taken him north toward Swanton, the most direct route to Canada, but swamps along the way could bog his men down, so he abandoned that option.

A day after visiting with the Governor's wife, Young threw on a jacket and went once again to rent a horse from Fuller's stable. This time, he took a road that meandered northeasterly out of St. Albans. It took him through gentle countryside and across a covered wooden bridge spanning the sluggish Black Creek at the little village of Sheldon. He stepped down from his horse and led it across the bridge.

"We should burn this," he said half aloud. "That should stop pursuers."

He rode on, pulling up again just before another covered bridge over the shallow Missisquoi River at Enosburg Falls to water his horse and eat the lunch he'd brought along. He cupped cold water in his hands and splashed it on his face, shivering. The horse drank his fill.

Young pulled a paper sack from his saddlebag and extracted a thick roast pork sandwich the cook at the hotel had made for him that morning. After dipping a metal cup into the cold, clear stream, he sat with his back against a tree beside the bridge. Although it was late in the season, the few red and yellow maple leaves still clinging to the trees presented a spectacular backdrop.

While Young ate, he recalled the conversations he had had with the Governor's wife and others of the town. Decent people, going about their daily lives, many of them worrying about their husbands or sons away in a war they believed was not of their making. Living in their quiet corner of the world, they were oblivious to what those husbands and sons were doing to the South. Or to what it meant to be a Southerner.

Why should they care about the Southern way of life? They claim it is a war over slavery. Slaves, yes, there are slaves all over the South. Our entire economy is built on slavery. It has been with us for hundreds of years. The South's economic system would collapse without it.

These Northerners, smug in their lives so far away from us, forcing us to bend our knee to them, sending their kin to put us down, to burn our homes and destroy our crops and molest our women. The South will not bow before such men.

He lingered beside the stream. Thoughts of his Kentucky home and his family brought on a fit of melancholy and he forced himself to think only of his mission as he remounted his horse. He continued toward the little town of Berkshire, stopping just short of the international border with Canada. He estimated he had ridden about eighteen or twenty miles.

Satisfied this was the best route, he retraced his path, arriving back in St. Albans just before dusk to return the rented horse to Fuller.

The stable owner smiled and commented: "You are a natural with horses, Mr. Clyde. It's rare to see a man who loves them the way you do." He brushed the horse's flanks. "I can't tell you how many times riders have brought their horses back to me frothed with sweat and breathing hard, but the times you've taken a horse from here, I can see how careful you have been. It's a pleasure to do business with you. I hope I can be of service again, sir."

Young smiled. "Why, thank you, Mister Fuller. I'm sure I will be calling on you again."

He handed Fuller his payment and asked the stable owner, "How many horses do you have?"

"I have seven, all of them in the best of condition."

"That is certainly a good thing to know," Young replied.

Yes, a very good thing to know. He patted the neck of one of the horses in its stall and left the stable.

The next morning, Young rose early as usual and washed and shaved from the bowl and pitcher on the room's commode. He read some passages from his Bible and then went downstairs for breakfast, eating alone. He bought a copy of the *St. Albans Messenger* and returned to his room, sat on his bed, and once again went over the plan. So many men to rob the banks. Enough to round up horses. Some to force the people on Main Street onto the

Green. And, yes, prevent men from running up from the foundry and the railroad station to stop us. What have I forgotten?

He went over the plan yet again.

Restless, he rose and looked out the window at the cloudy sky. The weather had not improved. Just before noon, he joined Collins and several others for lunch and told them to have the rest of the men join him in his room that afternoon at 2:30. He would go over their assignments a final time.

Back in his room, Young felt the tension of the last few days ebbing from him. His men were all present. Everything was in place. It was time for the cavalryman from Jessamine County, Kentucky, to do what he was sent here to do. And he was ready.

Just after 2:30 p.m., the men entered the Tremont House one or two at a time and mounted the steps to the second floor. The clerk watched as man after man climbed the stairs. He wondered, only briefly, what was going on. He soon lost interest and turned his attention to an article in the magazine he had been reading, his fingers strolling through the remaining strands of hair on his head.

Young greeted each of his men solemnly as they crowded into the room. Now, he was wearing the uniform of a Confederate officer, tailored especially for him in Montreal. A few of the men whistled softly.

"Well, Bennett! Look at you!" Sam Gregg said.

"Don't you look the picture of a Confederate officer!" Collins chided.

A few sat on Young's bed. One removed the newspapers from the chair next to the bed and took a seat. The others stood, cramped together. Ten of them carried large haversacks.

Young called for them to be quiet. "Today is the day, men. If this mission works, and I know it will, Mister Lincoln will have to withdraw some of his army from the South to protect towns like this one all along the border with Canada."

Murmurs of approval swept the room. Young repeated each step of the plan to be certain his men understood their assignments. He would oversee the action mounted on a horse he had assigned Marcus Spurr to take from Fuller's stable.

Collins was to head the four-man team that would rob the St. Albans Bank. Although he was a captain, outranking Young, Collins had agreed to join the group for a chance of some excitement and a way to get back at the Yankees who had held him captive.

"I cased the bank this morning, Bennett," he said. 'There are only a few people working there and we can take care of anyone who comes in. Maybe we can relieve them of some of the money they plan on depositing in the bank."

"What, commit armed robbery of helpless civilians?" cracked William Tevis. The others laughed. William, his brother, Squire Tevis, and Marcus Spurr were the others on Collins's team.

William Huntley, who went by the name William H. Hutchinson, said he planned to enter the Franklin County Bank alone, chat briefly with one of the tellers, and when his fellow raiders came in, they would all pull their pistols from under their long coats and rob the place.

"Don't wait too long before you three get inside," Young told Daniel Butterworth, John Moss, and John McGinnis. Young looked at Huntley. "I don't want you getting killed in there." Huntley nodded his agreement.

Wallace headed the team whose target was the First National Bank at Main and Fairfield Streets.

"I don't anticipate any trouble there, Bennett," said Wallace, who had gone to the bank the day before, ostensibly to change a large bill to smaller ones. While he waited for the clerk to count out his money, Wallace carefully noted the layout of the bank and its vault. Joseph McGrorty and Bruce, members of Wallace's team, agreed that their part of the raid would go off without a hitch.

Young had assigned George Scott, Charles Swager, Samuel Gregg, and William Moore to round up horses. They were to unharness every horse on Main Street from their wagons and then empty the stables. He told them not to shoot any of the horses' owners unless they tried to prevent the animals from being taken. Before dismissing the men, Young told them that during his talks with townspeople, there appeared to be few weapons that could be used against them, but he cautioned there might be more. One by one the Confederates left the room to take up their positions.

Satisfied that all was in place, Young opened a bureau drawer and strapped a double-holstered gun belt around his waist. He picked up two six-shot 1851 Navy Colt pistols. Before his men arrived, Young had loaded both cap and ball revolvers. He checked them carefully and holstered them. He donned his long, gray overcoat and pulled a full-length gray cape over it.

With his uniform and the weapons concealed, Young left the room and walked down the stairs. He nodded to the clerk behind the counter, pushed open the door, and walked to the middle of the muddy street. He looked up and down the street and saw his men doing their assigned jobs. Several stood outside the banks they would rob, waiting for the word. Others were rounding up horses from the stables and unhitching horses tied up along the street. Two men were guarding the heads of Champlain and Kingman Streets that led down to the railroad station and foundry. One raider has already begun herding people on Main Street over to the Green.

Time to make it official.

Young pushed his coat open, withdrew both pistols and shouted: "I take possession of this town in the name of the Confederate States of America!"

Marcus Spurr rode up on a horse he'd taken from Fuller's stable, leading a second mount. Young holstered his pistols and swung up into the saddle. He saw Scott and Swager bringing unsaddled horses from Fuller's place and from another stable farther along the street.

At gunpoint with their hands in the air, owners stood by helplessly as Gregg and Moore unhitched horses on Main Street.

The raid that Young had planned so meticulously was underway.

St. Albans would be changed forever.

CHAPTER 3

Danville, Kentucky
Spring, 1862

BENNETT Young stood in the middle of the room he had rented in Danville, Kentucky, while he studied for the ministry at Centre College, three blocks away.

He stared at the folded-up mattress on the bed across the room. That bed had been occupied until that morning by a friend, Joshua Todd. Joshua was leaving, as so many were, one by one, sometimes by twos and threes, even though classes were not yet over.

They were gone to war. Gone to fight, some for the North, some for the South.

Bennett still smarted from Joshua's remarks spoken earlier in the day.

"What's the matter, Young? Scared to fight?"

The look on his roommate's face and the scornful remark turned a youthful friendship to ashes.

"Are you going to stay here while we fight to save the Confederacy?" Joshua taunted.

Young had pushed by him wordlessly and walked stiffly back to their room. Joshua's trunk was packed and locked and ready to be loaded into a wagon that would take him away from Danville and Centre College. His former friend returned to their room with a servant, and without looking at Young, the two hefted the trunk between them and left.

Young propped a pillow against his bed's headboard and settled back against it. He heard the sound of horses' hooves and the squeal of carriage wheels taking Joshua away.

It isn't fair, he thought. They are all going. The war is passing me by, and I am studying theology.

He reached into a drawer in his bedside table and withdrew a letter he had received from his father earlier in the winter. He reread a passage he knew by heart: *You are only eighteen. My youngest son. We shall hear no more about enlisting.*

Nevertheless Young had raised the issue every time he wrote home after that, his letters growing more passionate. But each time his father wrote back, he did not mention the subject.

Young returned the letter to its place.

It isn't theology I need now, he thought. I need to fight those murdering Yankees.

He looked at the clock atop the table and sighed. Time for class. He threw his legs off the bed and strode down the stairs and out into the street, walking over to the two-story red brick college building.

The weather was mild this early spring day. Centre College still rang with the voices of students and their professors, but Bennett Young's heart was somewhere else. Somewhere he could learn the art of war and avenge the death and destruction that Union forces were inflicting on the South.

Later, as night fell, Young turned down the wick of his oil lamp, plunging his room into darkness. He slid between the sheets. Soon, the few remaining classmates at Mrs. Magruder's rooming house settled into their own beds and all was silent. Young stared into the darkness.

"I cannot rest while these murderers and thieves are destroying us," he muttered, "I have to fight them."

But as he lay there, his thoughts turned from war to the profession for which he was preparing. His heart ached at the contradictions that plagued him more and more. I'm studying for the ministry. How can I think of vengeance when the Lord says vengeance is His? How can I kill or maim another human being, no matter what his crimes? How can I reconcile these conflicting acts? He weighed and measured the disparate thoughts over and over, and it was hours before he slept.

Newspapers reported the defeat of Confederate forces at Fort Henry and Fort Donelson that past winter, and at Shiloh where the ground ran red with the blood of both sides. The most devastating blow for the South was the death at Shiloh of the Confederacy's best commander, General Albert Sydney Johnston. The cost in lives was already casting a pall in homes throughout the South, as it was in the North.

Life for Young at the Presbyterian college in the Blue Grass region grew increasingly difficult as more students withdrew to join the fight. From a newspaper article one mid-April, Young read of the exploits of General John Hunt Morgan, the scourge of Yankees in Kentucky and Tennessee.

Young's heart leaped as he read of Morgan and his Second Kentucky Cavalry, most of them expert riders from well-off Kentucky families, raiding as far north as Louisville, destroying Yankee military supplies, tearing up railroad tracks, capturing hundreds of Yankee weapons and hundreds of Yankee soldiers. The article went on to say that during each raid, young men flocked to join Morgan, swelling his division's numbers.

The next morning, Young packed his clothing and his books and hired a carriage to take him twenty mile north to his home in Nicholasville. As he waited for the carriage to arrive, he realized this might be his last summer at home for a long time.

The carriage rolled up to the Young family's brick house, built some fifty or more years ago. A white stone drive lead to the two-story house framed by soaring white columns. Young paid the driver and walked up the wide steps, entering through the front door. His father was just descending the stairs when he saw his son.

"Bennett! You're home!"

Young looked up. He wanted to blurt out his intentions right there and then, but he swallowed the words before they formed.

"Hello, father. Yes. It's so good to be here."

The two embraced, and as he held his father, Young's heart sank. *How can I tell him? What will he say? What will mother say?*

"So, you are home for the summer. Do you have any plans?" the elder Young asked.

"Nothing terribly demanding," Young lied. "I thought I could give Robert and Lank a hand around the place, if you would like." Young could see that the war had not touched his own family here.

His father heaved a sigh of relief. "That would be fine. I want to clear that field across the road and fence it. I plan on buying a few more horses. That might be a project you can work on with your brothers. It might take all of you a few months, working together."

Young smiled. "Sounds good to me, father. Where are they? Where are my sisters?" He looked around. "Where's mother?"

"The boys are working in the large shed. Seems they hit a boulder and broke the plow last April and they're just getting around to fixing it. As usual," the elder Young sighed. "Your sisters are with your mother. They took the carriage over to our new neighbors. Did I tell you in my letters that some folks bought the old Christiansen plantation? Your mother and Mrs. McRitchie became friends right away. She and the girls have been over there several times the last few weeks helping to get the family settled in. But they should be along soon. Come, let me help you with your baggage."

"That's all right, father. I can handle it." Young picked up his things.

That evening, Josephine Young served a lavish dinner to welcome her youngest son home from school. At the table, Young teased his brothers over the plow incident.

"You think you can do any better, mister preacher?" Lank shot back, grinning. "You don't even know how to harness a horse."

"Is that, so? I bet I can harness Glory faster than you can." Young turned to Robert, Jr. "Tomorrow we'll do it and you can time us."

"Deal," said Robert.

"I will bet on Bennett," said his sister, Susan.

"All right, I will bet on Lank," sister Josephine chimed in.

"Deal, eh?" their father said, looking darkly at Robert. "I think you've been making too many deals with those rascals in Lexington," he said, his gaze stern on his namesake son.

The table fell silent. Robert hoped to avoid any further discussion of his losing bets on the races. At that moment, their mother entered the dining room with a steaming plate of sweet potatoes, followed by one of the house staff carrying a plate heaped with sliced roast of beef.

Young broke the uncomfortable silence. "How is Daniel, father?" he asked.

"He's well. He'll soon be leaving the church at Georgetown to become the minister in Salvisa."

"Is that a larger church?" Young asked.

"I believe it is. We hoped he could get home this summer, but I guess the move will be taking up all his time."

"Well, then it appears I am stuck with these two," Young said. "Perhaps I can prevent them from breaking anything else this summer." Lank roared, punched his brother on the shoulder, and the two embraced.

"It's good to have you home, Bennett, even if you are the kid."

Later that evening, Lank and Robert left for town to attend a dance. Before they left, their father chided: "Don't you boys get any ideas about joining up, now you hear?"

The two stopped.

"No plans there, Father. Not while those Drater sisters are still around," Robert said. Laughing, the two ran out.

The summer passed swiftly. Young grew hard working in the fields alongside his brothers. As the days shortened and cool weather arrived, he heard of more friends leaving for the war, and he grew ever more restless. He knew his father had noted the changes in him, but Young could not muster the courage to tell the man he would not return to college but was going to join up.

His dissatisfaction grew stronger as he followed the war in the newspapers and by talking with friends.

When he read of General Robert E. Lee's crushing defeat of Burnside at Fredericksburg on December 13, Young was even more determined to go.

One evening soon after, he knew it was time to tell his parents. He had ridden Glory into Nicholasville where he saw a broadsheet calling on all able-bodied men to join Colonel Leroy Cluke, who was organizing a regiment, the 8th Kentucky Cavalry.

The broadside said the 8th would join General John Hunt Morgan's division in Tennessee. Young's heart surged. This is where I want to be, he thought. In action, not sitting around safely at home.

Before dinner, Young walked out to the veranda to gather his thoughts and plan how he would tell his parents he was going to enlist. He faced a bleak sun as its fading light drifted through the oak and beech trees at the far edge of the field. He shivered, wondering if he was reacting to a chill in the air or to the knowledge that what he was about to tell his parents would hurt them deeply.

He wrapped his arms around himself and watched the sun go down, seeing it as a symbol of the end of a major part of his life. His father came through the door and stood next to Young.

"I am joining the fight, father."

"Don't, son."

"I'm eighteen. I have to do this." There. It was said.

He saw the stricken look on his father's face.

"When?"

"As soon as I can. Tomorrow." Young cringed inside to see his strong father slump into a nearby rocker, avoiding his son's eyes.

"Your mother. This may be more than she can bear," the elder Young said, his voice shaking. Young realized that, although the news had devastated his father, the man's first thought was for how it would affect his wife. This was the man Young had looked up to all of his life, the man who had taught him to tell the truth, no matter the consequences.

And now, Young was determined to go to war. His parents' dream of seeing him follow his brother Daniel into the ministry would have to wait.

His face still ashen, Robert Young rose to his feet.

"I will tell your mother."

With a heavy heart, Young watched his father enter the house. Long minutes passed before his mother joined Young on the veranda, followed soon after by her husband. Her tear-swollen eyes revealed her dismay at the news.

"Mother," Young hesitated. "I...I know this is hard, but I can't stand by any longer." His voice near a whisper, he declared. "I must go."

"Oh, son," she replied, pressing a handkerchief to her eyes. Young went to her, enveloping her in his arms, his face buried in her graying hair. She sobbed and held her son tightly. He knew that anything he said would be inadequate, but he had to try to explain.

Softly, he said, "I know you don't want us, any of us, to fight this war, Mother. On either side. But...," and his voice wavered. "Yankee armies are here in Kentucky and Tennessee and

Virginia...killing and maiming and burning homes, destroying whole cities and towns."

He suddenly realized his voice had risen. "I'm sorry, mother. I feel strongly about this. I have to help stop them." His mother stood back, a hand on his arm.

"Is there nothing I can say that will change your mind?" Her eyes met his, her face drawn.

"No. I have thought long and hard about this, mother. I have to go."

Her arms dropped and she said, softly, "I didn't raise you for a soldier."

She turned and went back into the house. Soon, Young could hear her sobs coming from the sitting room.

Alone in his room later that evening, Young stared out the window across the fields that spread around all sides of the family home. His thoughts raced. He would give anything not to hurt them, to follow their wishes, but the war waits out there and he must be a part of it. He saw his brothers coming in from the fields. They'll take care of the family and the farm until I get back.

Early the next morning, after a solemn breakfast, Young went to the stable and entered Glory's stall. He patted her on the neck and spoke softly into her ear.

"We're going on an adventure, old girl," he whispered. Glory snickered and turned her head toward him. A dark bay Tennessee walking horse, she was a gift from his father on his graduation from Bethel Academy. He gave her a carrot he had taken from the kitchen.

Young brushed her down before slipping a navy blue saddle pad over her back. He hoisted her saddle up and onto the pad, then pulled the stirrups down and tightened the girth. Satisfied, he backed Glory out of the stall and led her into the wan sunlight.

Standing beside her husband, his mother handed Young a satchel of food.

"I don't know if they will feed you today, son. Here's something to eat just in case." She paused and with her head bowed, bade him farewell. "Take good care of yourself."

She embraced her son, sobbing again. Young kissed the top of her head.

Don't worry, Mother. I'll be back." His father reached into a pocket of his jacket and handed his son a small leather-bound book. It was the elder Young's Bible.

"I was going to give you this when you graduated, but...." Young looked at the book and smiled. He slipped the well-worn Bible into his saddlebag.

Father and son hugged each other until Young loosened his grip and stepped back. His father extended a hand and the two held the handshake. Tears welling in his eyes, the older man said quietly, "God save you, son."

"You take good care of yourself, hear?" Robert said, his emotion writ plainly on his face. Young and Lank embraced, and the girls hugged him, tearfully.

"I will write to you," Josephine said.

"I will, too," Susan said, wiping her face of tears.

Young nodded a final goodbye, swung up into the saddle, and rode Glory down to the dusty road. He didn't look back.

CHAPTER 4

Nicholasville, Kentucky
Fall, 1863

Young rode alone for the few miles into the center of Nicholasville. He approached a merchant wearing a heavy coat and sweeping dust off the wooden sidewalk.

"Excuse me. Can you tell me where Colonel Cluke's camp is?" he asked.

"Out the old turnpike, about a half mile or so," the man said, indicating the way." He leaned on his broom. "You fixin' to join up?"

"I am, sir, indeed," Young replied. The man shrugged and resumed sweeping. Young turned Glory toward the old turnpike and soon came upon a field shared by a small herd of cows and a forming military encampment, its new white tents gleaming in the sunlight. A few yards away he saw a larger tent. Attached to it was a sun-bleached wooden board on which were scribbled the words "Recruiting Station."

Young dismounted and got in line behind three other men still wearing their civilian clothes. When his turn came, he stepped up to a rough plank table set on saw horses. A young man, wearing three red stripes on both sleeves, looked up at Young, a look of extreme boredom on his face.

"Well? I take it you are here to join up."

"Yes, I am. I mean yes, sir."

"I'm a sergeant, mister," the man replied, scowling. "You only say sir to officers."

He handed Young a sheet of paper. "Remember that. Now, fill this out, if you can write. If you can't, just sign your X at the bottom. I'll fill out the rest."

He turned his face away and spat on the ground. Young turned to see four more recruits in line behind him. He was determined to let this sergeant know he was educated.

"I can write," Young said, trying to hide his annoyance. This was not the way he imagined things would be. He would learn the ways of war and fight with his comrades who would become his life-long friends, and he would return home a hero into the arms of his family. He scowled, filled in his name and his home address, and listed his parents as next of kin. Nearly through, he paused, looked at the sergeant, and signed with a flourish before handing in the sheet. The sergeant looked the page over and handed it back.

"Go with this man," the sergeant ordered, pointing to a newly minted soldier standing at stiff but awkward attention.

"Next!" the Sergeant barked.

Young followed the recruit as he'd been instructed. He noticed the boy's wrinkled uniform, still smelling as though it had just come from the factory. At a table nearby, another man in what Young assumed was an officer's uniform looked up as the two approached. The officer reached for Young's paper and looked it over.

"Private Young. Welcome to the 8th Kentucky. I am delighted to see you."

"Thank you, sir," said Young, standing at what he hoped was attention. He didn't know if he should say more.

The officer nodded.

"Most of the men with General Morgan are Kentuckians, many of them college-educated and from good families such as yours. Some up fromTexas and Tennessee, too. You will be in excellent company. Listen, learn, and do your duty. Now, I'll send you to Corporal Granger," he said, pointing in the general direction that Young was to go. "He'll find you some gear and a tent. You'll be sharing it with another man."

The officer looked up at Glory and added, "Oh, by the way, all our troopers ride their own horses, even Colonel Morgan. So you don't have to worry about finding someone to ride her home for you. Take her to the corral down there." He indicated with a wave of his hand in the direction of a fenced in field. "They will feed her and take good care of her. Dismissed."

Young saluted clumsily and walked Glory to the corral. A trooper led them inside a gate where dozens of horses fed on hay or nibbled grass, and Young unsaddled her. Carrying the saddle, blanket, and harness, he went in search of Granger. He passed a row of pup tents whose occupants were folding clothing and checking out newly issued gear.

"Can you tell me where Corporal Granger is?" he asked one man. The trooper pointed down the row of two-man tents.

"Go to the end, turn left. You'll find him," the man said.

Young made the turn and spotted a tall, dark-haired trooper with two yellow stripes on his sleeves. He was cleaning a carbine.

"Corporal James Granger?" Young asked. The man looked up, his dark eyes centered on the new arrival.

"That'll be me. And who are you, lad?" Granger asked. Young saw a man hardly older than he calling him "lad."

"I'm Bennett Young, sir. Assigned to your company." He immediately regretted calling the corporal "sir."

Granger ignored the faux pas.

"Welcome, Young." He waved a hand toward another soldier standing nearby. "Private Thomas here will show you where you will be issued your uniform, a carbine, and the other things you will need. Report back to me when you are finished."

"Thank you, corporal," said Young. Walking beside Thomas to the quartermaster's depot, Young asked him: "Have you been with General Morgan very long?"

"Little over a year," Thomas replied. "Seen a few things in that time." He said no more and Young hesitated to ask what those things were.

Thomas walked them toward a group of tables piled high with blouses and trousers and other items. A trooper looked Young over, assessing his size. He handed him a butternut-colored blouse and trousers of the same color; two pairs of long johns; two pairs of wool socks; a slouch cap; a wool blanket; a gum blanket covered on one side with India rubber; and a long-sleeve, calf-length white garment. Young took them and laughingly placed the cap on his head. He had expected to be issued a kepi, the round, flat-topped, stiff-visored cap worn by soldiers on both sides of the war. He asked Thomas what the white garment was.

"That's a linen duster. That piece of clothing and this gum blanket will be your best friends, behind your horse and carbine. Oh, and your socks," Thomas replied. "When it rains your gum blanket will keep you dry, well reasonably anyways. And when it's hot and dusty, the duster will keep your uniform clean, or at least as clean as you will ever see it after you've ridden for a while."

Young nodded. Apparently wound up now, Thomas went on. "Some of us were sent up here from Tennessee by General Morgan to help organize this regiment and get you down to join him when he gets back. We won't be in this camp very long. The Federals will find out about us soon enough, so we must get to Tennessee as quick as we can."

Young's pulse quickened. With Morgan! That's where I want to be, he thought. Thomas walked Young to the paymaster's table where new recruits signed their names and home addresses. That settled, they returned to Granger, who extended a leather tobacco pouch. Young shook his head.

"Thank you, but I don't smoke."

Granger nodded, stoking his corncob pipe with rough-cut tobacco.

"You're probably better off," he said. He changed the subject. "We'll be moving south once we have enough volunteers, so you'll spend a lot of time in the saddle. When we camp, you'll get drill training along with the other new men. If you like action, you've come to the right place." He scratched a match on the stock of his carbine and lit the pipe, looking over it at Young. "Now, I'll show you to your tent."

As they approached a row of tents, a young recruit, Samuel S. Gregg, emerged from one of them, shaking out a pair of trousers. He looked up as Granger and Young approached.

"Bennett?" Gregg asked.

"Sam!" Young replied. He shook Gregg's extended hand. "I didn't know you had joined up." He turned to Granger, "Sam is a neighbor of ours."

Granger nodded. "Well you two ought to get along well."

He left.

"I joined four days ago, so I guess I'm a veteran now," Gregg chuckled. "I'm glad we're going to be tent mates. Oh, wait. My gear is all over the tent." He gathered his things to make room for Young's belongings. Young unrolled his new blanket inside the tent and lined his side of the small space with clothing and his horse's saddle and bridle.

"I'll try not to take up any of your side, Sam."

"That's all right. Plenty of room." Gregg said, then asked: "What brings you here now?"

"I want to fight," Young replied quietly.

"From what I hear, we are going to get a belly full of that. More than a belly full, I reckon." Young finished stowing his gear, and seated inside the tent, changed into his uniform. He had trouble pulling the pants over his hips, but he finally managed and emerged from the tent.

"Kind of tight," he said.

Gregg looked down at his own waist. "Mine, too, but the sergeant said they'll fit better after a while. I hope that don't mean they're gonna starve us." He laughed.

That night after muster and supper, Young crept into the tent and lay down. He shifted around trying to find a place where his hip bone wasn't boring into the ground. Aware of Young's discomfort, Gregg told him: "Fold your spare trousers and put them under your hip. Makes it softer. Granger taught me that."

Young folded his extra pair of trousers and did as Gregg suggested. He lay there, his mind racing through the events of the day, leaving his parents and brothers and sisters, joining up, experiencing the excitement of a military camp, the veterans shepherding the recruits around, getting them settled. He turned toward Gregg who already had fallen asleep. He smiled, feeling happy to be there. His eyes grew heavy and eventually he drifted off.

Before the sun rose over the trees at the edge of the nearby woods, the sound of a bugle snapped Young awake. He sat up, bewildered.

"That's reveille, Bennett. Time to move," Gregg said. The two heard a kick against the side of their tent.

"All right, you two, get the hell out of there and fall in!" roared a voice outside. Carrying their boots, the two men scrambled out. Frost lay over the grass and tents all around. Young and Gregg could see their breath as they hastily pulled on their boots.

"Stand at attention next to me," Gregg whispered. "Sergeant McCarren's a son-of-a-bitch in the morning." He grinned and then snapped to attention as McCarren approached. The skin of the sergeant's face was like rawhide parched from too many days driving herds from South Texas to northern cattle yards. His mouth turned down as though he had just eaten something disagreeable. His arms seemed too long for his body, and his back was bent slightly from years in the saddle. Young immediately knew this was a man not to be crossed.

He looked Young up and down.

"You're the sorriest son-of-a-pup I ever did lay eyes on."

Young cringed. He balled his hands into fists and almost raised them, but Gregg nudged him with an elbow. Young's anger ebbed quickly and he gathered himself.

"You got your shirt buttoned wrong and your fly buttons are open. Jesus!" Young reddened at the look of disgust displayed on the sergeant's face. "Get yourself dressed properly. Go with this here sorry son-of-a-bitch down to the latrine trench and then to the chow line."

The sergeant took two steps back and looked left and right down the row of tents whose occupants were lined up just as Young and Gregg were. He shouted "Dismissed!" and turned and walked away. The men moved toward the latrine to start their day, one that would launch all of them on the adventure of their young lives.

Young and Gregg sat with the others at mess, wolfing down balls of corndodger and sipping bitter hot coffee from tin cups. As he ate, he wondered what he had gotten himself into. He bit off another piece and chewed pensively.

"I get the distinct feeling Sergeant McCarren doesn't like me," he said to Gregg.

Steam wafted up from Gregg's cup and he blew on the rim before carefully sipping his coffee. He grimaced at the bitterness.

"Sergeant McCarren doesn't much like anybody, not even himself," he said. "Just keep your mouth shut when he is on you and you'll be all right." Gregg sipped more coffee and continued. "The sergeant came over from another regiment to train the men here. Rumor has it he hit a recruit once, broke his jaw. I don't know why they would assign him to train more recruits. Guess it's the way of the Army. Anyways, just don't cross him."

As the days wore on, Young hoped to get home for a few hours or at least enjoy a visit with his parents before leaving Nicholasville. But, as the rolls filled with volunteers, Colonel Cluke was anxious to join Morgan in Tennessee.

Morgan had won a major victory at Hartsville, Tennessee, at the beginning of the second week in December, riding and fighting during ice and snowstorms. His men captured 2,000 Federal prisoners, two Parrott guns, and took the overcoats from shivering Yankee prisoners for his own men. After moving to Murfreesboro, Morgan was promoted to brigadier general by Bragg, with his commission handed to him by President Davis, who had arrived in the town a few days before. Morgan's second-in-command was promoted to full colonel.

A few days later, the word came down to Young's platoon to prepare to move south in the morning. Morgan and his men were soon to depart on what later became known as the Christmas Raid.

As the first light of dawn brightened the eastern horizon, the bugle sounded, rousing the men from their sleep. Young stretched and looked over at Gregg who was still asleep. He shivered from the cold as he leaned over and nudged Gregg awake.

"Time to rise, Sam."

"Oh, God," Gregg groaned. "I don't want to face this day. We are in for a long ride."

He scratched his belly and crotch.

"Oh, hell, might as well accept it."

Young rose and stepped outside the tent. The sun was barely up and a heavy frost sparkled on the grass. The men in adjoining tents were already packing their gear and clothing inside their blankets, then tying the blankets with rope at both ends.

Young asked a passing sergeant why they were not taking their tents along.

"When you're raiding there won't be time to put up and take down a tent. Your oil coat or blanket will be your tent, soldier," the man said and moved on.

A smell of coffee drifted his way and Young realized he was hungry. Gregg advised him to eat as much as he could.

"And stick a couple of biscuits in your pocket," he suggested. "You never know when your next meal is gonna be." Gregg smiled. "Another good notion from Corporal Granger."

Good advice, Young thought.

After breakfast, the men of the newly formed company mounted their horses, and with Colonel Cluke and his staff officers leading the way, the 8th Kentucky Cavalry, Confederate States of America, paraded past a reviewing stand filled with town notables, parents, wives, and girlfriends.

Before heading south, the men were allowed to say goodbye to their families. Young found his.

"Look at you, a soldier," his mother exclaimed, but without joy. Young hugged her.

"Shush now, Mother," his father said, taking his wife's hand.

"We don't have much time," Young said. "I want you to know I'm doing the right thing and…" he put his arm around his mother's shoulder. "… I will be back."

He embraced his father and his brothers and sisters. They talked briefly until a bugle sounded.

"Time to go," Young said. His family crowded around him, said their final goodbyes, and watched as he rejoined his company. The soldiers, new and veteran alike, mounted up, their uniforms a sea of gray and butternut. They turned south and rode away, not always in formation. Young turned for a final glance at his family.

With Cluke at the head of the column, the brigade began the one-hundred-thirty-mile march to Morgan's encampment at Alexandria thirty-five miles east of Nashville, where the new men would get more training, and where Morgan and his top commanders were planning their next foray.

Southern Kentucky was coal country and a hotbed of Confederate sympathizers. Many of those who scratched a living from the mines had relatives south in Tennessee and Alabama, some who already had faced the horrors of war. After camping for a night, Cluke and his new regiment rode up the long rise toward Halls Gap, then on to Waynesburg and Pulaski, where they were greeted by the residents of those small towns with cold well water and breads and cakes the townspeople could ill afford to give away, but give away they did, wishing the cavalrymen well. The column skirted Somerset, a larger town that held a Union garrison and supply depot.

Riding beside Young, Gregg commented, "I guess Colonel Cluke doesn't want to tangle with any Yankees, not yet anyway with this bunch of green horns." Young nodded, half wishing for a battle, but knowing he still needed to be taught how to fight. Finally, just south of Strunk, the regiment crossed the state line into Tennessee. It was not just a case of crossing from one state to another. To their minds, they had crossed an international boundary.

"This is Confederate territory. No Yankees around here," Gregg said.

After camping overnight, the 8th Kentucky continued south, a hard ride to Alexandria, arriving at Morgan's camp on a mid-December day, an hour before sunset. Young had expected to see Morgan, but the fabled raider was still in Murfreesboro where, on December 14th, he had married Martha Ready, the daughter of a prominent Kentuckian. President Davis and all the top generals of the Army of Tennessee—Bragg, Hardee, Breckinridge and Polk—were present. Lieutenant General Polk, also an Episcopal bishop, performed the ceremony.

Young and Gregg found their tent site several rows behind the first on a large field and stowed their gear, talking as they did.

"I wish I could see Morgan," Young lamented.

"Yes, it's too bad. I hear he's still up in Murfreesboro. Married some lady up there."

The two crawled inside their tent, pulled a thin blanket over themselves and immediately fell into a deep sleep.

The days passed, long, grueling, seemingly never-ending days, with Sergeant McCarren riding Young and the other recruits unmercifully. During carbine practice one cold morning, McCarren stopped behind Young, who, flat on his belly in a line with half a dozen other troopers, missed hitting the target twice.

"See that thing down there shaped like a man? That's a target," McCarren said loud enough for the others to hear. Some of them sniggered. McCarren cast a baleful eye on them and they returned to shooting. "See if you can hit the damned thing."

"Yes, sergeant," Young replied.

"Stand up, Private," McCarren ordered. Young turned to rise, accidentally aiming the barrel of his carbine at the head of the man lying next to him.

"Young! What the hell're you tryin' to do?" McCarren grabbed the carbine from Young's grasp. "Stand up!" Young scrambled to his feet and stood at attention, red-faced.

"We got Yankees killin' us, Young. We don't need you doin' it!" McCarren shouted. To Young it seemed the sergeant always screamed. "You had this weapon aimed at that trooper there!" McCarren pointed to the man lying on the ground.

"I...I didn't realize."

"Quiet!" McCarren thundered. He took two steps, his face only inches from Young's, his Texas accent deepening. "Trooper, I'm gonna be on your arse every minute of every day as long as I'm in this sorry outfit, which is going to be too damned long as far as I'm concerned! Now, get back down there and don't aim that weapon at anybody else or I will kick your arse all over Tennessee!"

Shaken, Young could only respond, "Yes, sergeant."

While McCarren taught Young to shoot, it was Granger who continued teaching him what living in the field was all about. Granger demonstrated how to stuff whatever grass he could find inside a spare shirt to make a pillow. He showed the men how to clean a carbine and keep their clothes mended. He also warned them to boil any drinking water they took from a stream, no matter where.

Young drilled endless hours with the other recruits, with McCarren riding him every inch of the way. He learned infantry as well as cavalry tactics, grew hard and lean, and commented to Gregg: "My trousers fit a lot better these days."

He itched for a fight.

CHAPTER 5

The Christmas Raid
December 23, 1862

MORGAN and his top officers arrived at camp from Murfreesboro on December 20th. The men learned that their colonel had been promoted to brigadier general and awarded the thanks of the Confederate Congress for his surprise attack that defeated federal forces at Hartsville on December 7th. The next day Young caught a glimpse of Morgan and Colonel Basil Duke, Morgan's second-in-command and brother-in-law, who also had been promoted.

The two commanders sat astride their horses to watch the men of the new regiment drill. To Young, Morgan seemed like an animal ready to leap on its prey. The man sat straight, his eyes sharp, missing nothing that happened around him. His long, black mustache curled to the lower sides of his handsome face, his goatee as black as his mustache.

When Morgan took his cap off to acknowledge a salute from his officers and men, Young noticed his hair was receding slightly, but it was long, curling against the back of his neck. Young was suitably impressed with his leader, vowing to follow him through whatever awaited them.

The hard days of drill and cavalry maneuvers had turned the fledgling 8th Cavalry into a cohesive fighting force and Young grew restless, eager for action. Late on the afternoon of December 21st, when Young and the rest of his company had finished carbine practice, Sergeant Granger called his squad together.

"We're moving out in the morning. After breakfast, prepare to move when the order comes down. Dismissed!" He turned and walked away.

"Did you hear that, Bennett?" Gregg asked. "We must be going back to Kentucky!"

"I heard, Sam." Young breathed.

At dawn on December 22nd, a chilly morning heralding stormy weather, the two worked with practiced swiftness wrapping their gear.

"Workin' keeps ya warm, doesn't?" Gregg said. Young nodded, feeling a bit warmer than when he awoke.

Then they waited. An hour passed, then two. Young frowned, wondering.

"What do you suppose is holding things up?" he asked Gregg.

"I don't know," his friend replied. "Maybe Bragg's sent us a change of orders to stand down. Wouldn't surprise me."

General Braxton Bragg, commanding the Confederate Army of Tennessee, was retreating south after a fierce battle with Union General William "Rosey" Rosecrans's forces at Perryville. Young and his comrades heard through the rumor mill that Morgan had earlier conferred with Bragg, who worried that Rosecrans was preparing to carry on the fight through the winter if necessary, instead of going into winter quarters. Bragg and Morgan were aware of a series of Federal stockades that had been built and fortified along the Louisville and Nashville Railroad from Nashville, Tennessee, to Louisville, Kentucky. Two large wooden trestles just thirty miles south of Louisville, although defended, appeared to be the weakest points along the rail line. If each trestle, about five hundred feet long and one hundred feet high, could be destroyed, they would cut Rosecrans's supply route for months.

Finally, as the temperature hovered near freezing, Sergeant McCarren shouted for the men to mount up. The entire camp was abuzz with excitement. Word that Morgan and his 3,100 troopers were about to leave had quickly circulated in the town and the surrounding area. Before long, large numbers of townspeople arrived bundled up against the cold to see the men off.

The company commander stood in front of the assembled troops.

"All right, men. Listen. We are riding back into Kentucky and we...."

The men interrupted with cheers, welcoming the news of going home. If not home, at least back to Kentucky, the home state of many of Morgan's men.

Their commander paused and then said, disgust plain in his voice, "As you know, General Bragg is moving back toward Chattanooga." Snickers emanated from some of the assembled troopers. "All right, all right. We have an important job to do and I know y'all are up to it. And one more thing. General Morgan just got married."

Cheers went up from the assembled mass of men, many of whom had heard rumors their general was to wed. The only thing that affected Gregg was news that they were in for a long, grueling march back to Kentucky.

He groaned. Young stifled a laugh.

"A lot better than sitting around here doing nothing," he countered. We are going to see some fun, Young thought, but it isn't going to be easy, especially in this weather.

The lower ranks didn't know the entire plan. Morgan had been ordered by General Bragg to guard his army as it withdrew south under pressure from General Rosecrans. If Morgan could accomplish his mission by riding hard to Elizabethtown and destroying the railroad bridges, it would slow or stop the Union commander. It would give Bragg time to deploy his Army of Tennessee to protect Chattanooga, a vital rail city about ninety-five miles southeast of Nashville on the Georgia border. Morgan's raid also was timed to coincide with General Nathan B. Forrest's romp through western Tennessee where he was to harass General U.S. Grant, who was threatening the Mississippi River city of Vicksburg, 160 miles south of Memphis.

Before saddling up, the men were issued their usual three days of cooked rations. They would heat them at meal times as best they could or eat them cold. Farriers were busy shoeing horses, and each man was given two extra horseshoes and nails. For those who didn't have them, a new saddle blanket, a blanket, an oilcloth coat, and overcoat were issued. The men were allowed one change of clothing and were happy for that, because they knew cold and sleet and freezing rain could come at any time. Those with shotguns were issued a dozen and a half shells each and those with carbines, forty rounds of .52-caliber apiece.

Before leaving Alexandria, Tennessee, new troops joined Morgan's brigade, swelling his ranks to 4,000 men.

Young and his comrades of the 8th were joined with the 2nd and 3rd Kentucky Cavalry Regiments, and with an artillery battery of two twelve-pounders and two six-pounders under the command of Colonel Basil Duke. The 10th and 11th Kentucky Cavalry Regiments, along with the 14th Tennessee, left camp under the command of Colonel William C. P. Breckenridge.

Young gripped the reins resting on Glory's mane and swung up into the saddle, eager to return to Kentucky. He suddenly felt an immense feeling of pride as he looked down the line of horsemen, some whose mounts were new and unused to their riders, skittering around, being pulled into line by hard tugs on their reins.

As the regiments unfurled their flags, the cheers from hundreds of onlookers buoyed the men's spirits. With bugles blaring, the mounted soldiers swung into line. As he passed a line of onlookers, Young heard one older man comment to a young girl at his side: "Have you ever seen such a beautiful sight?"

"Oh, it's so exciting, Grandpapa!" the little girl replied, waving. Young waved, too, and heard a cheer from back in the column as Morgan galloped forward along the line, a feather in his cap bowing to the breeze. He would lead his men into Kentucky, having bid goodbye to his new, young wife.

That night the troops reached the Cumberland River at Sand Shoal, crossed over without resistance, and the next morning moved north again, covering thirty miles through rough and hilly country. They stopped less than an hour for lunch and to water their horses at a stream. On the march again, they rode five miles and then two companies lead by Captain Tom Quirk were sent to determine conditions in Glasgow up ahead. The rest of the Rebels rested after having ridden a full ninety miles at the blistering pace Morgan favored.

"It's Christmas Eve, Bennett," Gregg said, as the column stopped for the night.

Young replied, "I know."

He pictured his family gathered for Christmas Eve dinner, the house decorated festively, a tall tree lit with candles that as a boy he feared would catch the tree ablaze and burn everything down, including his presents.

There would be no dining hall feast or festivities this year, but Young and the men boisterously enjoyed a meal of beef and chicken and fresh bread that the 2nd Regiment had taken from a Union sutler. The unlucky fellow had been captured, along with his twenty-Percheron team and a large wagon groaning under the weight of provisions the he had hoped to sell to Yankee soldiers. The men of the 2nd shared the bounty with others of Morgan's cavalrymen.

Gregg boiled some dried corn they had scavenged from a nearby farm, as Young and the others roasted the beef and chickens over a hand-made spit. Despite the cold, Young basked in the warmth of the fire and a belly full of real food.

Popping the cork out of a bottle of hard cider, Gregg offered it to Young, even though he knew his friend did not drink spirits. Young waved it away and shoved a forkful of nearly blood-red beef into his mouth. The long ride had made him hungry and he ate as though he would not have another meal until this raid was over. He wiped the juice from his lips and belched.

"Merry Christmas," Gregg said as he took a pull from the bottle that set off a coughing fit. "By gum, that's good stuff," he managed between coughs. "Merry Christmas. At least it ain't snowin' or rainin'."

They finished eating, scraped off their tin plates and readied their blankets for the night. Gregg lay his head on his saddle, his thin blanket and oilcloth over him, and took another swig from the bottle. Young watched his friend finally drift off to sleep, the bottle nestled in his arms.

Young pulled his blanket and oilcloth up over his head. He slept restlessly, shivering much of the night as the temperature dropped. Nicholasville and Christmas were a long way off.

Rumors swirled through the Rebel camp that they were now in territory that was heavily defended due to the importance to Union forces of the Louisville and Nashville Railroad. The line carried food and supplies to the Union Army in Nashville and farther south. Federal forces had built stockades along the railroad's length, and they were heavily manned.

When they awoke the next morning, Young and the rest of Company B learned that Tom Quirk had run into an advance guard of the Union's 2nd Michigan Cavalry when he led the two companies to reconnoiter Glasgow the night before. The Michigan troopers were so taken by surprise that they were slow in returning fire from the Rebels, who killed one man and wounded two others. Quirk lost an officer and a soldier but, outgunned, the remaining twenty Michigan men surrendered. The Yankees were questioned, names and home towns listed, and then they were paroled.

Christmas morning brought rain mixed with hail. The Rebel cavalrymen finished cold what little was left of their feast from the night before and mounted up again, resuming their ride north on the pike toward Munfordville.

"Damn, this weather," Gregg scowled, slouching in his saddle. He tried to pull the collar of his oil coat around his neck, but the rain seeped down, wetting his tunic and chilling him. Ten miles north of Glasgow, one of the men in Young's company said he overheard a messenger from Breckenridge say that fifty skirmishers ahead of the main Rebel column had run into Federal troops. Captain Quirk had led a charge straight at the Yankees. At the top of a rise, with a high fence on each side of the road, Federals opened fire. A Yankee company hit Quirk's men from the right flank.

"They were at point-blank range before they began firing," the messenger had related. "Two of our men were wounded. Five were captured, and the rest of them scrambled over the fences and skedaddled to a scrub oak thicket. I hear Captain Quirk suffered a head wound. I hope he'll recover."

Quirk had been wounded. Word soon circulated through the Rebel force that, as his head was being bandaged, Quirk told his commander: "I've a head built in County Kerry. It's been roughed up with shillelaghs enough so a couple of bullets are but mere trifles."

Wishing to avoid a more serious skirmish, Morgan ordered his two columns to continue forward several miles to a shallow crossing on the Green River. Young kneed his horse into the swift-flowing water and crossed without incident. The Rebel force camped that night in dank woods just north of Hammonville. They had ridden to just fifty miles south of Louisville.

The next morning, Morgan ordered Breckenridge to destroy the nearby Bacon Creek railroad bridge. The structure was situated just north of the small town of Munfordville and was defended by a handful of Yankee soldiers. Rebel artillerymen wheeled a captured Parrot gun into line, loaded and fired two rounds into the wooden bridge stockade, shattering wood in all directions. They fired several more shells, but still, the Yankee defenders refused to surrender.

A disgusted Morgan sent a flag of truce to the stockade to let the men know it was he and his raiders attacking them. Shortly after, one of the defenders tied a white flag to his rifle and shoved it out a window, waving in surrender.

Morgan's men captured a half dozen Yankee soldiers and burned the bridge and the stockade. His men tore up tracks and heated the rails over a series of hot fires and bent them, making them useless for making repairs once they'd left. Before moving on, the Rebels paroled their Yankee prisoners.

Young asked a corporal who'd been guarding the prisoners what parole meant. The corporal said that so far, neither the Confederate States nor the United States had prison camps large enough to hold the ever-increasing number of prisoners being taken, so captured men of one side would be held briefly then exchanged for an equal number of prisoners from the other side, providing they agreed not to return to the fight. Young wondered how many men on both sides would go back to the fight once paroled, regardless of what they'd promised.

The Confederates soon arrived at Elizabethtown, a small community on the Louisville and Nashville Railroad line. When he saw Morgan's men, the commander of the Union force in town sent a soldier out under a flag of truce. The soldier was brought into the Rebel lines and taken to Morgan, where he handed over a message written on the back of an envelope.

Elizabethtown, Ky., Dec. 27, 1862.
TO THE COMMANDER OF THE CONFEDERATE FORCES.
Sir, I demand unconditional surrender of all your forces. I have you surrounded, and will compel you to surrender. I am, sir, your obedient servant.
H. S. Smith, Commanding U. S. Forces

"We'll see who's surrounded," Morgan snorted, showing the note to his top commanders, who laughed derisively. He sent the Yankee courier back with a note demanding the Federal defenders surrender instead. Receiving no answer, he sent a second message and again Smith refused to surrender. Morgan sent a third message, offering the Yankees time to remove their women and children before the attack. After waiting for a reply and receiving none, he ordered the town shelled and attacked.

Some of Morgan's men had flanked the village and carefully worked their way in to the streets. By the time the two units met at the center of town, the Yankee defenders had thrown down their rifles and surrendered. Young watched as Yankee troops emerged from their positions, hands in the air. The Rebels had captured 652 Blue Bellies. Once their names, ranks and units were recorded by Morgan's men, the Yankees were paroled.

The prizes Morgan coveted lay only six miles ahead—two long trestles, one a thousand feet long, and the other 900 feet, both ninety feet high. They were considered the most valuable of all the bridges of the Louisville and Nashville Railroad. Because of that, both were heavily garrisoned with Yankee infantry ordered to make a last ditch stand.

The next morning, Morgan's brigades surrounded the two wooden trestles at Muldraugh's Hill and their stockades just north of town. They offered the Federal defenders a chance to surrender. The Yankees in one stockade came out with their hands in the air, but the other decided to fight it out. Morgan shelled them. Having had enough, the defenders waved white flags from the battered stockade and emerged with their hands up.

With their defenders under the control of Rebels, the bridges were torched. Soon, flames licked high and engulfed both structures. Watching the conflagration, Young marveled at how the flames grew. *This is worth all the misery, the days and nights since we left Tennessee behind us*, he thought.

Then he realized he had not yet killed a Yankee. Would he be able to pull the trigger and kill a man? Killing is against all he believed in, but this was war. He might have to. He tried not to think of it while he watched the flames consume the bridge.

Word filtered down that Morgan was more than satisfied with his men's work. It would be many months before the Federals could rebuild these bridges and restore service from Louisville to Nashville. Rosecrans's plans would be set back, giving Bragg time to deploy his army in Chattanooga.

The men had advanced 170 miles through enemy territory and had destroyed 2,300 feet of bridges. Now, Morgan had to get them safely back to Tennessee.

But it was getting late and the weather had turned colder, with the temperature dropping below freezing. The commander ordered his troops to bivouac for the night at the mouth of Beech Fork on the Rolling Fork River. The men covered themselves as best they could and shivered through the night.

"I hear the Yanks have got eight thousand men in Lebanon, just hankerin' to get at us," said Granger, huddled under his blanket and oil coat on the freezing ground. "Eight thousand to our two thousand."

"It's going to be a long trip home," Young agreed, pulling his blanket tighter around him. He wondered if the Yankees were regular Army troops who had faced fighting before or untrained militia. I don't think I want to meet any of them, he thought, shivering.

"If the ginrul is thinkin' of fightin' it out with that many Yankees...," another Raider, Charles Swager, said quietly, his voice trailing off. He groaned once and then lay quiet. During the night, a Rebel scout learned that Union Colonel John Harlan, who commanded a brigade of five infantry and cavalry regiments, was approaching their camp. Morgan rousted the men and they began crossing the swollen Rolling Fork River just before dawn.

Harlan's advance guard began shelling the rear of the Rebel column while Duke was helping the last of the men and their horses cross the river. Young and his company waited patiently for their turn. They saw Colonel Duke swing his horse around to survey the raiders crossing the stream when he was hit in the head by a tiny piece of exploding shell that swept him off his horse. Some of his men lifted Duke and placed his apparently lifeless body over the pommel of a horse and carried him across the strong current safely. They placed the colonel on the ground and watched over him while the rest of the men crossed.

As Glory emerged from the bitter cold river and scrambled up the bank, Young watched soldiers bundle Duke into a carriage and rush away. Young later learned from one of Duke's staff aides that the colonel was taken twenty miles northeast to Bardstown to the home of a friendly doctor, where he was placed on a pallet on the floor. Morgan's force followed.

The shell fragment had nipped of a small piece of Duke's skull behind his right ear. The colonel regained consciousness as the regimental surgeon sewed up his scalp. Young heard an aide say Duke gritted his teeth but didn't utter a word until after the surgery. When he did talk, he said only: "That was a close call."

The men around him heaved a sigh of relief. The surgeon ordered Duke to stay off his horse, so his men stole a buggy. With his head bandaged, Duke grumbled as he climbed into the buggy and lay on a feather mattress tucked under blankets. His head ached terribly, but he did as he was told: lie back as best he could. Word spread quickly to all the men in Morgan's command that the colonel was alive.

By mid-afternoon, Young and several scouts cautiously rode into Springfield, nine miles north of Lebanon. They found the town was not garrisoned by Yankees, but others scouted Lebanon, reporting back that several thousand Yankees were bivouacked there, and they heard that ten thousand or more were not far away.

As darkness fell and the temperature dropped even lower, Morgan ordered a forced march around Lebanon to avoid confronting the larger Federal forces.

While the main force skirted the town, Young joined Captain Quirk's scouts and two companies of the 2nd and 11th Regiments in a feint toward Lebanon, where they began driving the Yankee pickets into the garrison town.

Quirk ordered his men to stack fence rails and set them afire, fooling the Yankee troops into believing that Morgan's force was camped for the night and would attack at first light. But Morgan's brigade rode hard south toward Campbellsville, joined later by Quirk's scouts and the two companies. Young wondered what the Yankees thought when they attacked an empty "camp."

Trying to stave off the cold, some in Young's company wrapped cloth taken from stores in earlier raids around their throats. Others pulled their coats tight about their necks. Swager had caught cold and he shook as he rode next to Young and Granger.

"You hang on, Charles, we are going to make it back all right," Young said.

"I'm cold," Swager croaked.

"We all are, Charles," said Granger. "Here, take this and wrap it around your throat." He unwrapped a long scarf from around his neck and handed it to Swager. The brigade spent a dreary New Year's Eve camped outside the little town of Campbellsville. They were awakened at dawn and ordered to saddle up.

"I sure could use a cup of coffee," Granger moaned as he swung up into his saddle.

"Me, too," said Gregg, "even if it's chicory."

Young tried to keep his mind off such thoughts. What's the use. We don't have any coffee left and no time to build a fire and brew some even if we did. As they rode on many of the men dismounted and walked part of the way to keep their limbs from becoming frost-bitten. They stumbled along roads that had turned from mud to frozen clumps of sod.

The long column moved south, stopping only for thin rations and one more night of sleeping in the cold. They crossed into Tennessee on January 3rd, cold, miserable and nearly out of food. Their mounts were worn out.

When the weary cavalrymen had rested and refitted at camp in Smithville, thirty miles northeast of Murfreesboro, they learned there had been a second battle at Murfreesboro, which the Rebels called the Battle of Stones River. Union General Rosecrans's forces had repulsed two strong attacks by Confederate General Bragg, who was forced to withdraw, leaving Middle Tennessee under the control of the Yankees. They also learned that Lincoln had signed the Emancipation Proclamation, freeing the slaves.

CHAPTER 6

BACK at his base in Tennessee after the New Year, Morgan rested and refitted his command at Alexandria, thirty miles east of Nashville. Their Christmas raid, involving nearly a dozen clashes with Federals, had wrecked sixty miles of the Louisville and Nashville Railroad. They had captured and paroled 1,900 Yankee soldiers. Two of his men were killed, twenty-four wounded and sixty-four missing. They'd also stolen enough horses for every man who needed one to get a new mount.

Winter's grip gave way slowly, and the men enjoyed a warm spring of inaction, to recuperate and re-provision.

As the spring of 1863 faded, Young and the rest of his company learned that Morgan had received orders to invade Kentucky, to once again find and destroy railroad bridges. General Bragg's orders forbade Morgan from raiding outside Kentucky, but word swept through the lower ranks that Morgan was fed up with Bragg's timidity. He would disobey orders and invade Indiana and Ohio.

Morgan had sent a telegram to Bragg requesting permission to cross the Ohio River into Indiana. A few days later, an aide recounted what he'd overheard of events in a huddle with Colonel Duke. Morgan had sworn a blue streak when he read the telegram from Bragg.

"Damn his hide! He's refused me permission to cross the Ohio! While he retreats, he wants me to make a feint toward Louisville to cover his backside! Well, if this doesn't beat all!" The aide said Morgan had thrown the paper to the floor and stomped on it. Duke retrieved the crumpled telegram and read it.

"It says pretty plain what he wants us to do, John. You goin' to do it?" the aide mimicked Colonel Duke.

The aide gloried in telling what he had overheard. Stopping a few times to stretch it out, making his listeners urge him to go on, he said Morgan told Colonel Duke he'd do what General Bragg wanted, but when he was done, Morgan's raiders would cross the Ohio River and hit Indiana so hard, it wouldn't know what happened to it.

Hearing the news and uncertain that the aide had reported it correctly, Young walked off to be by himself. Morgan's a brave man, Young thought, staring at the night sky, but he's reckless. If invading Indiana is what he aims to do, we're in for a terrible time and it's going to cost us dearly.

But the planned raid was not to be.

Bragg telegraphed another order telling the young cavalry commander to ride into northeastern Tennessee, instead, to support General Buckner, who Bragg said was threatened by two large Yankee forces.

For Morgan and his troopers, this was a waste of time. For nearly three weeks, they rode east through the towns of Gainesboro and Livingston over poor roads that meandered through hilly and rocky terrain. They had little time to rest.

"Damn, Bennett," Gregg complained, "I'm so tired I fell asleep ridin'. We've got to get some rest pretty soon."

Young dug his heels into Glory's flanks to keep her moving.

"I know, Sam. I'm tired too."

He rubbed fatigue from his eyes and stretched his back as he rode. Is this what I signed up for, he wondered. I wish I knew what the top generals in this army were thinking. They sure would get a piece of my mind.

Morgan veered north into Albany, Kentucky, but he met only token resistance from Yankee forces. Nor was Buckner threatened. Intelligence Bragg had received was apparently wrong. The detour was costly for Morgan. His men and their horses were worn out, and much of the unit's food and supplies were used up. The Rebel raiders made their way westward again on narrow roads made slick by heavy rain. By nightfall on July 2nd, they camped at Monticello, Kentucky, about fifteen miles from the Tennessee border. The rain finally stopped.

Young, Gregg, and Granger were airing their gear to dry when a corporal came up.

"Granger, Young, and Gregg?" he asked. "You three are being transferred to Captain Tom Quirk's company as scouts."

"Well, this should be interesting," Young mused.

They quickly folded their clothing again, packed it in their blankets and reported to Quirk. There was little for them to do until Morgan received his new orders. The raid that had been called off so Morgan could assist Bruckner was on again. Morgan broke camp July 2nd, 1863, and he and his 2,460 men rode westward south of the Cumberland to Burkesville, Kentucky.

"I hear the Cumberland's flooded—half a mile wide in some places and flowing pretty fast," Quirk told Young and the others. "We need boats to get the wagons and supplies across. I want you boys to mount up and see what you can find upstream. And be careful. I'm told the river's covered with driftwood, some of it pretty big."

Young, Granger, and Gregg, along with six other scouts, cautiously rode a few miles north until they found half a dozen canoes at riverside.

"I've got an idea," Granger said, pointing to a long rail fence nearby. "We can take the fence apart and lash the rails to the canoes."

"Oh, you mean make them into floating platforms," Young said.

"That's right, I think we can make 'em strong enough to carry all the gear and the wagons, maybe even the Parrott guns and the howitzers, if they're broken down."

Young, Gregg, and the others began taking the fence apart. Using their Bowie knives, they cut hay and twisted the long grass together to use as ties to bind the fence posts together. Hours later, when they finished their backbreaking labor, they had put together three large platforms.

The scouts rode back to Quirk to report. Morgan brought his command upriver where horses and men could cross the swollen stream. Many of the troopers removed their clothing and held to their horses' manes or tails with one hand and to the canoe-rafts with the other, as they began the crossing.

Young nervously slipped out of his clothes and placed them and his carbine and cartridge pouch on one of the platforms. Luckily, the place they had chosen to cross was shallow enough to stand, so the men could push and pull the platforms and lead their horses across. Young and half the band had reached the far shore, when they heard someone shout, "Attack! Attack!"

A small Yankee force was upon them.

Young and a dozen other Rebels grabbed their carbines.

"Over there!" a Rebel shouted, motioning toward the riverbank to their right. Young snapped off a shot and watched the Federal troops duck. The other raiders joined in and charged the enemy, their Rebel yell echoing up and down the river.

"They're runnin!" Gregg shouted, firing after the fleeing troops.

The raiders waiting their turn to cross on the other side of the river whistled and shouted obscenities at their naked comrades on the far shore, who pulled on their pants and shirts as quickly as they could, taking the ribbing in good humor.

"I'm damned glad them Yanks didn't shoot low," one of them said.

The company heard that Morgan feared the Yankee patrol they had just scattered was part of General Frank Wolford's Kentucky Division, rumored to be nearby. But the Rebels met no further resistance as they advanced.

They were not as lucky as they rode north toward Tebbs Bend on the Green River at mid-afternoon July 3rd. Suddenly, they met stiff resistance from Union infantry. Quirk was hit in his left arm, the bullet shattering the humerus. Relieved of command, he was sent back to Burkesville for treatment, and Captain Tom Franks of the 2nd Kentucky was appointed to replace him.

After a hot fight, the Yankees withdrew and Morgan continued moving north. As daylight ebbed, Morgan knew his men needed rest, so he ordered them to camp overnight in the streets of the small town of Columbia. But there was no rest for Young, Granger and Gregg, who were sent to reconnoiter the Tebbs Bend Bridge at Green River.

They rode out in the dark of night. A few hundred yards south of a strip of land leading to the bridge, they heard the sound of axes and felling of trees. In the darkness, they couldn't make out how many Yankees were there or just what they were doing. Although the 25th Michigan, with 200 Union men, were outnumbered by Morgan's 2,460 rebels, they were determined to hold their position.

"Sounds like they're getting ready to welcome us," whispered Granger. The men led their mounts to a wooded rise and waited. The sound of chopping and trees falling continued throughout the rest of the night.

At dawn on July 4th, the advancing raiders saw what they had been hearing.

"Well, look at that!" Captain Franks said.

The Yankee soldiers were stacking trees into a breastwork, barring the way to the bridge. They had finished an abbatis, young trees tied side by side, their sharpened ends facing in the direction an enemy would approach, the points aimed waist high. Rifle pits and wire completed the defensive position.

The scouts rode back to Morgan to report the situation. Advancing to the same hill where the three scouts had spent the night, Morgan split his forces, sending most of his men to flank the garrison to cut off an avenue of retreat. He ordered his artillery contingent to fire one round into the breastworks. Its handful of defenders scampered back to their main group.

Young and the others watched as Morgan sent Lieutenant Joe Tucker forward under a flag of truce with a message for the Yankee commander demanding unconditional surrender.

Two blue-clad infantrymen escorted the Rebel before Colonel Orlando Moore, commander of the 25th Michigan Infantry, who read the note, smiled and told Tucker: "Lieutenant, if it was any other day, I might surrender, but on the Fourth of July, I must have a little brush first."

He wrote a note that Tucker took back to Morgan. It read: "It's a bad day for surrender and I would rather not."

Morgan reacted grimly. He directed a dismounted frontal attack. Colonel D.W. Chenault led his 11th Kentucky Regiment in a dash toward the breastworks, but Yankee fire decimated the attackers. When Chenault climbed the barricade, bullets ripped through his body, killing him instantly. The attack stalled and the Rebels retreated. Morgan ordered another attack. And another, sending his men eight times into the guns. Each with the same result.

Seeing the ground in front of the breastwork littered with his dead, Morgan hastily conferred with Colonel Duke, who seethed with anger. Those close to the two commanders heard Duke berate Morgan: "Dammit, John. What's got into you? We could have just bypassed 'em instead of this."

He pointed to the Confederate dead and wounded lying in front of the Federal defenses. Chastened, Morgan called off further attempts to breach the position.

"You're right, Basil. It was a mistake. I accept the blame."

His eyes reflecting the agony he felt, Morgan turned away from his second in command.

Under a flag of truce, he asked that he be allowed to retrieve his dead and wounded. The commander from Michigan granted the request. The Rebels suffered seventy-one men killed or wounded.

Watching as the dead and wounded were carried back, Young said quietly to Granger: "I'm glad I wasn't sent into that."

Granger nodded. Young wondered why his commander had attempted head-on attacks when he could have done as Colonel Duke suggested and skirted the position. Remembering what the aide had said about Morgan's plan to invade Indiana, Young feared his commander might really be losing his touch. He thrust the disturbing thought from his mind and tended to his horse.

CHAPTER 7

MORGAN'S men buried their dead companions and rejoined the rest of the column at a spot nearly a mile upstream where they crossed the river in ankle-deep water. Young, Granger, and five other scouts rode thirteen miles farther north to find out whether the town of Lebanon was garrisoned.

"They's about 500 soldiers just a'fore town and they got breastworks across the whole danged road," said a farmer they met on the road.

In an impressive show of his division's strength, Morgan lined his troops up in a long double column across the Campbellsville-Lebanon road, with his artillery in the center. He sent Lieutenant Colonel Robert Alston to the breastworks with a note demanding the commanding officer surrender, but the ranking Union officer, Lieutenant Colonel Charles Hanson, refused.

Word spread among Morgan's men that Hanson's 20th Kentucky Infantry regiment was protecting the town. Among the defenders were brothers and cousins of some of Morgan's troopers.

At mid-morning as the temperature rose into the high nineties, Morgan sent his messenger back to the town with another note. His hopes that the Yankees would surrender without a fight dashed, Morgan sadly wrote: "Remove your women and children. The town will be shelled."

With the courier back behind his line, Morgan ordered his artillery to fire on a brick railway depot where Hanson had concentrated his men. The shells exploded against the building shattering brick in all directions. Morgan decided the best action would be to send his men in. Along with the first wave of Rebels with the 8th Kentucky, Young rushed toward the town. Withering rifle fire pinned the regiment down in high grass fifty yards from the depot. Lying flat on his belly, Young gasped for air, sweat pouring off his face.

His heart leaped as he turned to see the men of the South's 2nd Kentucky, known for their street-fighting prowess, start moving in to join the action. At the sound of a bugler, the 2nd Kentucky attacked all the way to the depot, their Rebel yells piercing the air. Some drew their pistols and fired indiscriminately through windows, while others broke down doors and blasted their way into buildings. The Yankees quickly surrendered. As suddenly as the firing had started, a quiet settled over the town.

Morgan claimed another victory, but at a terrible personal cost. Just outside town, nineteen-year-old Lieutenant Tom Morgan, the general's younger brother, lay dead, his chest covered in blood. Tom had charged with the 2nd Kentucky's front line, cheering his comrades on when a Yankee bullet slammed into him.

While the surviving defenders were being identified for parole, the Morgan brothers buried Tom beside others killed during the attack. The battle cost Morgan forty killed or wounded. The Yankees lost three killed and sixteen wounded. Morgan took just over four hundred prisoners. They were paroled.

While the regiment awaited orders to continue with the rest of the Rebel divisions on a northward march, Young and Gregg saw Morgan walk away from his commanders to stand under a tree, alone. They watched as he took off his hat, bowed his head for a few moments, then stood erect and walked back to his men. Jauntily, he swept his hat back on his head and loudly declared he would feint toward Louisville and cross into Indiana, living off the land. He would carry the war farther north than any Confederate force had gone before.

The Rebels advanced twenty miles northwest, capturing Bardstown with little resistance. Three of the men and "Lightning" Ellsworth, Morgan's telegrapher, walked down Bardstown's Main Street to the Louisville and Nashville Railroad station. There, with guns pointed at him, the frightened local telegrapher handed over copies of telegrams telling that a major Yankee force was forming behind Morgan's column. Ellsworth estimated they were only twenty-four hours away. Among the messages was one reporting that Union forces were fortifying Louisville, fearing an attack by Morgan, and that hundreds of panicked residents had fled.

Morgan joined his men in the railroad station and instructed Ellsworth to pretend he was a Union telegrapher and send messages giving different headings for the raiders and increasing the size of Morgan's force to as much as 7,000.

To further confuse the Yankees, Morgan sent a small force as a feint toward the city. At the same time, he sent Young and Granger to scout for two companies he planned to send to the town of Brandenburg, Kentucky, on the Ohio River, where they'd look for a shallow place to cross. On the northern bank was Morgan's goal— Indiana. He was concerned that Brandenburg might be defended in force against possible Rebel incursions.

Before dawn on July 8th, the two companies and the scouts approached Brandenburg, stopping on a bluff overlooking the river. Light fog lay over the land and the river. Soon, the sun dispelled the milky haze and the town came into clear view. The scouts crept along the top of the bluff. Young whispered to his companion: "Looks pretty quiet.

"Doesn't look like any Yanks are down there," Granger said.

"No. Couple of men just went into a store. Looks like a bakery or something. I could use some fresh bread," Young said.

"Me, too. Let's just wait awhile, see if there are any Blue Bellies around."

They lay there for nearly half an hour as the sun rose higher, heralding another hot, muggy day. There were no signs of Yankee soldiers below them.

"Looks all right, I guess," said Granger. He and Young crept back to their own line.

"Very good," said Captain Harmon Turner, commander of one of the companies. "We'll take the town while you two ride back to General Morgan and tell him what we're doing."

At mid-morning, the two companies took Brandenburg without firing a shot. They captured a steamboat, the *John T.*

McCombs, and the mail boat, *Alice Dean,* and awaited the arrival of Morgan and the rest of his raiders.

Later, as Morgan ferried his army across the river aboard the captured boats, dozens of riflemen stepped out from behind haymows and houses on the Indiana side of the river and opened fire. The Rebels shouted taunts at the Yanks when they realized the Federal militia fire was ineffective. As Young's company waited their turn to cross, a field piece opened up from the opposite shore and a shell exploded near the wharf where a Rebel officer fell, severely wounded.

The first company of Morgan's men to reach the far shore quickly scattered the Yankees. In the midst of the movement, a gunboat came around a bend in the river. It was the Yankee river craft, *Elk,* on patrol. Its captain opened fire on the Rebels still crossing the stream, but from his Kentucky vantage point above the river, Morgan called in artillery fire on the *Elk.* Solid shot and bursting shells convinced the Yankee skipper to turn tail and steam back upstream toward Louisville.

Morgan brought the last of his men across the Ohio at midnight, turning a promise into reality. The first Confederates entered Indiana. But the surprise they'd hoped for was gone.

The raiders rode fifteen miles north toward the little town of Corydon. Out front of the brigade, Young and Granger spotted a dozen Yankee soldiers milling about. The scouts backed their horses into a row of trees beside the road and crept forward on foot. They observed little action among the Yankees up ahead.

Granger nudged Young.

"I think they're lollygaggin'," he whispered. "If they are pickets, I'd say they are doing a damned poor job of it. Must be local militia."

"Appears that way. Think there are any more around?"

"Don't know, but I'd guess if there are, they'd be up ahead near the town."

Young nodded. "Let's get out of here."

They crept back to their horses and quietly returned to the main body of troopers to report.

The main Rebel force approached Corydon about noon on the ninth and scattered the small group that Young and Granger had spied on, part of the same troop that had harassed them at Brandenburg. The Raiders pursued the Yankees toward town, but at the outskirts, they ran into a barricade of logs and fence rails placed across the road. Crouched behind were more Yankee militia.

Morgan ordered a mounted attack. Kneeling behind a tree, Young watched, amazed that the general would order an attack on horseback. Morgan usually favored having his men dismount and attack as infantry. The Rebel attackers ran into heavy rifle fire, a dozen or more men going down off their horses, dead or wounded.

Next to Young, Granger angrily muttered, "They can't jump the railings. It's slaughter."

Morgan and Duke conferred. They sent dozens of men to flank the barricade. Leaving their mounts behind, the men crept forward, and at a signal, they rose and rushed the town from the left and right, throwing the defenders into confusion. But more heavy rifle fire stalled the attack.

"These Yanks are tough," Granger said.

"They've regrouped. Must have some experience," Young said.

"Cover the company coming in from the other side of those trees," Granger advised, pointing to the left. When the Rebels emerged from the trees on the run, Young and the others lay down cover fire at the defenders. Young aimed at a blue uniform and pulled the trigger. The man fell backward as though hit by a blow from a fist. He crumpled to the ground. Young kept shooting, but his firing now was ineffective. Despite the adrenaline surging through him, he felt a stab of remorse.

My first Yankee. My first.

The Rebels surging in from the left stopped and hit the ground, their attack stymied. The Yankees were determined not to give up the town. Young looked around and saw two Rebel crews wheel their twelve-pound howitzers into place. They each fired once. One shell failed to explode but the other exploded on the town's main street, causing no damage. Still, fearing the Rebel guns could level the town, the Yankee commander, Colonel Lewis Jordan, finally surrendered the men of his 2nd Division, Indiana Legion.

But again victory was costly. Morgan lost sixteen men killed and thirty-three wounded. Angrily, some of his men virtually cleaned out the town, robbing the stores of bolts of calico, ice skates, women's hats and frocks. At gunpoint, some men forced the owners of the town's two mills to fork over $700 each.

Young and Granger sat under a tree beside a hotel where Morgan and a few of his officers took their places at a table in the hotel's dining room. Young lowered his head between his knees for a moment and then sat up, heaving a sigh.

Granger looked at him. "Are you all right Bennett?"

"Yes. Yes, I'm all right. I... just killed a man." He shuddered.

Granger put his hand on Young's shoulder. "Don't let it get you," he said. "It's always like this the first time."

"Yes. I knew this day would come and I wondered whether I could really kill someone. I did. Today. Oh, God."

At that moment, a waitress in the hotel dining room stood quivering, waiting for the Rebel officers to order. Young overheard her comment.

"General Morgan, I hear your General Lee has been defeated at the town of Gettysburg in Pennsylvania."

"What? What did you say, girl?"

"Our army beat Lee good and proper and he's retreating back to Virginia."

"Get me a newspaper," Morgan ordered one of his officers. A front-page report in the paper confirmed the girl's statement. Morgan threw the newspaper to the floor.

"This is bad news, gentlemen," he said. "I had hoped we could hook up with General Lee in Pennsylvania." He picked up the paper again.

"Look, here, this report says Grant has captured Vicksburg." Morgan stared out a window, the fingers of one hand twirling his mustache. He remained quiet for several minutes.

"All right," he said. "This changes things. It's time to leave. We will have to push on and find a river crossing somewhere. Let's go, gentlemen."

His subordinates groaned softly, knowing they might not get a solid meal for days.

CHAPTER 8

Young and Gregg were riding side by side when word came down the line that Morgan was going to invade Ohio, loop around Cincinnati, and race across the southern part of the state, still hoping to join General Lee in Pennsylvania. But Morgan had to get his men through this part of Indiana, marching a zigzag course northward and then eastward through nine other Northern towns.

Young soon began to feel the effects of the long days in the saddle, sometimes eighteen or nineteen hours. The Rebels met local militia in a few towns, but they beat them off as a duck would shed water. Still, the grueling schedule took its toll. Days after entering Indiana, Young's horse, Glory, gave out, stumbled, then fell. Young leaped from the saddle in time to escape injury.

He saw Glory's sides expand and collapse as she gasped for air, but her worn-out body could not rally. She looked up at Young, her eyes seeming to fade as he watched, and she died. He turned away, wiping a tear from his eye.

"I'm right sorry, Bennett," Gregg said, looking down at Glory from his saddle. "She was a good old girl."

Young said nothing as he cut the cinch with his bowie knife and tugged and pulled his saddle off Glory's inert body. He tenderly touched her head and turned to Gregg.

"Mount up behind me, Bennett," his friend said. "We'll see about gettin' you another horse."

Young loaded his saddle and blanket on a provision wagon, held his carbine in one hand, and Gregg pulled him up onto the saddle. Hours later, Young spotted a horse tethered behind a barn. He couldn't believe that some other trooper hadn't taken her. He found a cinch in a small barn nearby, saddled up, and fell in beside Gregg and Granger.

"Owner must have skedaddled when he heard we were comin'," Gregg said, chuckling. "Don't blame him."

The Rebels fought off feeble attempts by small militia forces hidden along the road who got off a few shots and then disappeared. The Raiders went through several small towns, deserted by their residents who feared they would be murdered in their houses by the Southern troops. But Morgan's provost marshals kept the men under tight control, though they overlooked some looting of shops. Looting food was allowed, but attacking innocent civilians could mean facing a firing squad.

In half a dozen towns, Young and the others in his company, like most of the entire troop, found easy pickings, stealing chickens from their coops. Some men captured pigs and slaughtered them. Others entered houses abandoned by their owners, helping themselves to food, some of it still warm on the stove. Others found freshly baked bread and shared it with their comrades.

Gregg and Granger emerged from a small white house north of Corydon with a baked chicken, a small pail of beans, and a handful of biscuits. Gregg ripped a leg off the chicken and handed it to Young.

"Oh! This is delicious!" Young exclaimed, savoring the first hot food he or any of the men had tasted in days. Squire Tevis extended the bucket and Young spooned out some beans and devoured two biscuits.

"Got any water?" he asked between bites.

"You're gonna have to get your own water, Bennett," Gregg said, but he was smiling.

Morgan's presence in Indiana had raised alarms in the upper levels of the Federal command, Lightning Ellsworth told Young and several others in Company B, taking his news directly from Union telegraphs he intercepted along their route. Ever since the Rebel Raiders had crossed the Ohio at Brandenburg, Union General Frank Wolford's 1st Kentuckians—known as the Wild Riders—were hot on their trail, Ellsworth said. The intercepted telegraph messages informed Morgan that other units had joined the chase.

Despite messages composed by Morgan and sent by Ellworth to confuse the Yankees, Wolford pursued Morgan's Raiders relentlessly. Still, Young, Gregg, Granger and the other scouts rode ahead time after time, reporting little or no Yankee opposition ahead of the main body.

Morgan's men swept through town after town in Indiana, emptying them of stores and supplies, ripping up rails and burning railroad cars as they went. In every town along the way, some of Morgan's men looted stores, and now the men wore linen coats taken off the backs of people or from shops in the towns they had passed through. One trooper, nearly six feet tall, wore a dressing robe and on his head, a large black sombrero with a long black feather suspended in a band. His black beard reached nearly to his waist and he sported an overgrown mustache to match.

Some had stolen calico and wrapped it around their bodies, others carried bird cages, and some wore ladies corsets around their waists. They looked more like a band of clowns out on a lark than a crack fighting force. Eventually, the Rebels grew weary of carrying the loot and tossed it away

Whenever they passed telegraph lines, Ellsworth tapped into them with his battery and sent more messages to confuse Federal authorities.

Young and Granger rode side by side.

"I swear, the general's got those Yanks so confused, they're goin' round in circles wonderin' where we are at," said Granger.

Young nodded, but he wasn't convinced. "I sure would feel better if we were back in old Kentucky."

In fact, Wolford was slowly closing the distance between his Federal troops and Morgan's Rebels.

As mid-day on July 13th approached, advance Rebel units crossed into Ohio at Harrison, a small, picturesque town northeast of Cincinnati. They were the first Confederate troops to enter that state, as well.

"Lightning" Ellsworth intercepted a telegraph message saying that General James Shackleford's cavalry had joined Wolford's Wild Riders. Cavalry units from Illinois, Indiana, Ohio, and Michigan were sent to cut the Rebels off. But Morgan's ingenuity saved him again. Within an hour he saw all his men safely across the Whitewater suspension bridge in Harrison and ordered it set ablaze.

To further stymie his enemy, he cut the telegraph wires. As Wolford's cavalry pounded down a hill just west of town, they saw flames and heavy smoke pouring from the bridge. They also saw a long line of Rebels headed away from them to the east. The frustrated Federal commander shouted epithets at the backs of the retreating soldiers, but he had to find another way across the stream.

The raid that Morgan had so hoped for, and all chances of joining General Lee, had degenerated into a race for survival.

Morgan's inventive telegrapher intercepted more Yankee messages and passed on word to the Rebel general that more than 100,000 home guards from four states were soon to join the chase. Several times, Morgan split his command, sending companies off in different directions to confuse Union commanders.

At one point, Young and Granger were chosen to join a dozen other scouts for a feint toward the town of Hamilton north of Cincinnati, while the main body turned south toward the city. As he approached Cincinnati from the north, even though Morgan ordered the telegraph lines cut, he knew news of his presence on the outskirts of the river city would spread by word of mouth. Panicked citizens and Union military commanders would call frantically for more troops.

"I'll bet the general ain't the least interested in getting bogged down in street-by-street warfare," Granger said.

Morgan reunited his forces and made a giant eastward loop around the city. He hoped to ride directly east 150 miles to safety in western Virginia. Little did he know that a large section of Virginia had split off to become West Virginia. Loyal to the Union, it eventually became the thirty-fifth state.

The Rebels rode eastward day and night, stopping only briefly to rest and water their horses. Some men, exhausted, fell asleep while they rode. Dozens fell from their mounts, others tied themselves to their saddles. Unlike in the Blue Grass country of Kentucky, where prize Thoroughbreds were found by the hundreds, Ohio's farms relied on ungainly, overfed workhorses. The draft horses the raiders had stolen in various towns along the way were not fit for cavalry duty, and the rigors of a long march across Ohio were too much for them. Many died, dumping their riders in the dust.

Young's horse collapsed under him just before nightfall on July 15th, as the column rode through the prosperous little town of Batavia. He managed to leap free of the falling beast, twisting his ankle as he landed in the dirt.

"You all right, Bennett?" Granger called to Young, who sat beside the road rubbing his ankle.

"I think so. My foot caught in the stirrup and I couldn't get it loose."

Granger dismounted and helped Young to his feet.

"Use my horse," the corporal said.

"Thank you, but I think I can walk on it all right."

Despite the pain, Young walked with the advancing column eight miles to an area west of Williamsburg before Morgan's foragers rejoined the column with twenty fresh horses in tow. Young got one of them.

Morgan finally halted the column, its men exhausted, its horses barely able to walk. They had covered twenty-eight miles. Along that distance, they had derailed a train and captured 300 recruits who tumbled from the cars, some injured badly. Unable to feed them, the Rebels listed their names and sent them off to nearby Camp Denison on parole.

Once again, Young and Granger were sent out with other scouts under Captain Thomas Hines's command, this time riding south toward the Ohio River to find a crossing into Kentucky. They covered twenty miles as fast as their mounts could carry them. When they reached the Ohio River, they glumly saw the water rushing by, nearly bank-full. There would be no crossing here.

"Might as well get back," muttered Captain Hines.

"Must be raining 'way east of here," Young said. "Otherwise, where's all that water coming from?"

Hines agreed. "Mount up, men, let's go back."

Through the sweltering days and stifling nights the Rebel column went on, losing men through exhaustion or illness. Duke reported to Morgan and said he was not certain just how many of his men remained. At every stop for rest, the gunners worked on their pieces, trying in vain to clear fouling from the barrels. Morgan rode ceaselessly back and forth along the column, encouraging his men to keep moving, assuring them safety was only days away.

Unknown to the General, the Yankee cavalry regiments pursuing him had gained ground. After passing through Jasper on July 16th, Morgan ordered another all-night march. Forty-five exhausting miles later, harassed by Yankee militia who sniped at them from concealed positions in woods, the column passed through Jackson, about fifty miles short of Portland, Ohio, and a river crossing at Buffington Island.

Here Morgan split his command again to confuse the pursuing Yankees. Duke led a large group north, and Colonel Adam Johnson went south. Meeting little resistance, the two separate commands regrouped after midnight on July 17th, west of Rutland.

Just after 1 p.m. the following day, the raiders stopped at Chester, eighteen miles from Pomeroy, on the banks of the Ohio. The long journey under constant sniping from militia and regular Union cavalry had stretched Morgan's column out for more than a mile. Many of the horses had collapsed along the way, and their riders were now walking, some falling to the ground from exhaustion, unable to go another step.

Advance Rebel units subdued Chester by about one o'clock in the afternoon. Morgan rode back and forth along the line of his strung-out command, encouraging them onward. Once they'd regrouped, Morgan ordered a two-hour rest. Young and his comrades wearily fell to the ground, thankful for at least a brief respite.

Morgan sent scouts out again, this time to find the best ford across the river. Although his bones ached and his eyes were heavy from lack of sleep, Young rode with the other scouts toward Pomeroy, about seven miles away. The nearby river was still at flood stage. Hours later, they rejoined the brigade, still waiting at Chester. The general stood by his horse as Young approached.

"How does it look, son?" Morgan's face was drawn with fatigue, but he still seemed alert and ready for a fight.

"I'm afraid the river is too high to cross at Pomeroy, sir," Young said wearily. "It is pretty well guarded, too." Morgan was displeased.

"What do you think? Should we push on toward Buffington Island?"

"Well, sir, if the water is high at Pomeroy, it most likely is just as high at Buffington, Island."

"All right. Thank you, son." Morgan turned to Duke, who, without a word from his general, waved the column forward. Young rode along, desperately wanting to lie down on the soft ground and surrender to sleep. Granger and Gregg rode along with him, their eyes heavy with exhaustion, silently pushing their bodies beyond limits they thought they could endure.

Now, as they approached Pomeroy, part of General Henry Judah's Yankee cavalry attacked. Judah's troops had been rushed upriver by boat in an attempt to cut Morgan off, but Morgan's carbines beat off the attack, and the column moved on, protected by hills on both sides of the road.

The main van of Raiders made it to Portland, adjacent to Buffington Island, where they planned to cross the river. A heavy fog shrouded the area. Morgan had occasionally conscripted locals to travel with the column to serve as guides, but he had none with him now, and without their help, he feared crossing the rushing water at night. He was especially concerned about how he would get nearly 200 wounded men to the far side in the blackness.

Duke conferred with Morgan and placed the 5th and 6th Kentucky regiments into position to attack a redoubt that commanded a defensive position over the ford. From civilians living nearby, Duke learned that 300 Yankee infantry with two artillery pieces had manned the redoubt. Morgan decided to wait until morning, when he hoped visibility would improve and make it easier to dispose of the Yankee defenders.

Fog still shrouded the river as dawn broke on Sunday, July 19th. The men of the two regiments crept forward to capture the redoubt only to find it abandoned, its two cannon lying upended below a bluff where the retreating defenders had pushed them. The Rebels cautiously pressed on to reconnoiter. As Morgan brought the rest of his command up, the fog rapidly dispersed as if an invisible breath had been exhaled across the valley. Now, the Rebels could see their situation and Young knew the division was in mortal danger.

With no warning, musket fire raked the entire division from behind and from atop a bluff to their left. Judah's 24-pound-guns were mounted on two boats, the *Moose* and *Imperial,* and they weighed in, shells exploding among Morgan's men, killing and wounding dozens. Morgan realized that the Union cavalry, led by

Generals James Shackleton and Edward Hobson, had finally caught up with him after the long chase across Ohio.

Murderous fire now spewed at them from three sides. This was not a place Morgan wanted to be. His exhausted men bravely fought back, but they were out-manned and out-gunned.

The Ohio River runs nearly north and south at Buffington, and the valley the Rebels found themselves in was about a mile long, with the widest point some 800 yards across at the southern end. Toward the north, the bluff angled close to the riverbank, leaving passage there through a narrow ravine.

Disembarked from their boats, Judah's entire force poured into the valley. Duke beat off one charge, but the Yankees regrouped and charged again.

Young and the men around him in the open field fired as fast as they could load, while smoke from their carbines partially obscured the advancing Yankees. Some fell, but Young was not certain if his shots were telling.

Yankee artillery shells exploded among the Rebels, lifting men up off the ground, some with limbs and heads sheared off. Frightened by the noise of the shelling and the intense rifle fire, horses reared, kicked, and ran around aimlessly, further endangering the Rebels. Other horses lay dead or dying on the field.

"Fall back! Fall back! Up the Valley!" came the cry from Young's left. He and Granger pulled back with the others, fleeing from the enemy whose advance seemed unstoppable.

Young's legs felt as heavy as posts. He looked around to see if he could spot Gregg, but in the confusion and the smoke, his friend was nowhere in sight. Young remained on his feet, keeping in line, helping to prevent the Yankees from flanking and gunning them down from another angle.

Like angry hornets, bullets zipped past him. Men down the line screamed and fell. His mind raced with thoughts he could not control. *Is this the end? Am I going to die here?* He reached for more cartridges. His fingers touched the last two. All along the line of retreat, firing dwindled as others in Morgan's command ran out of ammunition.

Closer to the bluff, the other Rebel companies were under heavy rifle and artillery fire from up the hill and from the gunboats on the river, now joined by a third, the *Allegheny Belle*. Exploding shells continued to take a heavy toll. Minnie balls whistled a tune of death through the air. Gray clad men fell in twisted heaps, their glory days over.

The numerous skirmishes and fights the Rebels had undergone as they fought their way across Ohio had depleted their ammunition. Their artillery lacked shells and the cannon bores were so clogged with powder residue they might have exploded had the guns been fired. The fatigue of the long and hazardous trek from Cincinnati to Buffington Island had taken a final toll on the men.

Heavy Yankee rifle fire from the bluffs cut down more of the beleaguered Rebels, and Judah's men charged across nearly level ground. Yankees manning the heavy artillery on the boats fired as rapidly as they could.

With enough ammunition, the Rebels might have stemmed the Yankee attack, as desperate as their situation was, but the end was inevitable. Young fired his last cartridge and ran, crouching, with the survivors of his company toward a depression in the field ahead. They fell into it and lay low. Unknown to the mass of Raiders, Morgan and Duke had hastily conferred, their horses close to each other despite the danger all around them. Duke urged Morgan to retreat up the valley with whatever men he could gather, while Duke fought a rear-guard action.

"No! I won't leave my men," Morgan shouted angrily.

"John, it's all over! You've got to get out of here! Take as many men as you can and go up the valley!" Duke shouted in return. Morgan surveyed the battle scene. He knew Duke was right, as usual.

He ordered five of his company commanders to round up what men they could and follow him. Under fire, the Rebel officers rounded up nearly 1100 men from different regiments. Young was among them.

The men leaped into their saddles and charged up the remaining quarter mile of the valley under heavy rifle and artillery fire from two sides. They squeezed through the narrow passage at the end of the valley, just over a thousand men making their escape.

Duke watched as his commander fled away from the carnage. Shot and shell still rained on the remaining Rebels. Duke hailed a nearby trooper and sent him with a white flag tied to his gun barrel to the nearest Yankee force—the 7th Ohio Cavalry. Seeing the white flag, the Yankee fire lessened, then became sporadic and finally stopped..

For a few seconds, the sudden quiet startled the men, but the moans and screams of the wounded shattered the silence. Smoke gradually drifted away and the commander sent an escort headed by a junior officer to accept Duke's surrender. The time was approaching 7 a.m. The battle was over. The famous raiders were defeated, their 1100-mile raid from Tennessee into Kentucky, Indiana, and Ohio over forty-six weary and danger-filled days was at an end.

Along with hundreds of Morgan's men seeking an escape, Young galloped north, rounding a wide bend in the Ohio River, searching for another way across.

Chased by Yankee Generals Shackleford and Wolford, Morgan and his diminished command stopped at a narrow part of the river. Bellevue, West Virginia, lay on the opposite shore.

Morgan ordered Colonel Adam Johnson to take the first group across, four abreast, despite the high water. Just as the first Rebels reached the far side, the Yankee gunboat *Moose* hove into view downstream. Young watched helplessly as the Yankee gunners shelled his comrades in midstream. Plumes of water erupted as the shells hit in the midst of them, killing and wounding many. Some of the wounded, screaming in pain, slid down into the water to die of their wounds or drown.

Young shuddered as he saw bodies float away. Still waiting his turn in the column, he saw Morgan knee his horse into the river, encouraging his men to keep moving. A shell exploded near the commander and he turned his horse back to the Ohio shore. Despite urging by some of his men to escape while he had a chance, Young was filled with pride to see Morgan return to his men.

Morgan surely knew his remaining command might soon be surrounded with their backs to the river. He saw a group of low hills and drove his men toward them. Young was placed with Colonel Roy Cluke's command, ordered to gather as much dry firewood as they could. After night fell, Morgan told them to light dozens of large campfires and then, with his men in columns of two, they rode away into the night.

The Yankees surrounded the fires, and as dawn broke they attacked, expecting this to be Morgan's final battle. But the wily Rebel leader had steered his men west away from the river, through unsettled hills and valleys.

Dozens of men now fell asleep in the saddle or dropped off their horses to sit on the ground, refusing to go farther. Morgan rode up and down the column, urging the men on. They reached the town of Zaleski, thirty-five miles west of the Ohio River, early on the morning of the 22nd. The Confederates poured through the town, panicking the residents, who locked their doors and hid in their cellars.

The Rebels turned northeastward, crossing the Muskingum River near Eagleport after a brief skirmish with Shackleford's cavalry, but Wolford placed his men across the Rebels' path in the low hills beyond Muskingum. Morgan veered away but the Yankees captured more than 100, leaving Morgan with only about 700 tired men, some still mounted, but others afoot. Exhausted, dog-tired, his horse stumbling occasionally, Young wondered how long it would be before Morgan's luck would run out, and his own with it.

Next morning, the 24th, they learned from a farmer near Cambridge of a ford called Coxe's Riffle, near Stubenville. The remaining Rebels rode as hard as they could through Harrisville and Smifhfield, stopping to rest at Wintersville only five miles from the Ohio River. Morgan sent two scouts out to find the main Yankee force. They returned after a few hours and reported that a large force believed to be Shackelford's and Wolford's cavalry was moving toward them from the south. Morgan ordered his men back into the saddle again.

In Wintersville, they stole food from a store and then changed course, heading northwest to Richmond instead of Stubenville on the Ohio. The fleeing Rebels ate what they could in the saddle.

His hunger assuaged, but near exhaustion, Young wanted only to stop and lie down to sleep, but he doggedly rode on. Hours later, Morgan's legendary luck returned, if only briefly, when a group of militia, thinking the Yankee cavalry were Rebels, fired on them. The blunder cost the Yankees an hour, allowing the Confederates to escape again. But dozens of the fleeing Confederates who were on foot stopped walking, sat down, and fell asleep, not caring if they were captured.

Their ranks thinned to about 600 men, many exhausted and running out of ammunition, the Rebels fought scattered skirmishes with Yankee militia as they pushed on toward Salineville. Nearing the town, the Rebels fought a running battle with troopers from the Union 9th Michigan Cavalry, losing 200 more men. With his once-proud command now reduced to fewer than 400 men, Morgan ran into a small group of home guardsmen headquartered in Lisbon, Ohio.

Young watched from his exhausted horse as Morgan sent a trooper with a white flag of truce to the guardsmen, promising not to attack if they let him and his men through peacefully. The guardsmen agreed.

On the way across, Young and many of the others saw the dust of a large force off to their right in a nearby valley. Morgan sat quietly on his horse for a few minutes, surveyed his remaining men, worn out and nearly out of ammunition. Young overheard him ask the commander of the guardsmen if he would accept his surrender.

Surprised, the officer, James Burdick, accepted but asked: "Under what conditions?"

"On the condition my officers and men be paroled to home," Morgan replied. Burdick stammered. He did not understand the situation, not being a regular Army officer.

"I have a right to surrender to anyone," Morgan insisted, demanding an answer.

"Yes," Burdick replied.

It was 2 o'clock in the afternoon of July 26 when Morgan tied a white handkerchief to a riding stick that Burdick was holding and told the Yankee guardsmen commander to ride with two of his own officers and inform the regular Federal troops that Morgan had surrendered.

Yankee Colonel George W. Rue rode his horse carefully through the surrounded Rebels sitting and lying on the ground until he reached Morgan and several of his officers. Morgan told him he had already surrendered. Rue said nothing, but Young could see the Yankee officer felt cheated out of capturing the infamous Rebel leader and his men.

The Yankees disarmed the 364 Rebels and corralled 400 horses. Young handed his carbine and his horse's reins to one of the regular Yankee troopers and slumped in the shade of a tree with other Raiders to await developments. He tried to swallow, but dust had cloaked his throat. He yearned for water. *It's over*, he thought wearily. *Now we're prisoners, and who knows where we will be sent, to what prison.* He tried swallowing again, but only gagged.

A Yankee sergeant walked by, his bayoneted rifle at the ready.

"Well, you got us, Yank," Young said, his body sagging from exhaustion. "Gave us quite a chase you did."

The Federal sergeant scowled.

"Shut your stinkin' mouth, Reb, and fall in with the others over there." Young rose wearily and walked to a group of prisoners.

"Are the wounded being given treatment, Sergeant?" he asked another Yankee.

"They will be, soon's we can," was the curt reply. Young and his comrades sat sweltering in the sun for what seemed like hours. Finally, Yankee water wagons arrived and the captives had their first drink since earlier that morning. Young gulped water from a tin cup. It tasted like ambrosia. He was grateful to be alive.

Although the Indiana-Ohio raid was a disaster for Morgan's Raiders, its results were far-reaching. Union General Ambrose Burnside had been forced to split off thousands of his troops to chase Morgan, delaying his movement on Chattanooga to join General William Rosecrans. That delay was a major contributor to Bragg's winning the battle of Chickamauga in September, the only major Confederate victory in the West.

Morgan had destroyed an estimated ten million dollars in federal military stores, equipment, telegraph lines, and railroads. He inflicted more than five hundred casualties and captured some six thousand Yankee soldiers, paroling all of them.

But for Young and his comrades who had survived, their grand adventure was over.

PART TWO

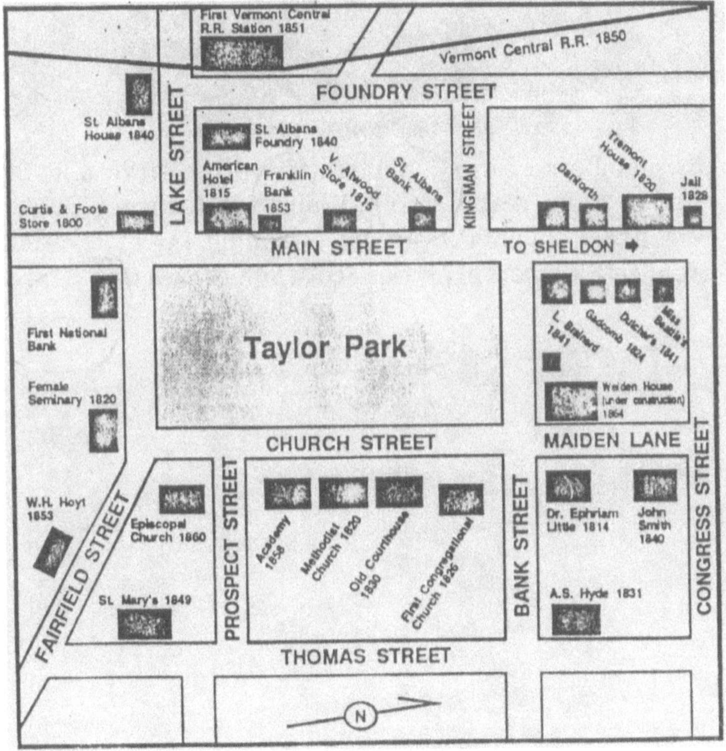

Map of Downtown St. Albans, 1864

Six members of the Confederacy's secret service, at the time of trial: (seated, l to r) William Hutchinson, George N. Sanders, Bennett H. Young. (standing, l to r) Reverend Stephen F. Cameron, George Scott, Squire Tevis.

Captain George Conger

Ann Eliza Brainerd Smith
(from James Murphy)

The Tremont House

Looking north on Main Street in the direction the raiders took to escape. The Brainerd Building is on the corner of Bank Street and Main.

The Sheldon Bridge (since replaced) that was said to have been burned as the Rebels fled to Canada.

Frank Leslie's Illustrated sketch of the interior of the St. Albans Bank, the teller being confronted by Young's raiders. There may have been fewer raiders in this particular bank, in reality. (image on book cover)

Photos provided courtesy of the
St. Albans Historical Society and Museum

CHAPTER 9

MORGAN was imprisoned in Columbus, Ohio, but Young and his fellow captives were marched under heavy guard along the Ohio River to a levee where they were to be put on boats and taken to other compounds. The men would not be paroled. That system was abandoned by both sides. They'd found that men taken in battle and paroled were rejoining the fight, just as Young suspected when he first learned of the practice.

They were a sight that amazed and delighted the Ohioans, who had gathered to watch the Rebel prisoners embark. Some of the onlookers hooted and hurled invectives as the newly captured prisoners shuffled aboard in their ragged uniforms.

"Kill the murderin' scum!"

"Shoot 'em all. Kill 'um!"

Some threw rocks that hit several Rebels until guards shooed the crowd away with bayonets affixed to their rifles.

Young and the other enlisted men were taken to Cincinnati, but only for a short time. They were marched under heavy guard to the railroad station where a train made up mostly of empty cattle cars awaited to take them nearly 100 miles to Camp Morton in Indianapolis.

"Looks like we'll be ridin' all over the country," Young grumbled to no one in particular as the crowded train slowly made its way out of Cincinnati.

By the time they arrived at Indianapolis, nearly a dozen of Morgan's men had died of their injuries. The wounded who could still walk were helped down from the boxcars by their comrades and were told to line up in columns of two, heavily guarded by Yankee troops. They marched slowly north through the city to the prison camp, a former fairground and Yankee Army training camp. Now it was overcrowded with Rebel prisoners, some held captive there since the fall of Forts Henry and Donelson in 1862.

Young entered the gate and took in the scene. Thousands of Rebel prisoners in ragged uniforms milled about in front of several long barracks. An overwhelming odor filled his nostrils and it wasn't long before Young discovered the source. Latrines had been dug, used, filled, and replaced with more latrines all over the area of the camp.

None of the prisoners seemed to pay any attention to the stench.

"They've been here a long time," Young muttered, nearly retching.

Inside the barracks, he discovered there were no empty bunks and was told to sit wherever he could find space on the wooden floor. Few of the men lying or sitting on the bunks bothered to look at the newcomers. Young saw one prisoner supporting the head of another, prompting the weaker man to sip some water. The reclining man's emaciated body told Young he would not survive much longer.

Early in the morning a couple of days later, two guards came in bearing a stretcher. They went to the bunk where the prisoner who had been given water lay, unmoving. The guards grabbed the body by the arms and legs, placed it on the stretcher, and carried it away. Young stared after them.

How many times have they done this? he wondered. That could be me one day.

Young walked outside. A line had been drawn around the inside perimeter of the camp, and when Young first settled in, he had asked another prisoner what the line was for.

"It's the deadline." The prisoner spat the words "Cross that line and them guards up there will shoot you dead."

Within minutes, another prisoner, bent over from malnutrition, his cheeks gaunt and eyes wild, had stumbled toward the line.

"No more! No more! No more!" he screamed as he crossed over. A guard raised his rifle and shot him. The Rebel crumpled to the ground where his legs twitched for a few moments before he became still.

"Bastard!"

"Murderer!"

The prisoners shouted and shook their fists. Other guards raised rifles and pointed them toward the men, who soon turned away.

Young and the other men from Morgan's group remained at Camp Morton for weeks before they were transferred. One cloudy morning they were ordered to gather their few possessions and line up outside the barracks. Several hundred men were marched to a nearby railhead under heavy guard. There, they boarded cattle cars for the long ride north to Camp Douglas in Chicago, another dreaded prisoner of war camp.

The Yankee guards did not feed the men aboard the train, although they were allowed to keep their tin cups, plates, knives and forks. As the train rumbled north, the men remained silent, worried about what awaited them. They had heard rumors that the Chicago camp was worse than Camp Morton.

Young closed his eyes, but sleep escaped him. Once during the trip, the train stopped and the doors opened. Guards handed salt beef and water up to the prisoners while other guards stood ready, bayonets affixed to their rifles. Once fed, the men were locked inside the cars again, and the train slowly picked up speed. Young sat leaning against the rough boards of his rail car and chewed the salty beef, swallowing it with sips from his tin cup.

Finally, the train slowed, lurched, and came to rest. Surly guards opened the cattle car doors. Young heard a snarl: "All right, Rebs, off the train."

Young looked out to see a long wooden fence. A short distance away, three soldiers with rifles and bayonets guarded the only gate through, and armed soldiers in blue walked along a parapet atop the fence.

Camp Douglas was a sixty-acre camp, located on the east side of Chicago near Lake Michigan. It was built on land donated by Senator Stephen A. Douglas, who had debated Lincoln over the slavery issue and lost the 1860 presidential election to him.

The prison had been a training camp for Union soldiers, as Camp Morton had been, but as the war progressed it was no longer the neat, well-kept place it once was. Now it was jammed with nearly 12,000 Confederate soldiers, heavily guarded.

Stiff after their long ride, the prisoners jumped to the ground, their utensils clanking.

"There's no place like home," Young cracked to a guard, who aimed a rifle at him in response. Young shuddered.

"Shut yer mouth," the guard snarled, motioning Young to follow the others through the gate. A guard detail marched the prisoners to one of several wooden barracks that stood in long rows inside the compound. It was a fenced city within a city. Inside the barracks, the walls were lined with narrow three-story bunk beds. On some of the bunks lay men, shrunken and half naked in the warm weather.

Young vowed he wouldn't be kept a prisoner long in this hellhole. That same night, he and several other prisoners crowded together to talk of escape.

"We have to get the lay of the land first," said Young. "If we want to get out of here, we have to plan carefully. We need to know the routines of the guards, when they come and go, when they order the lamps out, where the weakest spot in the wall is. We need to know how the food is delivered to the camp. We can't botch this, boys, or we will be here for the rest of the war. We could die here."

"We'll find a way sooner or later," another prisoner vowed.

As the days wore on, Young joined some of the healthier prisoners and spooned rations of watery soup into the mouths of sicker men. The Rebels sat by their comrades to comfort them in their final hours. Many died silently, separated from their homes and their families, alone within themselves.

Camp officials recorded every death as each day saw bodies being carried out of barracks throughout the camp. The death toll would grow to the thousands before the war ended.

Young and the men in his barracks watched and waited for any weaknesses in the Yankee routine that would allow them to escape. Alamanda Bruce found that weakness.

Once a week, a flour deliveryman carried 100-pound bags of flour into a storage building inside the prison where Bruce was working. On the return trip to his wagon, the man would carry an armful of empty bags and then repeat the process.

Bruce hid behind a pile of flour sacks, and as the deliveryman passed him to retrieve the empty bags, Bruce stole out to the wagon, covered himself with empty sacks, and rode out of the prison to freedom.

Guards discovered the prisoner gone when they counted heads the next morning and thereafter checked under the empty cloth bags as each wagon left the prison. Young hoped the sloppy guard had gotten his due after Bruce escaped.

One warm night, the prisoners were awakened by gunshots nearby. When Young peered outside, he saw guards carrying five bodies back into the camp. Men in an adjoining barracks had dug a tunnel under the perimeter fence, but when they emerged from their hole in an adjoining field, guards were waiting for them. When the prisoners started to run they were shot dead.

Although images of his slain countryman were hard to dispel from his thoughts, Young was not deterred. Several prisoners had begun another tunnel and he joined them, digging with rudimentary tools toward the wall. Weeks later, they estimated they were beyond the wall, and they dug upward.

The dirt roof over their heads collapsed on top of them and four diggers pushed through to emerge from the tunnel only to face rifles aimed at their heads. The guards had been tipped off.

Young emerged, and like the others, was immediately put in irons and returned to the camp. He was placed in solitary confinement where he received only one meal a day and a half bottle of water. He was barely able to sleep on the metal bed, only five feet long, its mattress thin, lumpy, and infested with fleas. Despite the size of the cell, eight feet by ten feet, Young managed to walk back and forth and get some exercise by bending and squatting.

Day after day, he sat on the dirt floor of the cell. If I stay here much longer I'm going to lose my strength, he thought, and that's been the beginning of the end for so many of my comrades.

Finally, after five days in solitary, guards opened his cell door. Light flooded in, and he threw his arm across his eyes to shut out the glare.

"All right, Reb. Come on out of there."

Young pulled himself up from the wooden floor and staggered out of the cell. The guards half-carried him back to his barracks where his friends greeted him.

One of them helped Young over to a bunk.

"I'm all right," he said. "Kind of weak, but don't worry, I'll get stronger."

Another prisoner handed him a biscuit that he'd hoarded. Young wolfed it down and guzzled a cup of water. As the days passed, he slowly regained some strength, exercising and eating the camp's rancid food.

He knew it would be impossible for any future mass escapes to succeed, so Young turned his thoughts to a possible nighttime escape, one prisoner at a time. But the camp's curfew kept prisoners confined to their barracks after eight o'clock in the evening. That night, after guards completed muster to count prisoners, Young whispered to his bunk mates.

"We can't try for a mass breakout again."

They agreed.

"We'll all be killed," one said. "You were lucky they didn't shoot you when you came up out of that tunnel, Bennett."

"Lucky," Young shuddered. "We'll have to make our escape one man at a time."

"What do you have in mind?" his comrade asked.

"I have latrine duty tomorrow. I have an idea that might work."

Young explained his plan.

"But, I'll gladly switch latrine duty with any of you," he said. They all shook their heads. Young should go.

The next day, as Young was cleaning the latrines alone, a deliveryman entered the building. He gave the prisoner a cursory glance, and standing at the urine trough, began unbuttoning his pants. Young took advantage of the moment to overcome him, take off his coat and hat, and drag him into a small closet at the far end of the building.

Fearing the man might cry out, Young gagged him with a strip of rag he found in the closet.

"I'm really sorry to inconvenience you this way, my Yankee friend," Young said. "But I need that coat and hat more than you do."

The man shuddered, fearing he might be killed. He tried to yell, but the gag across his mouth muffled the sound.

"Don't worry," Young assured him. "I'm not going to kill you. We're soldiers, not murderers."

The man nodded his head rapidly, as though he agreed with the Rebel prisoner. Young locked him in the closet and donned the man's coat, pulled the hat down over his face, and left the building. He climbed up to the wagon seat and drove toward the gate.

With steady nerves, Young turned his face away from the guard as he approached. Busy unwrapping a package of hardtack he planned to eat with his steaming coffee, the guard glanced only briefly at the approaching merchant. Recognizing the man's battered hat and coat, he grunted, "Pass."

Young held his breath and drove through the gate.

CHAPTER 10

WHILE in Camp Douglas, Young learned that Chicagoans sympathetic to the South had helped hundreds of escaped prisoners travel safely to Canada, and he heard of an address where he could shelter until it was time to move on. He drove the wagon northward taking it slow to allay suspicion.

Once out of sight of the prison, he abandoned the horse and wagon and walked away, leisurely at first and then, certain that he was not being followed, he quickened his pace. He made his way for twenty blocks, stopping at a house whose number he had memorized. Young and the other prisoners had been briefed on how to get to safe houses, based on information smuggled into the prison.

He knocked on the front door and waited. The door opened and a middle-aged woman looked him over suspiciously.

"Yes?" she asked.

"May a hungry wanderer enter?" Young said, using the code words the prisoners were told to use if they were lucky enough to escape.

"It is a cold and bitter day," the woman replied, watching Young carefully.

"It is that. But Spring cannot be long now," replied Young, completing the greeting.

Satisfied that Young was not a soldier or policeman, the woman stood aside to let him enter. She glanced quickly up and down the street, then shut the door and locked it. The warmth of a coal fire in the fireplace swept over Young.

"Warm yourself there for a few minutes," the woman said. She looked Young up and down and sniffed.

"You'll also need a bath and a change of clothes. I'm sure those are full of lice. I will burn them. And you are sure to have lice in your hair so wash it thoroughly."

Embarrassed at his appearance and odor, Young blushed.

"Yes, ma'am," he murmured.

"I will draw your bath now and then you can have supper," the woman said.

Young tried to stand as far away from her as he could in the small room. She took no further notice.

Minutes later, she called to him. He entered the bathroom and saw steam rising from a copper tub. The woman set a pair of pants, a shirt, and clean socks on a table beside the tub.

"You're tall, but I think these will fit you," she said. "Come to the kitchen when you are dressed."

"Thank you ma'am," Young said.

He shut the door and undressed, placing his foul, lice-laden clothes on the floor in the corner. He dipped a hand in the bath water to feel its warmth, then eased himself into the tub, heaving a sigh as the warm water enveloped his body. He slid down until the soothing water covered his neck and shoulders.

He rested his head on the back of the tub and lay there, luxuriating in the warmth surrounding his body, trying to recall the last time he had a bath. He could not remember. Then he sat up and soaped his body and rinsed the months of dirt and grime away. He thoroughly washed his hair, soaping and rinsing it several times.

All the while, his thoughts kept returning to the prison. He wondered if any of his companions had escaped. He frowned, remembering the bodies that were carried back into the prison after the first tunnel fiasco he'd witnessed.

The hard days and nights riding with Morgan were past now, but Young realized he missed them in a perverse way. Months of inactivity in prison had only whetted his appetite for action. The South was in dire trouble, and he yearned to return to fight once again. How grand it all had been. How Morgan and Duke and the rest had raised so much havoc wherever they went. He wanted to do it all over again. Could he find Morgan again? Soon, he dozed off.

Consciousness slowly returned and Young felt the chill of the water. He wondered how long he had slept. He emerged from the bath and reached for a large towel, then tried on the clothing the woman had provided. The shirt fit well, but the pants were a little short. He didn't complain.

As he entered the kitchen, the odor of a home-cooked meal almost overwhelmed him. The woman indicated a chair and Young sat

"Where are you from, young man," the matron asked.

"Kentucky, ma'am."

"Oh, I have welcomed several Kentucky men in this house," she said. She set a plate before him, but the portions were small. "I've fed several of your comrades who have escaped and found they could not keep large portions down. There is more, if you want it."

Young began to eat, chewing and swallowing carefully, savoring the meal.

"This is so delicious. I have not had a meal like this since..." he paused. "Since I can't remember. Or a bath, either." He ate more dinner then pushed his plate away, satisfied.

"It's all right, young man. I don't want you to be sick", his hostess said.

Pouring coffee into Young's cup she went on, "You will wait here for the carriage that will take you to safety. It's a long journey, more than 230 miles east to Detroit, then across the border to Windsor, Ontario. We have safe houses along the way where you will sleep and be fed."

Young sipped the coffee and wiped his chin.

"Thank you, ma'am," Young told her. "But I'm afraid I cannot pay you."

"It's all paid for by your government. We have rescued hundreds of Confederates and helped them return home by way of Canada," she replied.

She paused a moment. "Now, let me warn you, when you get to the border, you will be asked where you live. Just say you live in Detroit. Do not volunteer any information unless the border guards ask. Let the driver do most of the talking."

Young nodded.

"I was with..." Young started to explain, but the woman raised her hand to cut him off.

"I don't want to know any more about you or what you have done or how you got here." She paused and her glance softened. "It's better for both of us, don't you see?"

Young nodded.

"I am going now to fetch the driver who will take you."

Hours passed and Young fidgeted as he always did when he was anxious for action. Finally, the woman returned and pointed out the front window. Young saw a double-seat carriage and a driver waiting for his passenger.

"Go now, and God be with you," the woman said. She handed Young a leather pouch. He heard coins jingle as he gratefully pocketed it.

"I don't know how to thank you," he said. "Tell me, what is your name?"

She placed a finger on her lips. "The less you know the better, remember? Now, go."

She touched his shoulder. "Good luck."

The four-day ride to the border was uneventful. Along the way, Young tried to talk with the grizzled old driver, a farmer whose gnarled hands had forced him to give up farming and move to the city. But the old man uttered words of one syllable, revealing little if anything about himself or his part in escorting Confederate escapees out of the country.

They stopped at a safe house on the first night. The driver knocked on the solid wooden door of a two-story, wood-framed house beside the road.

An elderly woman opened the door and eyed the two men on the carriage.

"Could two weary travelers find sustenance and rest this night?" the driver asked.

"Can you pay for it?" the old woman asked.

"I have but little money," the driver replied.

"It will suffice," she said.

The signal given and returned, she added. "Come, I will make you some supper."

Young climbed down from the carriage and stretched his legs. Inside the house they met an elderly man seated in front of a fireplace with logs ablaze. Young presumed he was the woman's husband. He nodded once then left the room for the evening.

The two travelers ate a meal of dried beef boiled in onions and carrots, with crusty homemade bread and cups of coffee. Young was pleased that he was able to eat normally.

When they finished their meal, the woman told Young perfunctorily: "I do not wish to know your names or where you came from. I have only opened my home to two weary travelers who will be gone in the morning. Your room is upstairs. I'm afraid we have only one bed."

Young and his driver looked at each other, and shrugged. The two got into the bed fully clothed and pulled a blanket over them. Despite his weariness, Young played the events of the day over and over in his mind.

If it weren't for these good people, I don't know where I would be, he thought. I wonder what lies ahead. How much farther? Where will I be when we get to our destination?

Soon, his eyes closed and he was asleep.

After a breakfast of boiled oats and cream, crusty bread and strong coffee, Young took leave of the driver who was turning back to Chicago. Another driver took his place, and for three days, Young rode with other quiet men, sleeping in a different bed each night, sometimes sharing it with a driver.

Finally, after crossing over the narrow Detroit River, Young and the driver approached a small customs shed with a British flag waving from a pole beside the structure. A border guard looked them over carefully.

"Where do you live?" he asked the driver.

"Detroit."

The guard looked at Young.

"Detroit." With a dismissive wave of his hand, the guard sent them on their way.

The same day that he crossed the border, Young rented a room in Windsor, Ontario, counting out enough money remaining to pay for meals and lodging for another couple of weeks. The first night as he lay in bed, he weighed his desire to return to the war against continuing his education here in Canada. Before he drifted off, he decided on the latter.

The next morning, he caught a train for the long ride to Toronto. Once settled in at a rooming house, he wrote to his family in Nicholasville.

Dear Father and Mother:

I have escaped from a prison camp in Chicago and made my way here to Toronto, Canada, through the good graces of some wonderful and courageous sympathizers with our cause. I am safe and in good health, although I fear for the lives of some of the men I left behind. I would like to enroll at the theological college here and continue my studies. However, I have little money. If you could see your way to send me a bank draft, I would be most appreciative. I hope everyone there is well and I do miss you and my brothers and sisters terribly. Someday I hope I can return home and lead a normal life once the war is over. Please accept my best regards and warmest affection to you all. I look forward to hearing from you soon.

Yr. affectionate Son,
Bennett

He read the letter over. This is better, he thought. Mother and father will be happy that I have decided to continue studying. He sealed the envelope and walked out to mail it.

A little over three weeks later, Young received a letter from his father, who told him what a relief it had been to know he was safe. Enclosed was a bank draft that Young deposited in a Toronto bank.

He settled in and enrolled in the Theological Seminary at the University of Toronto. It was there that he met a fellow student, Gil McManus, a Canadian who sympathized with the South, and the two men became friends, eating together and, night after night, talking into the wee hours.

Young told McManus of his war experiences. The more they talked, the more Young realized he wanted to return to the fight, to find Morgan again, if his old commander was still alive. But he simply did not know how he could manage safe passage back to the South.

One evening over coffee at a local café, McManus told Young he knew of a man in the city who might be able to help him.

Young looked sharply at his friend. "You do?"

"Yes. He rents a room to a man with a Southern accent, a former Confederate officer, I believe. My friend tells me other men visit the house often and spend hours talking."

Young's spirits rose. "Can you take me to him?"

"Let me ask. I will call for you in the morning."

The next morning, McManus knocked on the door of a neat row house on a fashionable street. Young stood beside him.

"I will introduce you to James. Please don't ask his last name. He prefers it that way." Young nodded just as the door opened and a young man welcomed them.

"Good morning, Gil," the man said. He glanced at Young.

"James, let me introduce Bennett Young." Their host extended his hand.

"How do you do, sir," Young said. He saw a man in his mid-fifties, stout but not gone to fat, his hair black and long, his eyes dark brown.

"Please, come in, gentlemen."

The two followed their host into a parlor where, over coffee, he told Young that hundreds of American southerners had fled to Canada as the fighting engulfed their communities.

"There are also many Confederate soldiers here who have escaped from Yankee prisons." Young had learned that information soon after crossing into Canada, but he said nothing. James studied Young for a moment.

"There are Union spies here as well."

"I am not a spy, sir," Young replied, color rising in his cheeks. He showed James his pay authorization.

"No, I don't believe you are a spy, Mister Young."

James said his Southern tenant was usually gone during the day, but always returned after dinner in the evening.

"Would you like to meet him?" he asked. Young nodded eagerly.

"I will talk with him this evening and see if he wishes to speak with you," James said. The two bade their host goodbye and left.

A few days later, Young's landlady handed him a note that had been delivered to the house that afternoon. Young thanked her and retreated to his room to read it. A smile spread across his face.

That night, he and McManus returned to James' home where they were introduced to a tall, emaciated man who identified himself only as Malcolm Carroll of South Carolina. Young had seen other men who looked like this, men who had endured the horrors of Yankee prison camps. He shook the man's hand gently.

"I understand you were with Morgan," Carroll said, sitting down wearily.

"Until we were captured in Ohio, sir," Young replied. "What prison camp were you in?"

The man smiled grimly, indicating to Young to take a nearby chair.

"It shows that much does, it?" he said. "I was in Rock Island for more than a year...that's in Illinois...until I escaped. I am ever so grateful to my friend here for his generosity."

The two men talked while McManus and James listened silently. Young told Carroll that he was anxious to return to action, but he did not know how to get out of Canada.

"I would strongly advise you not to attempt to enter the United States and slip through the Yankee lines on your own," Carroll said. "Too many Southern men have been caught that way. May I suggest what may be a better plan of action?"

Young nodded. Carroll reached for a sheet of paper and wrote an address on it. He handed it to Young who looked at it and blanched.

The address was in Chicago.

"Go there. I hear there is a major action being planned that I think you might want to join. Don't ask me any more questions now." Seeing the man's color grow even more pale, Young thanked him and he and McManus took their leave.

Young went to an address in Toronto that Carroll had suggested to secure help with returning to Chicago. The man who answered the door did not reveal his name, but, after confirming Young's identity, he provided contact information for another Confederate officer who also had escaped from a Yankee jail.

Taken into the officer's confidence, Young joined a small group of ex-cavalrymen. He was given $100 in United States currency and helped to slip over the border and make his way to Chicago.

Safely across the U.S. border, Young rode a stage coach to the city. He stepped from the coach with mixed feelings about returning to the city where he had been held prisoner.

He found the next safe house and knocked on the door. A rough looking man of indeterminate age asked for identification and Young once again produced his pay authorization. His host led Young into a parlor where a man in civilian clothes stood with his back to the door. The man turned and exclaimed: "Bennett Young! How grand!"

"Captain Hines—sir!" A huge smile crossed Young's face.

"I'm glad to see you, Private. So you escaped Buffington."

"Well, sir, not exactly, sir," Young said. "The Yankees whipped us at Buffington Island. Oh, yes. Of course. You were there. What happened to you, sir?"

"I was eventually captured and sent to the Ohio State Penitentiary where General Morgan, Colonel Duke, and other officers were also imprisoned," Hines said, "Several of us, including the general, managed to chip through the rock walls of the prison. It took a us some time, but we got out."

"We managed to escape Buffington that day, but we were a sorry sight," Young said. "I was with General Morgan when finally he surrendered in Salineville in Ohio. I spent time in two prisoner-of-war camps, but I escaped from the camp here in Chicago and found my way to Canada, where I attended school for a time. But I want to get back into the fight now, sir."

"I'm delighted, Bennett, delighted. Please sit down and let's talk business."

Hines brought Young up to date. Back in Richmond, the captain had been appointed to organize and lead a widespread group of irregulars whose job was to sabotage Union facilities wherever they could and to burn major cities in the North, including New York.

Young paid close attention, anxiously waiting for the captain to say what he had in mind for Young himself. It wasn't long in coming.

"You will join a group of men I am assigning to free thousands of our people being held at Camp Douglas," Hines said.

Young groaned inwardly, his thoughts returning to the horrors he had witnessed as a prisoner there.

"The Democrats are holding their Presidential Convention on August 29th, and the city will be overrun with people, so there won't be much chance of you or any of your fellow escapees being recognized," Hines said. "Once the prisoners are freed, the ablest will be given arms and they'll join a group of Northerners who are opposed to the Lincoln administration. They call themselves Copperheads, or the Sons of Liberty. They claim their membership exceeds 50,000 men. If so, they could be a powerful force for the Confederacy."

Young's thoughts churned and he burned to ask questions, but Hines went on: "The Sons of Liberty, some of them veterans of the Union Army, will ride with us, capture the state capitols in Illinois, Indiana and Ohio, and create a new confederacy allied with our government. Then our men will ride south where they will fight again. Do you understand what all this would mean, Bennett?"

Young struggled to contain his excitement at the audacity of the plan and his own uneasiness about returning to Chicago and the camp. After all he had been through—fighting Yankees, freezing and shivering on the long raids, his escape from death at Buffington Island, and later his own capture, the prison camps where so many had died and where he had thought he would not survive—could he do this now? Maybe this assignment was the start of another chapter.

"Private Young. Are you willing to join this venture?"

Young returned to the present. "Excuse me, sir. Yes, I am willing, and yes, sir, your plan could mean the end of the war with the Confederacy intact."

Young knew he could not stay in Toronto while the war was still raging. He found lodging in the home of a family in Chicago whose sympathies were with the Confederacy and awaited orders to join the others who also were laying low in homes across the city. A few days before the Democratic convention was to open in the Amphitheater, Captain Hines called the men together.

"I'm calling off the action," he said. "The sons of bitches have been bragging all over the city about raiding the camp."

Seeing a puzzled look on the faces of the soldiers who had squeezed into the living room of a home not far from the prison camp, Hines explained.

"The Sons of Liberty. Bragging!"

Young could see Hines's hands balled into fists.

"I went to the camp yesterday. They're ready for us. It looks like they have added at least a company of veteran infantry and maybe more. There is no way we can overcome so many. And to add to the problem, more than half the men the Sons of Liberty assigned to the job have left the city."

He looked around. The men grumbled and protested, but Hines shook his head.

"No, no. I'm calling it off."

"Sir!" one man shouted from the back of the room. "We can still pull it off. There isn't a man here who didn't spend some time in that hellhole. We know every inch of the place. We can do it!"

"No. There's too many of 'em. Go back to Canada and wait for further orders."

Young left the meeting disheartened but determined to get back into the fight one way or another. He and the rest made their way back to Toronto the way they had come.

Unhappy and desperate, Young wrote to his father, asking for more money. He received another bank draft and a brief note from his father that the family was well. Young yearned to return home and decided that night to leave Canada as soon as he could.

He withdrew from the college and boarded a train, traveling east to Montreal. There, he crossed to the south side of the St. Lawrence River where he boarded a stage on the first leg of a long, arduous trip to Halifax, Nova Scotia. He would book passage south and travel by ship.

His two fellow passengers on the stage coach spoke no English, so Young had to be satisfied with looking at the scenery along the way or napping. The stage took them 115 miles to Quebec City, with two overnight stops along the way. The first was at a small hotel where his Canadian hosts, a husband and wife, greeted the travelers effusively in French.

"Do you speak English?" Young asked

"Oui, umm, yes, please, come in. My wife has prepared dinner for you and you have a bed in the loft. It is not a finished room, but the bed is large," the man said, noting Young's height. "And the mattress is comfortable."

Speaking French, the man assigned the other passengers to the other room with a double bed. Their host's wife served dinner for all three of them. Young turned down a glass of red wine. After dinner he did accept a cup of coffee and a piece of apple pie. Tired and wanting sleep, he rubbed his eyes, a signal that he hoped his hosts would notice. They did.

"Ah, monsieur, yes, you appear fatigued. If you wish to go to bed, just go through that door and up the stairs. Watch your head going through."

Young shed his clothes and got into the bed, laying his weary head on the pillow and was soon asleep. After a night's rest, he ate a breakfast of oatmeal, toast and coffee and awaited the next coach. Three more days passed uneventfully, and Young arrived in Halifax.

The stage stopped before a small hotel on the city's waterfront. Young considered for a moment then signed the register as Harold Clyde of Louisville, Kentucky. In his room, he unpacked his bag and then went downstairs to inquire about passage on a ship to Bermuda. From there, he would board a Confederate blockade-runner for the hazardous trip to Wilmington, North Carolina.

Back in Toronto, the Confederate officer Malcolm Carroll had recommended this route as the only safe passage open to Confederate soldiers and officials returning to the South.

Young slept soundly in his Halifax hotel room. At breakfast in the dining room the next morning, he noticed an older man sitting alone at a table near a window. The man had a high forehead and a long beard that matched his graying black hair. Thin, almost sickly, the man glanced up and noticed Young, then resumed eating his breakfast. Young overheard him speaking with a Southern accent while ordering coffee and made a point of leaving the dining room at the same time as this older gentleman.

In the hotel lobby, Young introduced himself. The man smiled.

"I am Clement Clay, sir," the man said, holding out his hand. "I'm glad to meet you Mister Young."

The older man's grip was firm. His penetrating eyes fixed on Young's as he made his apologies.

"I wish I could talk with you right now, but I have an appointment," he said. "Would you care to have lunch with me later today?"

Over a noontime lunch in the hotel dining room, Clay asked Young if he had arrived in town by ship from the South. Young said he came in overland but would be returning to the South soon.

"I'm hoping to get back home to Kentucky for a short visit and then to rejoin the fighting," he said. "But, I also have an idea that just might work,"

"So, you are from Kentucky, but not a Unionist?" Clay asked.

"My sympathies were and still are with the South," Young responded.

He paused, wondering who this man was and why was he was so interested in a stranger's story.

"I fought with General Morgan," Young said. The muscles of his face tightened as the memories of the last days under Morgan's command swept over him.

"Yes, an unfortunate end to a glorious chapter in the history of the Confederacy," Clay said.

"I spent some time in two Yankee prisons. The Yankees owe me for that," Young went on, grimly.

"I agree, Mister Young." Clay said. He paused and studied Young's face. "Forgive me for this, but could you produce some proof that confirms you are who you say you are? A document, perhaps?"

Their eyes locked. Young felt a cold chill run up his spine. Who was this man? Young felt that he must be of some importance, someone Young would not want to cross. Here in Canada, he could produce his papers without fear of being detained.

Young reached into his jacket pocket and pulled out his frayed pay authorization. He handed it to Clay, who studied it for a long moment.

"Thank you, Mister Young," Clay said, handing the paper back. "One can't be too careful. There are Yankee spies all over this part of Canada." He pulled a watch from his pocket and glanced at it.

"I'm sorry, but something has come up since we met earlier today," he said.

He slid the watch back in his pocket and thought for a moment. "Why don't you come to my room this evening? I would like to talk some more about your future."

Clay stood and walked out of the room. Young sat there for a long time, wondering just who this man was and what did he mean when he mentioned Young's future.

CHAPTER 11

THAT evening, Bennett Young knocked on Clement Clay's hotel room door. The older man smiled when he saw his visitor.

"Come in, come in."

Clay waved toward a wooden chair next to a single iron bed and closed the door.

"Have a seat, Mister Young." Clay grabbed a chair at a small desk, turning it around to sit facing his visitor.

"Do you know who I am, Mister Young?"

"No, sir," Young admitted.

"I am one of two commissioners appointed by the government in Richmond to represent the interests of thousands of fellow Southerners who have fled here to Canada to escape the fight. And I am here to attend to those who escaped from Yankee prisons," he said. "Men such as you."

Surprise was evident on Young's face. Clay laughed.

"I guess you didn't expect to run into someone like me, did you?"

Young shook his head.

"I'm just off a ship from Richmond, by way of Bermuda," Clay said. "I stopped at Halifax for a few days rest before boarding a stage to ride inland. As you can see, I'm not feeling well." He paused to gauge Young's reaction.

"From here, I travel to Montreal, then Toronto, and on to St. Catherine's, where I will rent quarters for an office." He shifted his legs and looked steadily at Young.

"So, you are anxious to do your part again, eh, sir?"

"Yes. Yes, I am," Young said. "But I have an idea, as I said at lunch. I think my idea could result in far greater benefit than me going off to get killed or wounded ...or taken prisoner again," Young grew excited as he spoke and had a hard time remaining in his seat.

"Tell me this idea," Clay said. Young leaned forward.

"I would like to organize a small band of veteran cavalrymen and lead a raid on northern towns along the border with Canada."

Clay raised his eyebrows.

"You know what the Yankees are doing to us in the South," Young went on, his anger growing. "I want to retaliate, I want revenge. But I think we can accomplish something much larger and more important. If the first raid succeeds, then we could make a series of raids on cities and towns along the entire border with Canada. That could force the Union to shift troops to those places and relieve the pressure on our armies in the South."

He paused for Clay's reaction. Receiving none, he continued.

"I could gather some of the men who were prisoners with me and make plans here in Canada to conduct a raid, perhaps take some town in New York or Vermont,"

Clay stared silently at Young, again wondering if he was a Southern patriot or an agent for the United States government.

"How would you manage such a thing, Bennett?" Clay asked.

"Sir, I can trust the men I would gather," Young asserted. "We fought with General Morgan, and we were prisoners together. They escaped as I did. Some went home through the lines, but others fled here to Canada. I can find them. If we plan this carefully, I know we can accomplish our mission."

Clay looked at Young. There was something about this young man that intrigued him. "Tell me more," he encouraged.

"Well, I don't have everything worked out, but I could scout some towns along the border in New York and Vermont, as I said, and see which ones would be the most vulnerable."

The idea was still forming in Young's head and he hoped he could come up with enough detail to convince Clay it was worth trying.

"The towns would have to be large enough to matter and close enough to the Canadian border for us to ride hard afterward and reach safety on Canadian soil." He warmed up to his subject.

"I would assign my men certain tasks—robbing banks and setting fire to some of the buildings in the downtown area to keep townspeople busy so they couldn't chase us. It would be a fitting reprisal for what the Yankees are doing to our towns and plantations back home."

Clay leveled his gaze at Young, who squirmed under the scrutiny. Did he suspect Young was a spy?

"What have you been doing in Canada since you escaped? What prison camps were you in?"

"Camp Morton in Ohio, and Douglas in Chicago, sir," Young said. "A number of us were taken to Chicago after Camp Morton. When I escaped, I went to Toronto to a safe house. For a time, I enrolled at the University of Toronto Divinity School where I..."

"You are planning to enter the ministry?" Clay interrupted.

"I was studying religion before I joined up with General Morgan, sir. But Yankee troops invaded my home county and pillaged and raped ...." Young paused, lowering his eyes.

"I'm sorry," Clay said softly. He waited for Young to regain his composure. "Are you still planning to finish your religious studies when we win the war?"

"I'm not sure, sir," Young said. "My brother is a minister, but after the things I've seen and done, I admit I am having second thoughts."

Clay stood. "I leave for Montreal in a few days. I would like you to come back to my room tomorrow at 10 a.m. I have something important I want to give you." With that, he bade Young good evening and saw him to the door. The next morning, Young arrived at Clay's room at the stroke of ten.

"Good morning, Bennett," Clay greeted him. "Have a seat, Now, sir, let me give you a little background. As I told you, I am one of two commissioners appointed by our government to represent our interests here in Canada. I'm an Alabamian. I served in the United States Senate for nine years and then later in the Confederate Senate for three years, after Alabama seceded."

Young gulped, realizing how important Clay was and how vital this man's support would be.

"The other commissioner, Jacob Thompson, has gone on to Toronto," Clay said. "What I'm going to tell you now is official." Young nodded.

"I have thought good and hard about our talk last night," Clay continued. "At first, I could not determine whether you were a true Southern patriot or a Yankee agent. There are many about."

Young's mouth opened but before he could speak, Clay raised his hand to calm his guest. "I have decided you are a patriot."

Young breathed a sigh of relief.

"I have some good news for you," Clay said. "At least I think it is good news." He handed Young a letter. "I wrote this early this morning. I am recommending your plan to the Secretary of War. I want you to travel to Richmond and present this letter to him. I am sure he will give your idea careful consideration. Now, do you have money enough for the journey?"

"Oh, yes, sir, I do. I received money from my father. I think it will do," Young assured him.

"Nevertheless," Clay pulled out a purse. "Here is money enough for your ship ticket and food on the voyage." Clay handed Young a sheaf of Canadian bills. "Good luck, Bennett," he said, shaking the young man's hand. "You certainly are going to need it."

Within days of his meeting with Clay, Young set sail for Bermuda. Shortly after he left, Clay departed for St. Catherine's. In Toronto, Thompson had already deposited three quarters of a million Confederate dollars in the Bank of Ontario, enough to take care of Southern business in Canada for some time to come. Clay rode a coach to St. Catherine's on the Canadian side of the Niagara River, where he set up his office in support of Confederates in Canada.

CHAPTER 12

TO REACH the mainland from Bermuda, Young boarded a steam-driven paddle-wheeler, the SS Syren, that ran regularly between the British-owned islands and Southern ports, daring the Yankee blockade ships to intercept it.

The first few days at sea were uneventful, but as the ship approached the Southern coast early one morning, fog lay thick on the water. A bit of luck, Captain Moffit pointed out to Young and other passengers.

"If we can't see the Yankee blockaders out there, they can't see us," he said. "But now, we'll just heave to and wait till the fog lifts and try to slip into port."

Young stood on the deck wishing the ship would get underway so he could get back on dry land and head to Richmond. He paced the deck. Just before noon, the fog evaporated and the ship was alone, rolling gently on the sea.

The captain ordered the below-deck crew to load hard coal.

"Why the change, Captain?" a passenger asked.

"We burned soft coal most of the way from Bermuda, sir," Moffit explained. "It's more plentiful and cheaper than hard coal, but as you may have noticed, it gives off black smoke."

The passenger laughed. "I had noticed, yes," he said. "I think my lungs are coated with it by now."

The captain went on. "A blockader could spot us easily with smoke pouring out of our funnel. Hard coal burns practically smokeless, and we need every advantage we can get."

Soon, the blockade-runner was underway again, its funnel clean of smoke. They made steady progress, but just when it looked as though they were clear, a lookout shouted: "Smoke! Dead astern, Captain!"

With a quick look aft, the captain put his lips to the metal voice tube and barked an order to the engine room: "All ahead full!"

The race was on.

They pushed hard through the sea, but as hours passed, the Yankee vessel drew closer. Fearing his ship would be captured or sunk, the captain spoke to the helmsman beside him: "Steady as she goes." He put his lips to the voice tube. "Engine room. Load soft coal. Be quick!"

Nearly within range of its guns, the Yankee skipper fired a shot from his bow. Crewmen and passengers on the blockade runner heard the shell explode on the water short of its target. Captain Moffit ordered a sharp turn to starboard behind a wall of coal smoke, then a turn to port.

With his target shrouded by smoke, the Yankee ship's captain stopped firing. Within a half hour, the blockade runner had passed through New Inlet on to Cape Fear River and reached safety. From there, it easily navigated the last twenty miles up to Wilmington.

Before he left the ship, Young spotted the captain on deck. He extended his hand.

"Well done, sir," the young Rebel said. "You have done a greater service to the Confederacy than you realize."

Although the captain raised his eyebrows at Young's comment, he did not ask for more information.

"Thank you, sir," the Captain said, gripping Young's hand. He chuckled: "If you've a mind to go to sea again, I would be proud to have you as a member of my crew."

"I'm a cavalryman, Captain," Young demurred. "I don't think I will ever get my sea legs. Best I stick to my horse."

In Wilmington, Young rented a room and spent a quiet night. The next morning, he boarded a carriage for the 250-mile ride to Richmond.

Tired and dirty when he reached the capital, Young took a room in the heart of the city. After a hot bath and a solid night's sleep, he walked down to the first floor of his hotel and asked the desk clerk for directions. A short walk later, he entered the Confederate White House.

After waiting what seemed like hours, an aide ushered Young into the Confederate Secretary of War's office and introduced him to Secretary James A. Seddon.

The secretary appeared to be about fifty years of age, slim, with a high forehead, a sharp nose and deep-set eyes. His hair was mostly gray and locks of it curled around his ears. He wore a pointed beard and drooping mustache, both also gray. He looked tired, Young thought.

"How do you do Mister Young?" Seddon said, extending his hand.

Young managed to stammer, "I, uh, I...mean, I am well sir. How are you?" He immediately regretted asking the question.

Seddon only smiled and introduced Young to his aide, Brigadier General William H. Stephens. Young saluted the general smartly who returned the honor, but more casually. Seddon invited the two to sit down. As he took his chair, Young realized he was in the office of the man who was responsible for the entire Confederate Army.

Have I made a mistake coming here? Will he ridicule my idea and throw me out of his office? Young tried to block out such negative thinking.

Seddon looked at him. "Tell me what you have in mind, young man."

"Mister Secretary, our commissioner in Canada, Mr. Clay, asked me to come here and share our ideas about raiding Yankee towns all along the border with Canada."

Seddon's eyebrows rose for a fraction of a second. "Raid Yankee towns?"

"Yes, sir. If we succeed, I am certain it will force the North to move troops from the southern battlefields to protect their northern towns. Just think!"

Young gathered his courage and went on. "It will reduce the Union forces arrayed against us and it will increase our chances of winning the war!" He paused, fearing he might have overstated his case, but he went on.

"I propose to scout out some towns in New York and Vermont close to the border with Canada. I want to lead the first raid with a small force of men against whatever town is deemed the best."

Seddon stroked his pointed beard, turned to stare out his office window for a few moments. He turned his gaze back into the room, looking toward General Carroll.

"General?"

"Private, how many men would you need to pull off this scheme?" the general asked.

"I think nineteen or twenty, sir," Young replied. "We don't plan to hold the towns. Just get in, do as much damage as we can, and get out."

General Carroll kept his gaze leveled at Young, who squirmed in his seat, sweat gathering in his armpits and rolling down his back.

"It could work, Mister Secretary," General Carroll said. "But the element of surprise must be scrupulously observed or it will surely fail. And we must assess what the reaction of the Canadian government might be."

Seddon nodded.

"Your idea has some merit, young man. But if President Davis approves this action, there are certain criteria you must abide by. One is that you cannot set up a base of operations or plan these raids from Canada. That would violate Canada's Neutrality Act, and we do not want to anger the British. You will have to plan your raid somewhere on Yankee territory."

Young thought for a moment. He recalled his stay with a sympathetic family in Chicago before the aborted raid on Camp Douglas.

"Sir, we know Southern sympathizers in Chicago who, I am sure, will provide us with a secret base."

Young's heart almost stopped when Seddon frowned. Is he going to turn me down? Have I come all this way for nothing?

But when he spoke, Seddon said: "I don't want another hair-brained scheme like that raid on Camp Douglas that never happened, Mister Young. How do I know you can carry off your raid?"

"I will recruit the best of the men I served with when I rode with General Morgan, sir, The size force I mentioned can easily infiltrate one of those northern towns and burn it. I know we can do it." Young's jaw set.

Seddon stared hard at the young man who'd brought such an idea to his office.

"If your plan is approved, you must control your men," he said. "There will be no robbing civilians or molesting women. But, if there is a bank that appears vulnerable, you may relieve it of as much money as you can."

Seddon hid a smile behind his hand. "All the money you take must be turned over to our commissioners in Canada. Every cent of it."

"Yes, sir. It's not the money I'm after," Young said. "I want retribution. I want those Yankees in their small towns to find out what war is really like."

Seddon observed Young in silence, liking what he saw and heard. He glanced at General Carroll, who nodded. When it came time for Young to leave, Seddon said he would let him know his decision within a few days.

General Carroll wrote a note authorizing temporary quarters for Young at an Army infantry unit in the city. While he waited for Seddon's summons, Young wandered about the city.

The war had not been kind to Richmond. Its buildings were run down and many of its residents were selling personal and household belongings on the streets to earn money to buy food. Others were reduced to begging.

This is what it all has come to, Young thought. Look at what the war has done to these people...and to others in worse condition. He vowed to avenge his people.

A few days later, a messenger found Young at his quarters and handed him an envelope. On the upper left corner were the words: Office of the President, The Confederate States of America. His hands shaking, Young tore it open. He mouthed the words contained in the letter. "You will present yourself to the Office of the President tomorrow at 9 o'clock in the morning." Young drew a long breath and exhaled it slowly.

"Yes!" he said.

Promptly at 9 a.m., Young entered the waiting room at the Executive Mansion in Richmond. He sat on a chair for twenty minutes watching a parade of people tromp in and out of Davis's office before a young male secretary beckoned him. He entered the President's office and saw a man of five feet ten or eleven inches tall, wearing a black suit, a white shirt and a floppy black bow tie. The man's wavy hair, once brown, was now mostly gray. A goatee graced his strong chin; his deep-set, piercing steel-blue eyes above prominent cheekbones assessed his visitor.

Young noticed that Davis's left eye was partly clouded, perhaps from some disease.

"Mister Young, I'm pleased you could come to see me this morning. Have a seat," Davis said.

Speechless, Young sat.

Davis rounded his desk and sat half on it, close to Young's chair.

"Secretary Seddon told me of your plan to raid towns along the United States border with Canada." The President's eyes were intent on Young, who felt the man was sizing him up.

"Yes, sir," Young stammered.

"Well, sir," Davis went on. "I was, at first, quite dubious of the value of such an enterprise. I must say you are a very young man to be given so much responsibility."

Young found his voice.

"Mister President, I served with General Morgan and spent months in two Yankee prison camps," he said. "I may be young, but I know I can accomplish this mission."

Davis studied his youthful visitor for a few moments more, then spoke: "You must be a resourceful man, Mister Young, to have survived all that."

He paused and rubbed his eyes. "Secretary Seddon was persuasive. So persuasive, in fact, that I acknowledge your plan has a great deal of merit. I have instructed the Secretary to grant your request and issue the proper credentials."

Young's face beamed.

"I do not have to tell you of the desperate situation we find ourselves in these trying days, Mister Young," Davis continued. "We have other secret operations going, which we hope will help turn the tide of the war, but I wish you the best of fortune. If you succeed, you will be doing your nation a very large service. Please report back to Secretary Seddon in the morning. He will expect you."

Davis stood up beside the desk. Young waited for him to go on, but then realized the interview was over. He rose.

"Thank you, Mister President. We won't let you down." Young could barely contain himself as he left the office. Once outside, he hurried back to his quarters and spent the day planning his return to Canada.

The next morning Secretary Seddon greeted him.

"Good morning, Lieutenant Young. I have some documents for you."

Young heard Seddon call him "lieutenant" and a chill went through him.

Was there a mistake? Did Seddon know who he really was? The Secretary handed him the two documents. Young glanced down at the top piece of paper—his commission as first lieutenant in the Provisional Army Confederate States for special service.

Now he understood!

The other papers contained instructions for the operation on the northern border. The main thrust was that he and his men were authorized to operate beyond Confederate lines as a military unit. His fledgling command was to be officially known as The Fifth Confederate State Retributors.

Young looked up at Seddon.

"Thank you, Mister Secretary. I swear to you we shall succeed in our mission."

"I wish you luck, lieutenant," replied Seddon. "When you return to Canada, report to Mister Clay for further orders. God speed."

Young saluted smartly and left to pack his bag for the return trip to Canada. Retracing his route, uneventfully this time, Young arrived in September and made the long trip overland again to St. Catherines to meet with Clay at the latter's residence.

The men conferred late into the evening. Past eleven o'clock, Clay reached under his bed and withdrew a valise. To Young's amazement, Clay counted out $1,000 in United States bills. As Young took the money, Clay also handed him a piece of paper.

"Please sign at the bottom," Clay said. "It acknowledges that you have received $1,000 to use for military purposes." Young signed where he was instructed.

"Good luck, lieutenant," Clay said offering his hand.

The next day, Young made the long trip by train to St. Jean-Sur-Richelieu, just twenty miles north of the Quebec-New York border. In yet another hotel room, he studied a map of northern New York and Vermont. His finger traced a path across the New York map close to the border. The only sizable town there was Malone, about ten miles south of Canada. This town had possibilities, he thought. He slid his finger across to Vermont and spied the towns of Swanton and St. Albans. He decided to visit them in person.

At a stop in Swanton, Young peered out the window of his railroad car and rejected that town. Too small. The next stop was St. Albans.

As the train pulled into the station, Young noticed the railroad foundry, alive with workmen. He stepped off the train and walked up a long block to Main Street where he turned a corner and stopped. Diagonally across the street to his right was a bank. He turned and walked north along Main Street past two more banks, one across from a large Green that sloped up to a parallel street lined with three churches, a school, and a courthouse.

Main Street was crowded with people. The busy village contained an important railroad junction for northwestern New England, and it was on the main passenger and freight line to and from Montreal, southern New England, and New York City. Close by the St. Albans depot, the foundry employed most of the men in town. Because St. Albans was so far north, there were no troops stationed here.

Best of all, the town's three banks were all within a block of each other. Easy targets. Young intended to relieve them of as much money as his men could carry. To create a diversion when they made their escape, Young planned to have his men torch buildings along Main Street.

Realizing he was in a thriving community, Young made his decision. St. Albans would be his first target.

He returned to the railroad station and caught a train to Montreal. As it pulled out on the track, he thought the decision he'd made was the right one. He went over his plan again and again. Rob the banks, guard against anyone coming up from the foundry. Grab horses, torch buildings, and get out of town.

"The North must pay for what they are doing to us," he muttered. Realizing he had spoken aloud, he looked around. The closest passenger, across the aisle was a corpulent middle-aged man Young took to be a salesman. Asleep, the man had one arm over a carpetbag. No one else was paying attention.

In Montreal, Young changed to a train bound for Toronto where he would recruit his men, all able-bodied veterans. Through his contacts with Clay, he sent messages to several men he had served with during his days with Morgan, especially Samuel Gregg. The men began filtering into Toronto within a few days, checked in with Young and then found rooms. When Gregg arrived, the two men embraced, pounding each other's backs.

"You're looking good, Sam" said Young.

"You, too, Bennett." The two friends chatted for hours, catching up on each other's activities since their days at Camp Douglas. Gregg told Young how he had knocked a guard over the head and taken his uniform, allowing Gregg to just walk out the gate of the camp.

"I lost a little weight after you escaped," he told Young. "Just the opposite of when you and I first met. Your pants were too tight. At the prison camp, mine were too loose, but I've got it all back now."

The next morning, the men gathered at the home of a Canadian family sympathetic to the Confederacy. Young told them they would filter into St. Albans one or two at a time and on the selected day, rob the banks and steal horses for their getaway. Collins, a captain accustomed to command, suggested that most of the men be assigned to robbing the banks and rounding up horses.

"I think you need only one man to prevent people on the street from running for help," Collins said.

"No, we'll need more than one guard. I shouldn't like to have the news get down to those fellows at the foundry too soon," Young insisted, determined to show who was in command. Collins looked at Young, first hesitating, then nodded his head in agreement. When Young finished talking, several of the men shook their heads and laughed at his audacity.

"By golly," said George Scott, a twenty-year-old Kentuckian who had escaped from the Chicago prison a few days after Young. "I think we can pull this off, Bennett – er I mean Lieutenant."

Young chuckled. "Enough of that, George."

Others were not so comfortable with the plan. Joseph "Gramps" McGrorty was the first to raise an objection.

"How do you expect to capture a town the size of St. Albans with twenty men?" he said. His tone reflected his disdain for the plan.

"I don't plan to capture it and keep it, Gramps," Young replied. "We will go there a few at a time, register at the hotels and at rooming houses. Then on the day of the raid, we strike fast and hard, hold up the banks, steal all the horses we need, torch some of the buildings and get out of there before they know what hit them. I chose St. Albans because it's a busy town and it has three banks close together. And it isn't far to the Quebec border."

McGrorty grumbled, "That's the most hair-brained idea I ever heard. In fact, it's crazy."

"Think about it, Gramps," Young replied. He needed McGrorty, a steadying influence among the others because of his age. Calmly he explained the plan again.

"We will have the element of surprise," he added. "We can't fail."

McGrorty pointed out what he perceived as a major flaw in the plan.

"What if there aren't enough horses? We going to have to run all around town looking for some?"

"We can't hire all the horses in the three stables here, Gramps. That would be too suspicious," Young countered. "We'll take horses that are on the street and steal horses from the stables."

McGrorty grumbled, then nodded his agreement to take part in the raid.

When a hush fell over the room, Young said, "I have orders not to plan the raid here in Canada, so no planning was done. Understood?"

His men nodded their assent, smiles crossing their faces.

"We shall meet again tomorrow in St. Jean, Quebec, for final instructions."

He smiled. "It's just a short train ride to the Vermont border. Make sure you are all there. Then we go to St. Albans a few at a time, so nobody there wonders what we're up to."

The men scattered to their rooms across Toronto. Young packed his bags and went to bed early. The next morning, he took the train to Montreal and another to St Jean, where he stayed overnight.

He arrived in St. Albans late the next afternoon, October Ninth, and registered at the American House, but he didn't like the accommodations, so he switched to the Tremont House on North Main Street.

A few days later, Young stopped in at the Fuller Livery Stables behind the hotel to look over the horses. Twice before the day of the raid, he rented a horse from Fuller and rode north out of St. Albans to scout out an escape route. He rode ten miles to Swanton, but decided against going that way, fearing swamps along the route might bog his men down. On another trip, he rode all the way to the Canadian border, first stopping at Sheldon, a small farming town only ten miles south of the border.

On the main street of the village, a few people stood in front of the Sheldon Bank, chatting. Near the bank, Young had noticed a covered bridge over a small stream called Black Creek. He smiled as he turned his horse south, thinking: Here's another bank we can hold up. And we'll burn this bridge once we're across.

By the time pursuers forded the stream, if they could ford it at all, he and his men would be well into Canada.

Back in his St. Albans hotel room, Young settled down to await the arrival of his men, satisfied that he'd done all he could do. One evening at dinner in the Tremont House's dining room, three women had approached him. He stood and nodded toward one of them, Henrietta Carpenter, with whom he'd had a few discussions about the Bible—at a public place, of course.

"Mr. Clyde," said another woman in her company. "I'm sorry to disturb you at your meal, sir, but I wonder if we may talk with you."

"Most certainly, Madame. How may I be of service?"

"I am Rachel Kimball. I believe you know Mrs. Carpenter." Young nodded. "And this is Mrs. Childs," Mrs. Kimball indicated with a wave of her hand.

"Mister Clyde, our church, the Congregational, is in need of a new minister, since our most recent minister was transferred to another community. Mrs. Carpenter informs us that you, such a pious man, are staying at the Tremont House and may be contemplating an extended stay in our community."

Young remained silent. She went on: "We, uh... we were wondering if you would be interested in accepting the post of interim minister. We cannot formally make the offer, you understand," Mrs. Kimball said, her hand fluttering before her face. "That would be up to the Board of Deacons, but I have it on good authority they would look favorably on you."

Young looked at each of the women in turn.

"I am honored by your confidence in me, but I'm afraid I won't be in town very long."

"Oh, that is a shame, Mister Clyde. Forgive us for being so forward."

"Not at all, Mrs. Kimball. I am quite honored."

"Well, good evening sir," Mrs. Kimball said. "Please, again forgive us."

"Of course. Good evening, ladies," said Young, as the women turned to leave. He sat down again, picked up his fork and looked out the window as the women passed. He nodded and smiled.

CHAPTER 13

**St. Albans, Vermont
October 19, 1864
The Raid**

A FEW minutes before 3 p.m. on Wednesday, October 19, Young and his men clumped down the stairs of the Tremont House, their pistols hidden under their jackets. Collins laughed as he turned to one of his fellow soldiers. "I just threw a bottle of Greek fire into the hotel washroom," he said, "They'll learn how to fry chicken before I come again!"

The others knew that Greek fire is a concoction of chemicals that bursts into flame when exposed to air. They chuckled nervously. On the sidewalk and the street, they walked toward their assigned positions.

Those who were to rob the banks hoisted knapsacks higher on their shoulders, their long coats buttoned. The men were in place guarding the streets coming up from the railroad station and foundry. Seeing that his men were in position, Young brandished his Navy Colt pistol and shouted to the few citizens walking on St. Albans' Main Street: "I take possession of this town in the name of the Confederate States of America!"

A passing townsman looked at him curiously and kept on walking. From somewhere inside the hotel, Young heard laughter. A piano player struck up a tune.

Marcus Spurr, assigned to steal a horse for Young, emerged from Fuller's stable with a saddled horse.

"Here's a mount for y'all, Cap'n!" Spurr shouted.

Young quickly climbed in the saddle and rode up and down the street, waving his revolver. Townspeople on the street and the wooden sidewalk finally realized that the crazy man waving his revolver was not so crazy. They were under attack!

Some of the Rebels, their .36-caliber Navy Colt revolvers in hand, herded a handful of people across Main Street to the Green. Most of the other raiders were outside the three banks. Collins, Marcus Spurr, Squire Turner Tevis, and two others casually walked into the Bank of St. Albans, a handsome, two-story building set back off the sidewalk behind a picket fence. Charles Bishop, the teller, was seated at a front window facing Main Street, counting and sorting bank notes. Seeing the men enter, he rose and walked behind the counter to wait on them. Two of the Rebels pulled out their pistols and pointed them at Bishop's head.

"Good Lord!" the frightened clerk exclaimed.

"We are Confederate soldiers come North to rob and plunder as Sheridan is doing in the Shenandoah Valley!" Collins shouted.

The clerk sprang toward the rear of the bank and into the directors' room where another clerk, Martin Seymour, was working on the bank's books. Seymour stood to find out what the ruckus was about.

The two men tried to close the door to the room, but Collins and Spurr leaped over the counter and slammed their shoulders against it, their pistols pointed at the bank employees.

"Not a word!" shouted Collins, "We want your money and if you resist, we will blow your brains out!" Shaken, the employees promised they would resist no more.

Other robbers rapidly gathered money off Bishop's table and out of the safe. Later, bank officials determined the Rebels had missed seeing $50,000 in St. Albans Bank notes in the vault and overlooked a drawer under the counter that contained $9,000 in bills. The Rebels did haul bags of silver from the vault containing about $1,500, but took only $400 because the coins were too heavy to carry.

Watching the robbers gather up the money, Seymour swallowed nervously and suggested to Collins: "Sir, since you are committing an act of war, perhaps you will allow me to inventory what is being taken so the bank can recover its losses from the United States government."

Collins chortled and waved his pistol at Seymour and replied, "Stand back against the wall and be quiet."

Spurr stood guard at the bank's front door when he heard a knock. He unlocked it and Samuel Breck, a St. Albans merchant, entered, oblivious to what was taking place. Breck was carrying $393 in a leather bag, intending to pay off most of a $500 loan the bank had given him and his partner, John Weatherbee.

Spurr grabbed Breck by the throat and told him he would kill him if he resisted. The robbers relieved Breck of the money and herded him to the back room with Seymour and Bishop.

Soon after, Morris Roach, a teen-age clerk for storeowner Joseph Weeks, entered the bank with $210 his employer had told him to deposit. The robbers took Weeks' money, too.

Shaking with fright, the boy cried: "But, but...Mister Weeks told me to deposit the money in the bank here. Now he's going to think I stole it!"

"Don't worry, son, I will give y'all a receipt for the money," Spurr replied.

Taking up a pen, he wrote on a piece of bank paper: "Mr. Weeks has this day made a generous contribution to the cause of the Confederate States of America in the amount of $210." He signed it: Marcus Spurr, Army of the CSA, and handed it to the youngster as he walked him back to the vault to join the others.

The robbery took less than twelve minutes, but before the men left, their pockets and valises stuffed with money, they made their captives take an oath. At gunpoint, Collins ordered the men and the boy in the vault to raise their right hands and repeat after him: "I swear on my honor I will do nothing to injure the cause of the government of the Confederate States of America."

Collins slowly waved his revolver back and forth. Shaking, the captives raised their hands and repeated the words. "And that I will do nothing to impede the escape from this town."

The men nodded their heads.

"Swear!" Collins ordered, waving his revolver.

"I swear!" the men and the boy replied in unison. "I swear!"

"Damn. Right!" Collins said. He turned to his comrades. "Let's go, gentlemen, time's a'wastin."

William Hutchinson was inside the Franklin County Bank on Main Street, next to the American House, while four other Confederates waited outside trying to remain calm. Hutchinson approached cashier Marcus Beardsley.

"Do you know the price of gold today?" he asked Beardsley.

"I'm sorry, sir, I don't know," Beardsley replied. "We don't deal in it."

Another merchant, oblivious to what was happening in the town, came in to make a deposit and Hutchinson asked the man if he would give him Greenbacks for two gold pieces. The merchant agreed.

As he left, four more Rebels, one of them Lewis Price, entered the bank and stood silently by a front window for a moment before walking toward Beardsley. The Rebels pulled out their pistols and without a word pointed them at the banker's head.

Shaking and incredulous, he listened as Hutchinson told him coldly: "We are Confederate soldiers. There are a hundred of us and we've come to rob your banks and burn your town."

Overhearing those remarks, Jackson Clark, a local sawyer, made a dash for the door, but Hutchinson blocked his way.

"Not so fast," Hutchinson told him, placing his pistol at Clark's head. "Get into the vault." He turned to Beardsley.

"You, too," nodding his head toward the vault door.

When Price and two other men began closing the door, Beardsley cried out: "Don't lock us in here, we'll suffocate!" Nevertheless, the Rebels closed the heavy iron vault door and locked it, to muffled cries from the men inside. The men were released unharmed a half hour after the raid by townspeople who had gone into the bank and heard them banging on the vault door.

In the two-story building that housed the First National Bank on nearby Fairfield Street, just seventy-five yards from the American House on Main Street, cashier Albert Sowles was taking a break. Eighty-nine-year-old General John Nason, a veteran of the War of 1812, and nearly deaf, was reading a newspaper at a desk near the back of the bank.

Rebel soldiers Caleb Wallace, a nephew of Senator John Crittenden of Kentucky, and George McGrorty, a Texas cowhand before the war, walked in the front door, drew their pistols and pointed them at Sowles.

"You are our prisoner," Wallace told Sowles. "If you resist, I will shoot you dead."

Alamanda Bruce and James Doty also entered the bank, pulled out their pistols and, seeing Sowles covered, cleaned out the vault, stuffing wads of bills into their haversacks and coat pockets and throwing government bonds to the other raiders in the room.

McGrorty spotted four bulging bags on the floor of the vault. Thinking they might contain gold, he ripped open three. They contained only pennies. It was later discovered that had he opened the fourth bag, he would have found gold.

All during the robbery, General Nason continued to read his paper, unaware of the drama happening around him. Later, after the Rebels had retreated to the street, Nason put aside his newspaper and asked Sowles: "What gentlemen were those?"

Approaching the bank to make a deposit, St. Albans resident William Blaisdell spotted armed men leaving the bank carrying heavily laden haversacks. He realized what was happening and fell on one of the robbers, knocking him down and trying to wrest the pistol from his hand. It was Hutchinson. Wallace turned and spotted Blaisdell pinning Hutchinson to the ground.

"Shoot him! Shoot him!" Wallace cried. But as the two men wrestled in the dirt, none of the robbers could get in a shot without hitting Hutchinson. Two of Young's men put their pistols to Blaisdell's head and ordered him to let go. Realizing he would be shot dead, Blaisdell gave up the fight.

Standing at the door to the bank, Nason shook his head, "Two upon one is not fair play." He descended the three steps, walked around Blaisdell and the Rebels and headed home, shaking his head. "No, sir, not fair at all."

The Rebels let Blaisdell go and he ran up the street toward Young. As three Rebels continued herding passersby to the park, villager Collins Huntington walked across Main Street to fetch his children from the school on Church Street, just above the park. Nearing the Lamoille Bank, he started to cut across Main Street when Young ordered him to join the others in the Park.

Thinking the man was drunk, Huntington ignored him. The Rebel leader fired one shot at the father, striking a rib. Grabbing his injured side, Huntington staggered, but a man grabbed him and helped him to the Green where he joined the other town residents. Huntington would survive the wound.

Young ordered Collins and two other men to get more horses. Fuller emerged from his livery stable, pistol in hand. Recognizing Young, he cried: "You!"

Young shouted to him: "I need spurs! Get them for me, Mr. Fuller!"

"No, damn you!" shouted Fuller, kneeling on the wooden sidewalk and aiming his pistol at Young. He pulled the trigger but it misfired.

Young pointed his Colt revolver at Fuller and laughed. "Now are you going to get me those spurs?"

Thinking quickly, Fuller dashed inside Bedard's harness shop near the livery stable, and ran out the back door, shouting the alarm.

"Rebels! Rebels! They're robbing the banks! They're killing people!" Fuller ran along the side street calling to his townsmen: "Somebody go get the men down at the Foundry! And weapons!"

A New Hampshire builder, Elinas J. Morrison, was supervising a crew building a new hotel on a side street. He heard the shouting and gunfire coming from Main Street and ran to the scene.

"What's happening?" Morrison asked the stable owner.

"They're robbing the banks! Rebels! A whole bunch of 'em!"

The two men hurried to Main Street. With his pistol reloaded, Fuller again took aim at Young, but one of the Rebels shouted, "Look out, Cap'n!"

As Young turned, three shots rang out. Fuller had ducked behind a pillar and escaped harm, but Morrison gripped his stomach and with his back against the door of Miss Beattie's millinery store, sank to the wooden sidewalk. Fuller knelt to help Morrison, but he could not stem the bleeding from the wound. Three men carried Morrison to a pharmacy a few doors away where the pharmacist treated his wound. The men then carried him to the Tremont Hotel.

As they were leaving one whispered: "Looks like he's goin' to die."

"Suit him right," one of the others said. "I hear tell he's a Reb sympathizer."

Morrison was known as a Copperhead, one of a large group that favored an end to the war and letting the South go its way.

Even as the shots rang out on Main Street, people elsewhere in the town were going about their daily activities, unaware that the war had come home.

Leonard Bingham was walking down Champlain Street from Main when he heard the shooting and turned to run back up to Main Street. He spotted a man in a Confederate uniform galloping a horse up and down the street, waving a pistol.

Quickly appraising the situation, Bingham waited until Young reigned in his horse just a few dozen yards from the First National Bank at Main and Fairfield Streets. With smooth timing, the Northerner grabbed for the reins and tried to pull the Rebel from his horse, but he lost his grip as Young turned his mount away. Realizing his plight, Bingham ran toward Wheeler's store for cover. Young aimed his pistol at the fleeing man and fired. Bingham sagged to the curb, a bullet in his back.

"Oh, God, I've been shot!" Bingham cried. As Young galloped away, two men hiding inside Wheeler's store ran out and lifted Bingham, carrying him inside the store where the owner brought them clean cloths to dress the wound. He also would survive.

With the Rebels starting to emerge from the banks, their haversacks stuffed with money, men who had run up from the foundry took cover wherever they could and fired on the Rebels with rifles and pistols, but their shots were ineffective. Other townspeople emerged from shops along the street, some loading their pistols and rifles.

A man fired down on Young from a second-story window but his shot missed. Young and the other Rebels blasted back with their revolvers. Broken window glass and splintered wood showered into the room, wounding the shooter.

The Rebels shot at a man running north on Main Street, intent on sounding the alarm to those who did not know what was happening. He was too far away for their pistols to have any effect.

A girl four or five years old wandered out of one of the stores near the shooting. Her mother screamed and ran out to get her, pulling her back inside. At the elementary school above the park, students and teachers eagerly watched the battle unfolding below on Main Street.

A few of the Rebels threw bottles of Greek fire against the wood-sided Atwood store and several other buildings, but because the exterior of the buildings were so wet from the previous night's mist, the fires only smoldered. Flames had emerged from the water closet at the Tremont House where Collins smashed his bottle of Greek fire, but the hotel staff had put it out.

While the raid progressed, the operator in the St. Albans telegraph office sent a message to Governor Smith at the state capitol in Montpelier. He tapped out: "Southern raiders are in St. Albans, shooting citizens and burning houses." He said he believed the governor's wife was safe at home.

As soon as he was finished, the operator slammed his office door shut and ran down toward the foundry, away from the shooting. The telegram confirmed: Governor Smith's worst fears had come true.

Firing from townspeople grew hotter, and from his combat experience, Young knew when it was time to retreat. Swinging his mount around, he spotted his men emerging from the three banks one by one, their satchels weighted down with money, Navy Colts in their hands.

"Men! The horses! Over here!" he shouted. "Mount up! Mount up!"

Some of the Rebels without mounts pulled harnesses off horses hitched to wagons on Main Street and mounted them bareback.

Up the hill, Mrs. Smith, the governor's wife, heard the shooting and went outside to determine what was happening. Just then a servant girl who had been shopping for food downtown ran up to the door.

"Rebels! They're robbing the banks and shooting up the town!" the girl cried.

Mrs. Smith went back into the house and emerged again, this time carrying a pistol. She stood on the front steps, expecting the Rebels to come riding up the street. Within minutes, a horseman came up the hill at a gallop. She cocked the pistol, but then realized the rider was her own brother-in-law.

"Ann! Ann! Have you heard? Oh," he shouted, seeing Ann Smith holding her pistol. "I guess you know. Rebels are cleaning out the banks, but our boys are giving them a fight." He dismounted and suggested she hand him the pistol. He checked the chamber.

"It's a good thing they didn't come this way," he told her. "There are no bullets in your revolver."

"Halt right there!" Rebel John McGinnis shouted at George Conger and his son, Stephen. When they heard the shooting, the two had grabbed rifles and run up to Main Street from Champlain Street.

"I'm a Confederate soldier here to rob your town and you're my prisoners!" McGinnis thundered. But Conger, a veteran Union officer home on leave to care for his invalid wife, knew when it was time to fight and when it was time to retreat. He decided to retreat.

"Come on!" he shouted at Stephen. The father and son ducked into a shop on the corner of Main and Champlain Streets and ran out a side door where they were met by some of the men from the foundry headed toward the shooting.

"Hurry! Hurry!" Conger shouted, pointing toward Main Street. "Rebels are robbing the banks and burning the town!" Grabbing whatever weapons they could from startled residents along the way, the foundry workers raced up toward the battle.

Back on Main Street, Young reared his horse and shouted to his men: "Form up! Form up in lines of four!" He fired shots in the air to discourage would-be defenders. Young spurred his horse to the front of the first line and shouted: "Ride, men! Ride!"

The Rebels kicked their horses' flanks and sped north toward Canada, their Rebel yells echoing off buildings along the way.

Just past Bank Street, north of the Green, raider Charlton Higbee sagged in his saddle, a bullet hole in each shoulder. James Doherty grabbed the reins of Higbee's horse and another Rebel helped hold him in the saddle.

"Hang on, Charlton! Hang on!" Doherty shouted. Soon, blood soaked the wounded cavalryman's shirt and jacket. But they were on the run.

CHAPTER 14

Captain Conger hastily took charge of the townsmen as the Rebels thundered north.

"All able-bodied men with horses, follow me!" Conger shouted. "We're going after those murdering Rebs!"

He organized a posse of fifty men armed with pistols, rifles, and shotguns to chase the fleeing raiders. Far from the village center, the raiders turned northeast on the Sheldon Road.

Two of the Rebels rode on each side of Higbee, who was bleeding badly and struggling to say in the saddle. About five miles out of town near Fairfield Pond, Young realized Higbee could not make it safely to Canada. He ordered the two riders helping the injured man to ride on with their fellow Rebels while he remained behind to seek help for Higbee.

Coming across a farmhouse a little way off the Sheldon Road, Young reined in the horses and helped the wounded man out of the saddle. Higbee sat on the ground, his face pale, his eyes rolling in his head. Young approached the house and knocked on the door. A woman of middle age answered and asked Young what he wanted.

"My friend has been shot and needs immediate attention. Can you help him?"

Unafraid, she agreed and helped Young walk Higbee inside her home, placing him on a chair.

"What happened?" she asked as she helped Higbee remove his shirt. Higbee grunted in pain. She examined his shoulders where the bullets went in and through.

Young said nothing. The woman nodded and lifted Higbee's arms one at a time. The Rebel cried out in pain.

"The bullets missed the bone." she said. "He is very lucky."

She heated water on her cook stove and bathed the wounds. Higbee groaned again, but bit his tongue, braving the pain.

"Are you all right, young man?" she asked. Higbee nodded, but sweat had broken out on his brow. "I will pour some alcohol on your wounds to prevent infection," she said, laying her hand on his shoulder to comfort him, then leaving the room.

"You're going to be all right, Charlton," Young said, but he wondered if Higbee would survive. The woman returned with a gallon jug of whiskey and a few clean rags.

"This will hurt a great deal, young man." She placed a rag in Higbee's mouth and told him to bite hard.

"Please hold him around the waist," she instructed Young. She generously poured whiskey onto a piece of cloth and placed it gently on the wound where the bullet exited from Higbee's right shoulder. Higbee screamed and his face lost even more color. She waited a few seconds and pressed the whiskey-laden rag onto the other shoulder. Higbee bit the rag harder this time, but did not scream again.

"Now," she said to Young, "I must bathe the wounds in back just like I did in front. So, help me bend him over. Yes, like that. Gently. Now hold on to him."

She bathed whiskey on both the entry wounds, then helped Young straighten Higbee so she could bandages the wounds with long pieces of cloth. Higbee groaned, his face white from the pain.

"That should help. I can't guarantee he will heal. What happened?" she asked Young again.

"I am sorry, I cannot tell you," Young said. "But I will pay you for your doctoring my friend, and if you will allow him to stay here for a time."

The woman wondered what she had gotten into, but the thought of helping a badly injured stranger and the money Young offered made up her mind.

"Certainly sir. He may stay here for a while. My husband has gone into Sheldon to get supplies. I expect he won't turn your friend out either."

Young handed her several folded U.S. bills.

"I would appreciate it if you would tell no one other than your husband that my friend is here. And thank you for your kindness."

"Of course," she said.

"All right," Young said. He turned to Higbee. "I must go on ahead, Charlton. You'll be fine here. This fine woman and her husband will take care of you."

"Yes, sir," Higbee said. "I'll be along directly."

Young helped the woman move his friend to a bed in an adjoining room where they propped pillows behind him so he could sit up.

With Higbee cared for as best he could manage, Young mounted his horse again and rode hard in a circuitous route entering Canada a few miles east of Frelighsburg.

While Young was finding medical help at the farm, his men had outpaced their pursuers. They rode in a pack toward Sheldon village, about nine miles from St. Albans. Just before the covered bridge that Young had seen when he scouted their escape route, they spotted a farmer on the other side of the stream driving a team toward them. His two horses pulled a wagon piled high with hay.

Collins galloped across the bridge and drew his pistol.

"We want your wagon!" he shouted "Get down off there before I shoot you!" The man gaped at Collins and his companions. Collins waved the pistol again.

"Get off the damned wagon! Get off!"

"I just loaded this hay! You can't take it!" the man complained.

"We have a better use for it!" shouted Collins. "Get down, damn it!"

Finally realizing the danger he was in, the farmer jumped to the ground. Collins and two other Rebels backed the hay-laden wagon onto the covered bridge. Collins unhitched the team and walked it back to the farmer.

"We intend to burn your hay in the bridge, sir," Collins said. "But we don't want to kill your horses." He handed the reins to the man.

Then he went back and touched a lighted match to the hay. It smoldered at first, and he struck another match. The hay caught fire. Smoke billowed out both ends of the bridge. The three Rebels leaped up onto their horses and thundered off toward the border.

Only minutes behind them, Congers and his men reined up at the bridge. By now, smoke was so dense no one could see inside. Two men leaped from their horses and cautiously made their way onto the bridge. They choked on the heavy smoke, but managed to push the burning wagon out of the structure so they could continue their pursuit.

Not so far ahead, Collins' horse foundered, and seeing a farmer riding toward him, he stopped as the others thundered by.

"Good day, sir," Collins said.

"Good day to you, sir," the farmer replied warily. He watched wide-eyed as the Rebels galloped past him.

"My horse is a little peaked," said Collins smiling. "I would like to swap mine for yours."

"You want to what?" the farmer asked.

"I want your horse. You can have mine."

"I ain't goin' to swap my horse for that nag," the farmer insisted. Collins drew his pistol.

"Now, would you kindly swap horses with me, sir?"

The man dismounted and handed the reins to Collins. Quickly mounting the fresh horse, Collins pounded off to catch up to his friends.

Congers and his posse approached a few minutes later. They saw a man standing there with the sweating and hard-breathing horse and opened fire on him, thinking he was one of the robbers. His heart pounding, the hapless man fled into a nearby alder swamp, bullets zipping past his head.

As darkness fell, the Rebels crossed over the Missisquoi River Bridge at Enosburg Falls, then galloped the final eight miles to the border.

Collins shouted to his comrades, "Spread out, don't stay together." They split up as they rode deeper into Canada.

When Conger and his men pulled up before a small marble sign with "Canada" the only word on it, he reined in his horse and stopped.

"We're at the border, men," Congers shouted to the fifty men who had chased the Confederates with him this far. "Do you want to cross into Canada and get those Rebs?"

Several men nodded and murmured, but twenty-eight turned their horses around and headed for home.

A few miles to the east, Young crossed the border alone and in the dark. He spent his first night in the woods, unable to sleep in the cold and damp. As the first rays of dawn crept over the horizon, he rose and mounted his horse again, but at that moment a passing Canadian farmer spotted him. Young told the man who he was and asked him if he had seen the others.

"I heard dat tree strangairs were a-rrested yesterday at Frelighsburg, about fifteen miles dare," the Quebecer replied, pointing down the road. Young was silent for a moment, thinking: I'm the commander of those men and I should surrender and help them the best I can.

He rode in the direction the farmer had pointed and soon came across a farmhouse. By now, he was shivering from the cold and realized he had not eaten since lunch the day before. He saw a woman peer out a window and then cautiously open the door as he approached.

"Monsieur?" the woman inquired.

"I'm sorry, ma'am, but I don't speak French," Young replied. "I'm a stranger in your country and I'm very hungry." He rubbed his belly, then pointed his finger at his mouth. "Could you give me something to eat?"

She turned and said something in French to her husband, who had just come in from his barn. He nodded his head.

Switching to English, she told Young, "Please, monsieur, come in."

Young entered the house, unstrapped his gun belt, and hung it on a hook next to the door. The woman looked apprehensive, but Young smiled and strode to the wood stove to warm his hands.

Apparently relieved that this stranger meant her and her husband no harm, the woman prepared eggs and ham and toasted home-baked bread with fresh butter. Young wolfed down the food and thought of asking for more when the door flew open. Conger, E. D. Fuller, owner of the livery stable in St. Albans, and three other men burst into the house.

"It's you!" Fuller cried, spotting Young. The Rebel commander jumped up from his seat but remembered he had left his pistols on a hook near the door. He leaped for the door but it was barred by two of his pursuers. Young struck out at the nearest man, but a blow to his head from a rifle butt drove him to the floor.

"Now, you murdering Reb," said one of his captors, "we'll take you back to Vermont and have a first-class hangin'."

"And maybe double it for stealing my horses," Fuller added." He giggled at the absurdity of his last threat.

The farmer and his wife protested, but two men grabbed Young, groggy and bleeding, and dragged him outside. Seated between the two in the back of a waiting wagon, Young feared he was on his way to a rope and a gallows in Vermont.

Another man sat on the wagon's tailgate, a shotgun across his lap. As the driver began the trip back to the border, Young jumped up and pushed the guard off the tailgate before he could bring his shotgun to bear on his prisoner. Young easily pushed the two other guards off the wagon, then leaped to the front seat and pushed the unaware driver off.

He grabbed the reins and drove off, but his escape was short-lived. Others in the posse caught up with him as the wagon careened down the road. With guns pointed at him, Young realized he would be killed if he didn't surrender again. He pulled up on the reins. Conger ordered him tied up this time, and the posse resumed its journey south toward the international boundary.

Just a few miles from the border, the posse came across a small group of British soldiers. A red-coated captain called to the Americans to stop. Seeing Young struggling against his captors, the officer demanded to know what they were doing.

Before Conger could explain, Young shouted: "Captain, I am a Confederate officer! These men are Americans. They've captured me illegally! Please order them to set me free!"

"Is this true?" the British captain asked Conger. "What is your authorization to come into Canada armed to capture this man?"

Conger fumbled for an answer, but realizing he was in Canada illegally, he quickly understood he would have to play on the sympathies of the British officer.

"Sir, this man led a raid on St. Albans, robbed our banks, and shot and killed one of our citizens," Conger said. "We only wish to take him back to the United States and try him for murder and robbery."

"And for horse thievin'," Fuller interjected.

"Well, sir," replied the British officer. "I am taking charge of this man." He suggested that Conger and his men accompany him to Frelighsburg, where other Rebels were being held.

"If you go there you may be able to take four Confederates across the border instead of one," the captain said.

Conger raised his rifle, still intent on taking Young, but he lowered it when he realized he was close to creating a major international incident. He turned to Fuller and the others. "Men, I think it would be prudent if we went to Frelighsburg to see what we can do."

Under guard, the posse rode eight miles to the little garrison town where the British were holding Swager, Wallace and Gregg. Taken to the colonel in charge, Conger insisted the Canadians surrender the Rebels so they could be returned to Vermont.

"I bloody well don't think so," the officer replied. "These men are my prisoners and I intend to hold them for a hearing. I would suggest, sir, that you and your men return from whence you came."

Conger stared long and hard at the British officer.

"Sir, these men killed a man in our town and wounded two others. They robbed our banks and tried to burn our town, and to make their escape, they stole our horses. I demand you release these men into my custody."

The officer stood and glared at Conger.

"Demand?" he said, looking down his patrician nose. "I remind you that you are in no position to demand anything. I shall not listen to another word. You are in British North America illegally, and unless you wish to create an international crisis between your government and Great Britain, I suggest you turn your horses around and go back home. If not, I shall arrest you."

He pinned Conger with his gaze and spoke again: "It just wouldn't do to have Americans roaming around the colony armed to the teeth, now would it?"

Realizing his position was untenable, Congers turned to his men.

"I could insist on taking the Rebels back to Vermont, along with the money they stole from our banks, but I don't want to be responsible for causing a war with Great Britain." His gaze fell on each of the men in the posse. One man snorted and, looking at the British officer, said clearly: "I'd like to call his bluff."

"Don't be a fool," Conger told him. "Do you want to die here? Or wind up in prison?"

The man shook his head, sheepishly. "I guess not, George."

He mounted his horse, kicked him in the sides and turned toward home. Conger and the others followed. Young heaved a sigh of relief.

The colonel ordered his captain to accompany Young and his men to St. Jean where ten more Rebels were being held.

Young and the three with him were greeted warmly when they were placed in a large cell with their comrades.

"We thought you might be dead, Bennett," said Alamanda Bruce, shaking Young's hand.

"I'm all right," Young replied. "How did you get captured?"

"They found us asleep in a tavern in Bedford, just north of here. Me and Spurr," replied Bruce. Young glanced at Marcus Spurr.

"They took a little over $36,000 we had, lieutenant," Spurr said.

The others told of their plights. Collins was asleep in a room at Bacon's Hotel in Stanbridge East when he was roughly awakened by constables at 1 a.m. Lackey was arrested on the sidewalk outside the hotel. The two men had $4,679 between them. Both Rebels had ditched their pistols once over the border.

"At least we didn't have to pay for the room," Collins joked to the delight of the other men.

Doty and McGrorty gave up $12,645. They had been asleep in a barn at Durham Flats. They were awakened at gunpoint by Justice of the Peace Henry Whitman, who had been alerted about the bank robberies.

Scott was arrested by a detective at the Farnham Falls railroad station. He was carrying $2,859. Squire Tevis, Swager, and Wallace surrendered $19,028 after being captured near Frelighsburg. Dudley Moore was arrested at Waterloo, and $2,002 taken from him.

"What about Billy Tevis?" Young asked.

"Last I saw of him, Bennett, he was wearing a woman's dress and boarding a train," Spurr said. "Damndest lookin' woman I ever saw even if he did shave off his goatee." The others laughed.

"I heard Hutch got all the way to Montreal before he was arrested," Scott said. "I hear tell he was carryin' $100,000." Young frowned at the news. But then he brightened when he heard that seven of his twenty companions had escaped capture. In his head,

Young had tallied the amounts of money the men said they held when captured. He realized it amounted to about $177,200. He wondered how much those who escaped capture had taken. He would eventually learn that the banks claimed a combined loss of $208,000.

CHAPTER 15

WHEN he learned of the Confederate raid on his town, Vermont's Governor Smith sent a message to the War Department in Washington. The news shocked the Union's top brass, who immediately telegraphed military units in states along the border with Canada to be on guard against further Rebel attacks.

Smith was told to find enough troops to guard St. Albans. He telegraphed Army officials in Burlington, who sent 500 men, mostly veterans at home convalescing from wounds, as well as newly recruited troops who'd been awaiting transport to the war in the South. The men arrived the next morning and set up camp on the same Green that had held town citizens under duress.

In the border county of Orleans to the east, William W. Grout, commander of state provisional forces, immediately issued a broadside that was hastily posted in village stores and post offices around the county. It read, in part: "A Rebel raiding party from Canada has entered St. Albans and murdered her citizens, and in obedience to the above order I call upon every man who has a musket or rifle to report at once for military duty during this emergency. Bring powder and ball."

Grout further ordered men living in the towns of Barton, Newport, and Troy in Orleans County close to the border to report to militia officers. Similar orders were sent to other officials in towns and counties nearby. In Northfield, eight miles south of Montpelier, lay the military college, Norwich University. Its commander sent cadets up to Newport and other towns. In villages all along the border, gun dealers did a brisk business providing weapons to civilians who feared their towns might be next on the Confederates' list of places to attack.

In New York, Major General John A. Dix, commander of the Eastern Military District, was attending a dinner when an aide entered the room and whispered in his ear. Excusing himself, Dix went into an adjoining room and dictated a telegram. It ordered Colonel Redfield Proctor, the top military official in Vermont, to send a company of troops to St. Albans and pursue the Rebels.

"Send all efficient force you have and try to find the marauders who came in from Canada. Put a discreet officer in charge. In case they are not found on our side of the line, pursue into Canada and destroy them," Dix's telegram said.

It was a reckless order that could well have sprung a Confederate trap. The United States and Great Britain had earlier signed a neutrality pact, the Webster-Ashburton Treaty. The United States would violate that pact by sending troops into the Canadian province—just what the Confederates wanted. As one official in Richmond put it, a war between the United States and Great Britain could mean peace for the Confederacy.

Also dining with Dix that evening was Lord Richard Lyons, the British ambassador to the United States, who had just recently returned from a visit to the Canadian Provinces.

When he returned to the dining table, General Dix told the diners about the raid and his action. Shocked, Lord Lyons asked the general: "Did your government authorize armed soldiers to cross into Canada in pursuit?"

"No, sir," replied Dix. "I have issued the order on my own responsibility." To cover his action, Dix replied: "This is permissible under the 'hot pursuit' section of the Webster-Ashburton treaty."

Lord Lyons was not convinced. "We shall see, sir."

He excused himself and returned to the British Embassy where he sent a telegram to Lord Charles Monk, the royal governor-general of the Province of Canada.

When Secretary of State William H. Seward heard of Dix's order, he exploded, but then after considering the situation, Seward smiled. He sent for Lord Lyons, and when the British ambassador arrived, Seward told him the Rebels' actions were a deliberate attempt to start a war. He demanded their immediate extradition.

Lord Lyons protested. "Mister Secretary, we are holding a group of men who used our territory from which they mounted a raid in your country and then returned to our province. We have every right to hold them and allow our courts to decide on whether they should be extradited. It is all spelled out in the treaty."

Seward knew he could only press his demand up to a point. Continuing to demand the British turn the Rebels over might tip the British Empire fully onto the side of the Confederacy.

At the White House, President Lincoln's secretary handed the President a copy of General Dix's order that had been telegraphed to the War Department shortly after it was sent to Colonel Proctor in Vermont. Lincoln stretched his long legs under his desk and heaved a huge sigh, shaking his head. Readily understanding the full import of General Dix's action, the President scribbled a note on a sheet of paper rescinding Dix's order.

"Run this over to the War Department and give it to Mr. Stanton himself," the President ordered. One of his secretaries, John Hay, complied.

Lincoln was coming around to believe the South would be defeated, but he also knew the United States could not fight the Rebels and take on the British Empire at the same time.

After his secretary left, Lincoln stared out the window onto Pennsylvania Avenue, his head resting on the fingers of one hand. He sighed once more. This is the most awful job any man could have, he thought. But he knew he had to busy his mind, to push back the debilitating depression that had plagued him for too many years before it could rise again. The war had to be directed as he had been doing since Fort Sumter. He had to concentrate his efforts on Ulysses S. Grant and the general-in-chief's grand design for defeating the insurrection.

CHAPTER 16

OVER the following weeks, the foray by Conger's posse into Canada created an international sensation. The State Department demanded British colonial officials in Canada turn the Rebels over to the United States, but in a letter from London, the British icily replied that Her Majesty's courts in Canada would decide the soldiers' fate.

Newspapers in the United States, including the *New York Times*, criticized the British and called for the Rebels' extradition for trial. George N. Sanders, a politically connected Southerner and self-described tactician living in exile in Canada, convinced the two Confederate commissioners there to allow him to retain lawyers to defend the prisoners. Sanders considered himself an unofficial Confederate commissioner in Canada, but he was looked on by some in the Confederate government as a troublesome manipulator.

Sanders was especially hated by Captain Thomas Hines, who'd been one of Morgan's company commanders before he was captured following Morgan's defeat in Ohio. Hines had been sent to Canada to recruit Confederate soldiers who had escaped there, gathering men to raid Camp Douglas in Chicago and free thousands of prisoners. Hines considered Sanders an opportunist who could only cause trouble for the South in Canada and the United States.

But Sanders was now in the middle of the St. Albans affair and had access to thousands of dollars Confederate Commissioner

Jacob Thompson had deposited in the bank in Toronto prior to the raid in Vermont. On his own initiative, Sanders hired John J. C. Abbott as chief counsel for the raiders.

Abbott, aged 43, was formerly solicitor general for Canada East. He, in turn, hired Toussaint Antoine Rodolphe LaFlamme and William W. H. Kerr. Both men were well-known criminal lawyers in Canada East. Sanders and the attorneys put lawyers all over the region on retainer to prevent the United States government from hiring them.

But they overlooked one of the best criminal lawyers in all of Canada, Bernard Devlin, who soon joined the prosecution team.

Acting for the Canadian government along with Devlin would be Francis G. Johnson, Stephen Bethune, Edward Carter, John Rose, and C.F. Edwards, all Montreal lawyers.

Asa O. Aldis, a justice of the Vermont Supreme Court, was sent to Canada to represent Vermont's highest court. American attorneys J. H. Dewey, D. R. Bailey, Myron Buck and H. G. Edson were to look after the interests of the State of Vermont; and Edward A. Sowles, also an American, was retained to represent the three sacked banks.

A day before the hearing was to begin, Devlin, a handsome, dark-haired son of Irish immigrants, summoned his top two assistants to his hotel room. On an oak bureau lay a pile of legal papers. He greeted the men. .

"Now then, gentlemen," he said. "I think the best strategy—in fact the only strategy—is to call for extradition on the basis that these prisoners are nothing but murderers and thieves."

The two young lawyers glanced at each other.

Devlin went on. "I know, I know, the defense most likely will claim the Rebels acted under orders from their government, thereby claiming their action was legal as an act of war."

"Do they have proof of that?" Edwards asked. "Any official documents from the Confederate government?"

"My understanding is that Mister Young claims to have a copy of his commission as a first lieutenant in the Confederate Army, and orders to raid towns along the United States border with Canada. He will claim those are his war orders."

"That very thing is included in the Ashburton Treaty," Rose cautioned.

"And we must not forget Great Britain's recognition of the Confederate States as a power at war with another nation," Edwards said.

"Yes," Devlin agreed, "but I think we can argue around those things. We can make a solid case that these men were nothing but robbers and killers who acted on their own."

If they proved that, Devlin added, Canada had no other course but to extradite the Rebels to the United States under the Webster-Ashburton Treaty. The treaty was signed between Great Britain and the United States in 1842. Among other things, it called for extradition of criminals seeking refuge in either country.

Rose and Edwards agreed this was a workable strategy.

While the lawyers were unwrapping their legal weapons in court, Sanders and his Confederate minions began a public relations war among Canadians in the province. Many, if not most, Canadians were solidly behind the Rebels, helped along by a story Sanders convinced the *Evening Telegraph* to publish, countering stories the Americans were supporting. Sanders spread the word that the Rebels were acting as soldiers under specific orders from the Confederate government, and it was not they who had committed a crime, but rather the Americans who illegally pursued them into Canada.

"The enterprise was conducted without unnecessary violence...," the *Evening Telegraph* quoted Sanders. "...and was accompanied by an open and public declaration at the time by those engaged in it, that they were acting as soldiers under the orders of the Southern Confederacy and pursuant to those orders." He referred to Young's statement as he emerged from his St. Albans hotel that he was capturing the town in the name of the Confederate States of America.

The *Montreal Herald* also wrote a series of articles clearly biased in favor of the Rebels, prompting a reporter for the *New York Times* to write that the two Canadian papers were publishing "inflammatory articles...that daily abound in utter falsehoods about the United States." The *Times* reporter was concerned that: "The Canadian judiciary may decide against us in the case and let the marauders go free."

Believing that public sentiment in Montreal was strongest in favor of the Rebels and that they would be safer away from the border, Sanders played his ace. He sent his men around to restaurants and stores to circulate a rumor that Union General Dix had dispatched a large force of troops to cross the border and take the Rebels back to the United States. The ploy found fertile soil among the Canadians. Incensed that Dix would order American troops into Canada a second time, Montrealers talked about organizing a militia to oppose any invasion. When no American soldiers crossed the border, the fears dissolved, but sympathies had been aroused in favor of the raiders.

A few weeks after their capture, Young and his men were arraigned in the St. Jean court before Justice of the Peace Michel Joseph Charles Coursol.

Before the arraignment, Coursol had ridden from Montreal to St. Jean to talk with the officials who captured the Rebels, and he also interviewed Scott, one of the raiders.

In court, the Rebels were informed of seven charges against them arising from the attack on St. Albans—three for bank robbery, one for murder, one for intent to murder, and two for assault. They pled not guilty to all charges.

Coursol informed the raiders that they were being transferred to Montreal for their safety after the rumor was floated that another posse was on its way to recapture them and return them to Vermont.

Young smiled. "Well, boys, it looks like we'll be a little safer away from this town."

Shackled, Young and the others were loaded aboard carriages and driven to the St. Jean train station, accompanied by two dozen guards. The officials even worried that sympathetic Montrealers might try to free the prisoners and help them escape from Canada.

When he stepped off the train in Montreal, Collins shouted to people at the station: "Here we are in the beautiful city of Montreal, ladies and gentlemen. Step right up and get your tickets to the trial."

But because most of the Montrealers did not speak English and didn't know what was unfolding, they simply gawked at the shackled prisoners and their guards.

Carriages transferred Young and his men to the city jail, where they were placed in adjoining cells. Young sat on the bench inside the cell he shared with two of his compatriots and wondered what lay ahead.

Instead of delivering the usual jail food at dinner time, their jailer, Louis Payette, told the men he had a special treat for them. Leading them to the jail's dining room, he turned to usher in four of his deputies carrying huge trays with plates of food piled high on them—sliced roast beef, turkey, mashed potatoes, baked butternut squash and, most unexpected, bottles of wine and beer to wash it down.

"Look at this, Bennett!" exclaimed Collins: "A feast to grace the tables of the best homes in the South!"

"My land!" exclaimed Young. "This is indeed a feast! I'd say a feast fit for kings!"

Young and his fellow prisoners took their plates and dug in. All the food had been prepared by Montrealers solidly behind the Southerners.

Mopping his chin of gravy, Young turned to Collins "Tom, I have a good feeling we are going to come out of this all right."

Collins laughed. "I think we might if this grub is any indication how they feel about us up here." Patting his belly, Young smiled.

Magistrate Coursol convened their hearing on November 2nd in the Montreal Police Court and immediately granted a delay. The Rebels' lawyers had filed a motion asking for a hearing before Judge Thomas C. Aylwin in the Court of the Queen's Bench in Montreal to determine whether Coursol actually had authority to hear their case.

In Judge Aylwin's courtroom on November fifth, the Confederates' lawyers presented a motion for a writ of habeas corpus, claiming Coursol's hearing was illegal. They argued that, because he was a Justice of the Session of the Peace—the full title of Coursol's office—the judge lacked authority to preside over a case of this importance. But Judge Aylwin called the defense claim "utterly ridiculous" and ordered the case back to Coursol's court.

Back in court, Young lifted his gaze to the crowd in the balcony, scanning the faces. He drew in a quick breath. There was his father sitting beside another man and a young girl.

The elder Young, a tall, well-built man, had aged in the two years since his son left home. Young caught his father's eye and smiled broadly, urging him by hand signals to come down to the courtroom. His father smiled and nodded. The girl sitting beside him smiled briefly at Young, too. Puzzled, he managed a weak smile in return.

The elder Young descended to the courtroom and opened his arms to hug his son.

"Bennett," he cried. "It has been so long, so long." The two held each other tightly.

"Yes, father," Young said. "I didn't think I would see you so far from home. I... I can't tell you how happy I am you're here. How did you get here? Where are you staying? What...."

His father gripped Young by the shoulders. "Easy. One question at a time. I learned you had been captured so I arranged the trip by train. ..." Before the man could finish, Young turned to a few of his companions who remained in the courtroom.

"This is my father. He's come a long way." Young introduced his comrades, who gladly shook hands.

"You've a good son," Swager told the older man before he and the rest of the raiders were led away by bailiffs. Young pleaded for a little time to spend with his father and the remaining bailiffs walked a few feet away, their eyes still trained on their prisoner.

"I want to know how everyone is at home. Has the war affected you?" Young paused. "Oh, please father, sit down for a minute."

The two sat on a bench. "I came by train from home. I arrived late last night, too late to visit you in the jail or to let you know I had come. It was a long dirty ride, but I'm here and I intend to stay with you," Young's father said.

A frown creased Young's face as thoughts of the trial and its possible outcome swept over him.

"Don't worry, Bennett." His father could see what he was thinking. "You have the best lawyers in this town. You may have lost this one, but you and your men have a good case. I'm sure Justice Coursol will free you."

"I hope you're right, father," Young replied. "I don't want to think about the alternative." He looked beyond his father, searching for the other people he had seen in the balcony.

"Who were those people seated with you?"

"He's the Reverend Stuart Robinson from Kentucky," the elder Young replied. "He's been in exile since he spoke out loudly against the Lincoln administration. He came here to administer to the religious needs of our people who fled here. And the girl is his daughter, Mattie."

"I see," Young muttered. He was struck by the girl's beauty and wanted to meet her. "I would like to talk to Reverend Robinson some time."

"And his daughter, too, I suspect," the elder Young said, clapping his son's shoulder.

"Well...yes," Young agreed. At that moment a bailiff took Bennett Young's arm to return him to jail with the others.

"I'm sorry, sir, but it's time to go," he said.

Father and son embraced again and Young was led away. He looked back.

"Take care of yourself, father." The older man nodded gravely. Young scanned the balcony again, but the Reverend and his daughter had gone. After Young left the courtroom, his father sat for a moment to collect himself before returning to his rooms. It would be a long stay.

The trial resumed December 13th, a cold and snowy day. Magistrate Coursol gazed around his courtroom from the bench. He stroked his long chin whiskers and smoothed his full mustache across his cheeks. He peered up at the gallery crowded with spectators, then looked at the prisoners and the lawyers for the prosecution and the defense. All were in place and ready.

"All right, gentlemen, let's begin."

Over the next week, a parade of prosecution witnesses, mostly from Vermont, provided details of the incident in St. Albans— how the Rebels had raided the banks and how much money they stole. Stable owner Fuller described how the Rebels had saddled his horses and led them out to the street for their companions to mount when it was time to flee.

"They took every last one of my horses," Fuller said. "I'm ruined!" He stopped and then blurted out an afterthought. "And they almost shot me."

Late in the afternoon, the prosecution rested and Coursol told the defense to be ready to put on its case the next morning. The Confederates' lawyers held a strategy session that night and agreed that Young should be the first to testify.

"He will be a powerful witness," Abbot told the others. Abbott realized the prosecution would most certainly challenge the authenticity of Young's copies of his commission as a lieutenant and the orders he was given by Secretary of War Seddon.

"If they do, I suggest Bennett ask the court for a recess," Abbott said. "We can send to Richmond for more copies." The lawyers agreed. Abbott went to the jail early the next morning to brief Young and the others on the strategy.

Shortly after 9 a.m., the magistrate turned to the defense lawyers lined up in front of their row of prisoners.

"Call your witnesses," he said. Abbott nodded at Young who took the stand.

"Lieutenant Young," Abbott said. "You are a duly commissioned officer of the Confederate States of America?"

"Yes, sir, I am."

"And do you have proof of your commission, sir?"

"I do."

"Please, would you read aloud your orders?"

Young reached in his pocket and produced two documents, which he read aloud: "You are hereby informed that the President has appointed you First Lieutenant in the Provisional Army in the service of the Confederate States to take rank as such from the 16th day of June, 1864. Should the Senate at their next session advise and consent thereto, you will be commissioned accordingly. Immediately on receipt thereof, please communicate through the Adjutant and Inspector General's Office your acceptance, or non-acceptance, of said appointment and with your letter of acceptance return to the Adjutant and Inspector General the oath herewith enclosed, properly filled up, subscribed and attested, reporting at the same time your age, residence when appointed, and the state in which you were born."

The paper was signed by James A. Seddon, Secretary of War, and dated June 16, 1864. Abbott asked that the document be entered as defense exhibit "M."

Abbott asked Young if he had any additional instructions from Secretary Seddon. Young unfolded the second document and read it at Kerr's prompting.

"Lieutenant B. H. Young is hereby authorized to organize for special services a company not exceeding twenty in number from those who belong to the service and are at the time beyond the Confederate States.

"They will be entitled to their pay, rations, clothing, but no other compensation for any service which they may be called upon to render.

"The organization will be under the command of this department to be disbanded at its pleasure and the members returned to respective companies." It also was signed by Seddon and dated the same as the first document. Kerr asked that the document be entered as defense exhibit "N."

Young told the court he was a Kentuckian and an officer in the Confederate Army at war with the United States. He said he was ordered to recruit up to twenty men and conduct a raid upon a northern frontier town. He chose St. Albans, Vermont, because it was close to the Canadian border and because the town's three banks were easy targets. His men were still enlisted in the Confederate Army. His government had authorized what he and his men did at St. Albans.

His voice rising with passion, Young turned to face Magistrate Coursol.

"The course I intended to pursue in Vermont, and which I was able to carry out but partially, was to retaliate in some measure for the barbarous atrocities of...," and he contemptuously sounded out the names of Union generals, "... Grant, Butler, Sherman, Hunter, Milroy, Sheridan, Gierson and other Yankee officers, except that I would scarce harm women and children under any provocation, or unarmed defenseless and unresisting citizens, even Yankees, or to plunder for my own benefit."

The crowd in the balcony rose to their feet in unison, applauding and shouting their agreement with Young. Coursol banged his gavel.

The young Confederate officer said he and his men were not fully prepared to defend themselves in the courtroom because the Union blockade of Southern ports prevented any communication with the Confederate government in Richmond.

Attorney Devlin leaped to his feet to object for the prosecution. Before Coursol could rule, Young hastily went on: "Therefore, your honor, I formally request a thirty-day postponement of these proceedings so further efforts can be made to obtain more official documents to prove my claims." Devlin again objected.

Coursol replied: "I shall consider your objection, Mr. Devlin."

He adjusted his spectacles to read Young's documents, but made no comment on the request for a delay in the hearing.

Marcus Spurr and Charles Swager testified that they joined the Confederate Army because they considered the United States their enemy. They made war against their former country because of those intense feelings. The spectators murmured their approval, prompting the magistrate to pound his gavel again.

Late in the afternoon, Abbott called Captain Thomas Collins to the witness box. The handsome Rebel was a commanding figure, tall, clean shaven with broad shoulders. Speaking softly, he told the judge he joined the Army as a commissioned officer and later he was promoted to captain. His voice rose with passion as he recalled the recent past.

"The Yankees dragged my father from his peaceful fireside and family and imprisoned him in Camp Chase where his suffering impaired his health," Collins said, looking directly at the prosecution lawyers. "They have stolen Negroes and forced them into their service, leaving their women and children to starve and die." His knuckles turned white as he tightened his grip on the witness box railing. "They have pillaged and burned private dwellings, banks, villages, and depopulated entire districts, while boasting of their inhuman acts as deeds of heroism and exhibiting their plunder in northern cities as trophies of Federal victories."

He looked around the courtroom. His impassioned words lay heavily on the spectators.

Recalling a discussion by the defense lawyers on the Ashburton Treaty, Collins said it was designed to prosecute murderers, thieves, and robbers.

"I am neither, but a soldier serving my country in a war commenced and waged against us by a barbarous foe, in violation of their own Constitution, in disregard of all rules of warfare as interpreted by civilized nations and Christian peoples."

This time, turning to face the bench, Collins claimed neither he nor his companions violated Canadian law. It was the Vermont posse that pursued them into the country who broke the law.

As for the raid, he said: "If I aided in the sack of the St. Albans banks, it was because they were public institutions and because I knew the pocket nerve of the Yankees to be the most sensitive and that they would suffer most by its being rudely touched." With contempt in his voice, he went on: "Federal soldiers are brought up at one thousand dollars a head and the capture of two hundred thousand dollars is equivalent to the destruction of two hundred said soldiers." Collins paused as the spectators cheered.

The magistrate rapped his gavel angrily. "One more outburst of this sort and I will clear the courtroom!"

With a slight smile crossing his face, Collins continued: "I thought the expedition would pay. I guess it did, in view of the fact that they have wisely sent several thousand soldiers from the bloody front to protect exposed points in their rear." Laughter rocked the courtroom and the justice again rapped his gavel, but allowed the spectators to remain.

After Collins sat down, Abbott addressed the magistrate. "Your honor, you have heard these gallant men speak from their hearts. They are truly patriots of their new country. I request you rule on our request for a thirty-day delay in further proceedings so we may communicate with officials in Richmond."

Instantly on his feet, T. G. Johnson, objected on behalf of the Canadian government.

"Your honor," he sneered, "if a continuance is granted and when the time is nearly over, the defense will ask for another and another until the men might go free."

His voice dripping with sarcasm, Abbott countered, "Any objection to a delay in these proceedings might come with some grace from the United States."

Standing erect and facing Johnson, Abbott continued, "But for the counsel for the Crown to have opposed it before the circumstances of the case could be examined is something truly astonishing and which could never have been expected in a country noted for its sympathy for political refugees." He insisted the Canadian government had no right to interfere in the case.

Laflamme rose, the fingers of both hands in his vest pockets as if he were probing for a piece of biscuit within them.

"The Crown has entered into a conspiracy with the United States. The purpose of kidnapping the prisoners from British territory where they were entitled to their freedom and to surrender them to their enemies who were awaiting their rendition, is not to do justice but to wreak vengeance upon them," he thundered. The prisoners, he concluded, had a right to all the evidence they could gather in their defense.

Coursol looked up from his notes. Without explanation, he said: "The court grants the defense request for a continuance until December 13th. Court is adjourned."

With a rap of his gavel, he left the bench.

CHAPTER 17

BACK in their jail cells, the prisoners joked and pounded each other on the back.

"That's one for our side!" Charles Higbee shouted over the din.

Alamanda Bruce and Marcus Spurr danced a jig, and finally too exhausted to continue, they flopped onto the cement floor, laughing.

"You're a helluva raider, but you can't dance worth a damn," Bruce mocked his partner. Spurr wrestled him onto his back.

'Get off me, you big galoot!" Bruce shouted.

"All right men!" Young called. "Let's settle down. The lawyers will be here soon."

Minutes later, Abbott, Kerr and LaFlamme entered the cellblock to explain their continuing strategy. Kerr said he would write a letter to President Lincoln asking that a courier be granted a pass through the union lines to carry a letter to Richmond requesting confirmation of Young's commission and orders for the raid on St. Albans.

"I think we also should write to Lord Lyons in Washington," suggested LaFlamme, "We'll ask him to speak to President Lincoln about allowing the courier."

"Lord Lyons is the British ambassador in Washington, isn't he?" Young said. LaFlamme nodded. He said he also would write to James M. Carlisle, a Washington lawyer, asking him to call on the American president and Lord Lyons, for the same reasons.

"I'm not sure any of this will do any good," Young said. Kerr agreed but said they had to try. He suggested writing to Lord Monck, the British Governor General in Canada, asking if he, too, would send a messenger to Richmond for the documents.

"All right," said Young. "We need those documents. If we don't get them, we'll be sent back across the border, and none of us wants that. Would you bring the written letters here so I can read them before you send them?" The lawyers nodded and took their leave.

In short order, Kerr brought the letters to Young at the jail. In the letter to Lord Monck, Kerr argued that the prisoners had a right to protection as belligerents, having taken refuge in neutral Canada.

"Since other efforts to get through to Richmond have been intercepted by the United States," Kerr wrote, "the prisoners have resolved to throw themselves upon Your Lordship's humanity in asking such assistance as may be lawfully afforded them in their attempt to procure from Richmond the evidence which will conclusively establish their innocence of such crimes as were reputed to them." Young liked the letter. He read the others and handed them back to Kerr.

"Thank you," he said.

While they waited for answers, the Rebels enjoyed the attentions of Montrealers, who feted them with lavish meals, wine, and beer, day after day. The largesse was paid for by Sanders using the Confederate bank accounts, although the prisoners did not know this.

Feeling puckish one evening after the letters had been sent off, Young wrote to the *St. Albans Messenger*: "Will you please send me two copies of your daily? During the present investigation, your editorials are quite interesting and will furnish a considerable amusement to myself and comrades." Smiling to himself, he continued: "You are somewhat abusive, but I have sufficient magnanimity to overlook your ire, feeling that in after years you will do me the justice to repair the wrong. I am extremely sorry I cannot visit your town and subscribe to your valuable journal in person. My business engagements in Montreal prevent my coming at present. Should you visit Montreal within the next few weeks, I will be found at Payette's Hotel and will be grateful to see you."

He reread his words and laughed heartily.

In a letter to the manager of the Tremont House, Young wrote: "You will probably remember that I was a guest at your house. I regret I neglected to settle my hotel bill. Nevertheless, I am enclosing five dollars drawn from the St. Albans Bank."

The others laughed when he read them that part of his letter.

Young also asked the hotel manager to remember him to Cyrus Bishop, the teller at the St. Albans Bank, who was forced to take the Confederate oath.

"Please tender my regard to Mr. Bishop in hopes he will bear faith and allegiance to the Confederate States of America, which he has so solemnly sworn to do. We have heard nothing of the old gent, president of the institution at the time we suspended him. I presume he is still faithful to the pledge and is firmly fixed in the old armchair. If so, tell the old boozer his sentence has now expired."

He also wrote that he had left behind a "ruffled shirt" and a flask of Old Rifle Whiskey, which he intended to use in case his ammunition was used up.

"It is warranted to hold uphill at one-hundred and fifty yards." He showed the letter to Collins. His companion chuckled.

"Why, that's mighty decent of you writing to your old friends in St. Albans, and pay your bill." He passed the letter on to the other prisoners.

"Old Rifle Whiskey?" Spurr laughed. "When did you take to drink, Bennett?" The others joined in joshing Young.

A day before their hearing resumed, the prisoners had a visitor, Reverend Robinson. The Reverend introduced himself and said hello to Young specifically. Young remembered seeing him in the balcony of the courtroom with his daughter.

"Good afternoon, gentlemen," the Reverend said. "I am here to determine if any of you wish me to write letters to your loved ones at home or if there is something you need that I might bring to you."

He looked around, but the men were quiet. "If any of you feel the need for prayer, I would be happy to oblige."

Young spoke up. "That's very kind of you, Reverend. I don't know about the rest of these rascals, but I could use some writing paraphernalia, pens and paper and such." Robinson said he would bring the things Young wanted on his next visit. A few of the others asked for personal items, socks and handkerchiefs.

The elder Young also visited his son several times while the Rebels waited for answers to their letters to Washington and Lord Monck.

Arriving at the jail on a cold day in December, Young's father said he would have to return home.

"I will send you money or anything you need," his father said. He reached through the bars and took his son's hand in his. "Don't worry, Bennett, things will turn out right in the end."

The older man choked up. "Goodbye son. God bless you and your men."

"Wait, father. I have some letters for mother and my sisters and brothers. Please see they get them." His father took the letters, squeezed his son's hand one more time, and walked from the cell block.

The court hearings resumed on a bitterly cold morning, December 13th. There had been no reply to any of the letters. It was rumored that Lord Monck wanted Young and his men extradited as quickly as possible to smooth relations with Washington. The prisoners entered the courtroom, dejected and fearful of the outcome.

The gallery was again filled with spectators who had come to the courthouse early, anticipating a release of the prisoners.

As he sat down, Collins turned to Young and whispered: "Don't worry, Bennett, it isn't over yet."

"Aye, Tom. But it doesn't look good."

Coursol gaveled the hearing to order. Abbott rose and immediately objected to Coursol's right to hear the case. The crowd erupted in applause and shouts of support. The magistrate pounded his gavel, threatening once again to clear the courtroom. He turned to Abbott.

"As judge of the Sessions?" Coursol asked, seeking clarification of the man's objection.

"As judge of the Sessions or in any other capacity in which you may sit," replied Abbott.

Devlin jumped to his feet. "This court's sole duty is to hear evidence, not to hear arguments about the law."

Turning toward Devlin, Abbott countered, "If the court has no jurisdiction, it has no right to hear evidence."

"The objection is to my jurisdiction in toto?" Coursol asked Abbott.

"Yes," Abbott insisted. "I deny your right to sit at all."

Looking down at his papers for a moment, Coursol stated: "I am obliged to hear any objections to my jurisdiction in this case."

Young's pulse raced and he reached over and grabbed Collins by the arm. The two friends smiled at each other. The other prisoners also stirred in their seats, thinking that something important might favor them.

Abbott launched into an argument that went to the heart of the Ashburton Treaty and its sections relating to extradition of fugitives.

"Your honor, the Ashburton Treaty between Canada and the United States is not legal, since the act of the Canadian Parliament of 1861 agreeing to it has not received Royal sanction." Abbott seemed to abandon the Rebels defense strategy that he and the other lawyers had based their entire case on so far.

"Therefore," he continued, "the act of the Imperial Parliament in London must prevail over that of the Canadian Parliament." He argued further that according to the Imperial Parliament, his clients could only be arrested by a warrant from the Governor General, not by a local magistrate such as Coursol.

"Therefore, your honor, your warrant being illegal, you cannot sit on this case."

The spectators erupted in shouts and applause.

"Free the prisoners!" they shouted. "Let them go!"

Coursol glared up at them and pounded his gavel. Finally, he spoke.

"You have raised a knotty question. I will take your argument under advisement and announce my decision this afternoon. Court is adjourned until 2 p.m."

Seated with the others in their cells, Young lay his head back against the stone wall and closed his eyes. This time he kept his thoughts to himself. *If we are freed, I shall return home and join a regiment somewhere. I'm needed.*

His thoughts darkened. *But if we are extradited, then our lives are forfeit; we will be strung up like sides of beef to swing on the end of a rope. All lost.* He shook off the dismal thoughts.

"Who has the time?" he asked.

"One thirty-five, Bennett. Not time yet," said Collins.

Just before 2 p.m., the prisoners, their lawyers, and the

spectators re-entered the courthouse. All eyes focused on the judge's chamber door, wondering what was happening inside.

They waited. The judge did not appear. After forty-five minutes, Abbott turned to Young.

"I think the longer he takes the better it will be for our side," he said. "If he were going to order extradition, he would not take so long."

"I hope you are right, sir," Young said.

"Bennett, what's going on?" Swager asked from his seat on the other side of Collins.

"I'm not certain, but Mister Abbott thinks the delay means we might be all right."

Finally, as the clock struck three, Coursol entered the courtroom. His ruling in favor of the Rebels nearly mirrored the words Abbott had expressed during his presentation earlier.

When the magistrate finished citing evidence presented on both sides of the question, he looked up and said, "I therefore declare that having no warrant from the Governor General to authorize the arrest of the accused as required by the Imperial Act, I possess no jurisdiction. Consequently...." his remarks were drowned out as a roar from the gallery shook the courtroom. He pounded his gavel for nearly a full minute, then glared as he continued: "Consequently, I am bound in law, justice and fairness to order the immediate release of the prisoners from custody upon all the charges brought before me."

He rapped his gavel once.

"Let the prisoners be discharged."

Young and his comrades leaped to their feet, hugging each other and shouting, trying to make themselves heard above the din.

Young turned to Abbott and took his hand, shaking it heartily. "You did it! You did it, Mister Abbott! Thank God!"

Spectators began scurrying around for the hats they had thrown in the air upon the magistrate's ruling. There was a mad dash for the stairs and the doors to let those waiting outside know the verdict. Reporters ran off to waiting carriages to take them to their newspapers.

Attorney Devlin strode angrily to the bench as Coursol readied himself to leave the courtroom.

"Your honor, I must protest your verdict," Devlin said. "You, sir, made your ruling without hearing the merits of our case." He gripped the magistrate's bench. "These men were charged with seven separate charges while they have been examined on only the one charge." He angrily told the judge he should have been allowed to present evidence on the other six charges.

"Would you discharge a criminal on six indictments because he was acquitted on one?" Devlin demanded.

"Having no jurisdiction in the one case, I could certainly have none on the others," Coursol replied.

As the full contingent of lawyers for the prosecution approached the bench, Coursol raised his hand: "Not another word on this. I have the weight of the responsibility of such a course, but I am bound as a magistrate to do what my conscience and duty direct, without regard to influence, feelings, or consequences."

With that, he turned and strode from the courtroom, leaving the unhappy lawyers for the prosecution standing dumbfounded and angry in front of his bench.

The magistrate also had ordered the return to the raiders of $86,950 that had been confiscated when they were captured. Anticipating such a ruling, the sheriff had packed the money in two bags and turned it over to John Porterfield, the Confederates' banker.

Still stunned by the verdict, the Rebels were hustled out of the building as a huge crowd that had gathered outside the courthouse cheered wildly.

Coursol was soon castigated by Canadian barristers for his ruling. In a letter to the *New York Times* printed on December 22nd, one writer signing only as "Englishman," called Coursol a disgraceful Dogberry.

He claimed Coursol could not have written the ten-page decision during the two-and-a-half hours while in recess. Instead, "Englishman" strongly hinted that the decision had been written beforehand by one of the defense lawyers.

CHAPTER 18

THE Southerners left the courtroom and quickly disappeared into the crowd, making their way to the homes of Confederate sympathizers in Montreal. Fearing the Canadians might still give in to demands from Washington and return him and his men to the United States, Young, along with Turner Tevis and Hutchinson—now recovered from his wounds—hired a hackney driver and headed for rural Quebec, east of Montreal.

"We have to get out of the country," Young told the other two when they climbed aboard the carriage. "I'm afraid the Yankees aren't going to give up so easily."

Young's words were prophetic. Edward A. Sowles, who represented the three St. Albans banks, had prepared a fresh warrant for the re-arrest of the former prisoners. He tried two judges who refused to sign it, but finally located Superior Court Judge James Smith in his Montreal home, who did. It was only a matter of making the arrests again.

Meanwhile, the elderly driver of the carriage carrying Young and his two friends flogged his ancient horse along a country road paralleling the St. Lawrence River, traveling eighty-three miles northeast to Trois-Rivieres, stopping at French-speaking homes along the way for food and shelter from the cold. At Trois-Rivieres, the Rebels hired a younger driver and a faster horse and sleigh.

"Now, we can make better time," Young said.

"I was sick of seeing the back of that old man," Turner Tevis griped.

Young was silent for long stretches. This is too easy, he thought. No one seems to be chasing us. He stirred in his seat, remembering the long ago flight across southern Ohio, when he was sure the fresh Federals troops would eventually catch Morgan and his exhausted raiders.

Two and a half days later, they arrived at Levis, just south of the river across from Quebec City, where they stopped to find quarters and dinner. Early the next morning, they boarded the sleigh again and headed for Riviere-Ouille, where they found rooms at a hotel.

Although they tried to remain incognito as they went from town to town, the French hotel owner realized who these men were and feted them at dinner. Resuming their journey early the next morning, the three men and their driver made their way through deepening snow to Riviere-du-Loup and on to St. Francis, just twenty miles from the Quebec-New Brunswick border.

Weary of the ride, the travelers entered the first inn they saw. As they signed the register, they heard a voice: "Well, if it isn't Lieutenant Young."

A Montreal constable, Marcel Ermantinger, and three deputies confronted them, pistols drawn. Shocked, Young and his companions raised their hands.

"What? How?" Young stammered.

"The same way you got here, lieutenant," Ermantinger interrupted. "By carriage."

He paused to smirk. "By two carriages, actually, before the snow. We pushed on looking for you and your friends, but until now we missed you."

Young sighed. "How did you know we would stop here?"

"I knew you would find your way here eventually. It was just a matter of time. And I had time to wait." Young recalled what he had been thinking after leaving Trois Rivieres.

"Yes," he said quietly. "Just a matter of time."

The next morning, Ermantinger and his deputies hired three sleighs to return the Rebels to Montreal. They had traveled three hundred tortuous miles and were almost within sight of freedom, only to be taken again.

As he settled in one of the sleighs between two deputies, Young thought about his recapture. How had this come to pass?

The same mistake, he thought. We made the same mistake twice. Had Morgan not gone into Indiana and across Ohio, slowing him down over the long distance, and if we had only ridden across Canada a little faster, likely we would not have been overtaken.

Back in the Montreal jail, Charles Swager and Marcus Spurr greeted their three compatriots.

"Bennett!" Spurr cried. "We thought you had made it safely out of the country!"

"Almost, Marcus, almost," Young replied sadly. The others described how they, too, were taken again.

His face grim, Young asked: "Did Collins and the others make it?"

"I don't know, Bennett," replied Spurr. Swager shrugged his shoulders.

Unknown to the recaptured men, Collins, Scott, Bruce and Doty had gone into hiding in a rural Quebec town. They fled Montreal in January and found shelter with sympathizers where they would remain until spring. Later in April they would reach Cape Breton to learn the war had ended and Lincoln had been assassinated.

Magistrate Coursol's release of the Rebels had created uproar in the United States and in Canada. Some newspaper editors in the northern border states called the ruling an outrageous act, charging Magistrate Coursol with simply going through the motions of a hearing while all along he had been paid to side with the Rebels.

The *St. Albans Messenger* thundered: "Judge Coursol has not only written himself down as an ass, but has laid himself open to the very serious charge of being bribed."

The *Burlington Free Press*, the *Burlington Times*, and several newspapers along the northern border seconded the sentiments of the *Messenger*.

A few days after Magistrate Coursol's decision, General Dix informed all his commanders in the New York Military District that American troops would be sent into Canada if any future raids by Confederates were launched from that country. Top officials in the Province of Canada and the United States warned that further United States' incursions into the British province would mean war between the two countries.

For a second time, President Lincoln countermanded Dix.

CHAPTER 19

DECEMBER 27, 1864, dawned cold and snowy in Montreal. The remaining Confederate prisoners, Young, Hutchinson Tevis, Swager, and Spurr, were fed and then escorted under heavy guard to Judge Smith's courtroom in the Superior Court.

As they entered, Spurr nudged Young. "Look who's here, Bennett."

He pointed toward Samuel Breck, from whom Spurr and the others took $393 that the merchant had intended to deposit in the Bank of St. Albans to pay off a loan.

Young turned toward Abbott. He pointed out Breck and told Abbott about the money.

The defense lawyer realized where the prosecution was going.

"It looks like they are again going to claim you and the others were nothing but robbers and thieves. This should prove interesting,"

Abbott turned to the other lawyers and they whispered together until the bailiff called the court to order and the judge entered from his chambers behind the bench.

Abbott muttered. "It's Judge Smith, the same one who signed the warrant for your re-arrest.'

"Is that bad?" Young asked.

"We shall see. We shall see," Abbot said.

A bailiff told Young and the other Rebels to take seats in the prisoner's box to the left of the judge.

The judge looked toward Devlin. "Is the prosecution ready?"

"We are, your honor," Devlin replied.

"The defense, Mr. Abbott?"

"We are, judge."

"Very well. Mister Devlin, call your first witness."

"We call Samuel Breck of St. Albans, Vermont, to the stand."

Abbott immediately leaped to his feet. "We object to this witness. The prosecution has obviously decided to make this a case of simple assault and robbery when it goes far beyond that."

The judge looked at Devlin.

"Your honor, we need only to prove that a prime facie case of robbery is needed for extradition of these prisoners according to the Ashburton Treaty. Mister Breck is a St. Albans merchant who was robbed as he entered one of the banks these men held up."

"That argument lacks credibility on the face of it," said Abbott, "As the record shows from the trial before Judge Coursol, these men declared when they entered the bank they were Confederate soldiers and that fact was upheld by the documents the leader of the Confederates, Lieutenant Young, presented to Judge Coursol. Those documents were given to Lieutenant Young as evidence he had been appointed a lieutenant in the service of the Army of the Confederate States of America and describing the mission he was ordered to carry out. I mean by that the raid upon St. Albans, Vermont."

The judge took notes on the arguments, and then looked up to announce: "Objection overruled. I will allow testimony by Mister Breck."

Abbott sat down and scowled, scribbling notes on his notepad.

In the witness box, Breck glanced nervously at the prisoners and shifted in his seat.

"Mister Breck, would you state your name and tell the court where you live, please?" Devlin instructed.

"My name is Samuel Breck and I live in St. Albans, Vermont."

"What is your occupation?"

"I am a merchant in St. Albans, Vermont."

"Where were you in the late afternoon of October 19, 1864?"

Breck wiped his lips with his hand. "I was in St. Albans...I mean I was in the Bank of St. Albans."

"And would you describe for the court what happened when you entered the bank?"

Breck again wiped his lips and uncrossed his legs.

"When I opened the door, I saw several men with guns pointed at the clerks. They seemed to be gathering up money and putting it in big satchels they carried. When I realized what was happening, I turned to run out of the bank, but one of the men... I found out later they were Rebels... grabbed me by the throat and held a gun to my head. He threatened to kill me if I didn't give him my leather bag."

"And did you give him the bag?" Devlin asked.

"Yes, sir, I did. The man was choking me." Breck's hand went to his throat as if to feel again the choking sensation. "And... and I thought he was going to shoot me."

"And what was in the leather bag you carried, Mister Breck?"

"I had three hundred and ninety-three dollars in it." His face grew grim as he recalled surrendering the money.

"And what was your intention to do with the money, sir?" Devlin asked, looking up from his notes.

"I went to the bank to repay a loan."

"So, you went to the bank to repay a loan, but the money was taken from you before you could transact your business, is that correct, sir?" Devlin asked.

"Yes sir. They just plain robbed me before I could give the bank the money."

"Who robbed you?" Devlin asked.

"They did," Breck said. "Those men there." He pointed to Young and the others.

The prosecutor pressed on. "Do you recognize any of the men seated at that table there who robbed you?"

Breck looked toward the defense table. "Yes, sir, that man there was the one who throttled me and took my money."

"Which one are you referring to?" Devlin asked.

"The second one from the right in the first row." Spurr shifted slightly in his seat and lowered his eyes.

"Let the record show the witness has identified Marcus Spurr as the man who robbed the witness of three hundred ninety three dollars inside the Bank of St. Albans, Vermont," Devlin said. "Thank you, Mister Breck. No further questions."

"Mr. Abbott?" the judge asked.

Abbott stood. "No questions, your honor." When Breck left the stand, Young wondered why Abbott did not question the witness.

The prosecution then called George Bettersworth, a Confederate refugee in Canada. He testified he had been jailed in Montreal for a few days on the belief by police that he was one of the Rebel raiders. Bettersworth testified he had met Young and Spurr while planning an attempt to free Confederate prisoners from Camp Douglas, and again in Toronto where Young had been studying for the ministry.

"When I first met Lieutenant Young, he told me about the raids being organized for plundering and burning northern towns along the frontier," Bettersworth testified. He said the prisoners told him while he was in jail with them they had robbed the three St. Albans banks and stole horses to make their getaway.

Under cross-examination by Abbott, Bettersworth conceded the prisoners told him the raid was in retaliation for atrocities being committed by Yankee troops in the South.

Checking his notes for a brief moment, Abbott asked Bettersworth: "Tell me, sir, were you in the war before coming to Canada?"

"Yes. For two years. I was captured at Pittsburgh Landing."

"That battle also is known as Shiloh, is it not Mister Bettersworth?

"Yes, sir. Named after the church there, Shiloh Church. We almost beat General Grant there."

"What year was that, Mister Bettersworth?"

"It was 1862, sir. April sixth and seventh. I was captured on the seventh."

"And did you observe Yankee soldiers involved in certain activity after the battle?

Bettersworth hesitated. "Do you mean what did they do there?"

"Yes," Abbott replied. "Tell the court what you observed."

"Well, sir, I seen some Yanks drinkin' and then they broke into houses and stole what they could get their hands on. Then they burned half a dozen houses and killed livestock." He paused, the realization dawning that he might be helping the defense.

"And did the Yankees steal anything of yours? "Abbott pressed.

"Yes, sir."

"Well, what did they steal, Mr. Bettersworth?"

Bettersworth looked at Devlin for guidance, but the Canadian lawyer's eyes were elsewhere. Reluctantly, Bettersworth replied: "I had fifty dollars wrapped in a handkerchief. They stole that. I was going to send it home."

"Did they take anything else?" Abbott asked, bending to check his notes.

"They took my boots."

Abbott straightened and told the judge he had no further questions. Devlin shook his head when the judge asked him if he wanted to cross-examine. Judge Smith adjourned the court session for the day after Bettersworth's testimony, saying he had other pressing business to take care of.

The Rebels were taken back to their cells. Abbott joined them later that evening.

"Do you think Breck hurt us today, Mister Abbott?" Young asked, picking at the roast beef and mashed potatoes the men were served.

"It's hard to tell. The judge overruled me, but if this is the only avenue the prosecution is pursuing, I don't think it will add up to much."

Young chewed a piece of beef, unconvinced.

"Mister Abbott, who they goin' to put in the box tomorrow?" Spurr asked. He extended a bottle of beer to the lawyer, who declined.

"I understand they are going to put the bank's lawyer on first. I'm not sure what the point is, but it must have something to do with their claim that the robbery is enough for extradition," Abbott replied.

"When are we going to testify?" Swager asked. Abbott assured the men they would get a chance to tell their side of the story once the prosecution ended its case.

"Well, gentlemen, enjoy your meal. I envy you that much anyway, eating the way you do. Better than some of the hotel restaurants here," the attorney joked. "Good night. I will see you in court tomorrow morning."

"Good night, sir," replied Young. "We'll be there."

CHAPTER 20

THE next morning, Edward A. Sowles stood in the witness box. Attorney Devlin looked at his notes. He had carefully thought out his line of questioning, seeking to bolster what he hoped was the judge's opinion, that the Rebels were common criminals.

"Mister Sowles, you represent three banks in St. Albans, is that correct?" he asked.

"Yes sir, I do."

"And those banks were robbed the afternoon of October nineteenth, and some \$208,000 was taken, is that correct?"

"Yes, it is."

Devlin got straight to the point. "Was robbery a crime in Vermont at the time of these holdups?"

Young stirred in his seat and scowled. Of course it was a crime, but nothing like you Yankees are doing in the South.

Sowles agreed it was a crime and the facts as they were so far presented constituted a robbery. Devlin sat, a grin of triumph on his face.

Abbott checked his notes. "Mister Sowles, in your opinion should a detachment of United States soldiers under the command of an officer in your army do like acts as those charged against these prisoners, your soldiers and officers being then in Georgia, would they be guilty of robbery?" Young sat up, all ears to hear what Sowles would say.

Devlin leaped to his feet. "I object!"

"Overruled. Answer the question, Mister Sowles," the judge said.

"I think not," said Sowles. "The Federal and the so-called Confederate armies were in the state of Georgia and that was the battleground," he said. Many in the courtroom knew he was referring to Sherman's massive attacks through Georgia.

"The State of Vermont is not in rebellion against the authority of the United States, but is a loyal state," he pronounced loudly. "Its citizens are not committing acts of treason. Many of those in Georgia are doing so. I consider the act of the prisoners as an act of robbery." Sowles stopped, hoping he had made his point. Young was not sure if he liked Abbott's questions or Sowles's answers.

"No further questions." Abbott sat.

Judge Smith looked toward the prosecution. "Do you have any more witnesses today, Mister Devlin?"

"No witnesses your honor. I do have some statements to be entered into the record. May I have a fifteen-minute recess to talk with my colleagues?

"Any objection, Mister Abbott?"

"None your honor. Actually, I was going to file a motion as soon as the prosecution rested, but I think this might be a good time."

"Very well," the judge said.

"The defense challenges your right to hear this case, your honor," Abbott said. He handed a clerk his written motion to take to the judge.

Not surprised at the defense strategy, the judge said: "I will hear your motion tomorrow. We will take a short recess now and then reconvene. This court is in recess."

Court resumed after twenty minutes at which time Devlin presented written statements from Vermonters who witnessed the raid and from the British officer involved in arresting the Rebels after they crossed the border. He then sat down, finished for the day.

One of the bailiffs approached Abbot and whispered in his ear. "Your witness is here."

Young and the others turned toward the rear of the courtroom to see a young man in work clothes enter and look around, confusion written on his face.

Abbott slid the fingers from both hands into his vest pockets and then stood to look at the young man.

"Your honor, I call George Stephen Conger."

The befuddled young man walked to the witness box.

"Would you state your name, please?" Abbott asked.

"George Stephen Conger."

"Where do you live, Mister Conger?"

Conger looked nervously around the courtroom and then at the judge, who was busy writing. "St. Albans, Vermont, sir."

"What occurrence did you observe in the city of St. Albans, Vermont, on October 19th, 1864?"

The young man looked anxiously at the prosecution table. "The first thing I saw was puttin' some fellows on the Green."

"By the Green, you mean the one on Main Street near the banks. Is that right?"

"Yes. They were put on the Green by force with revolvers at their heads. There was a guard set over them. I saw them taking horses off some double team. I then saw some ten or twelve of them coming out of the American House yard on horseback."

He gazed at the ceiling as though reliving the raid.

"The townspeople were running, some one way and some another. I heard the discharge of firearms. I discharged firearms myself on that day."

"Who did you fire at?"

The young man held his arms up as though he were sighting a rifle. "I fired at the raiders. I was armed with the breech-loadin' carbine. At the lower part of the town, just above one of the banks, I was firin' at the parties. I followed them down the street, firin' at them, about a quarter of a mile and kept firin' at them all the way."

"Was anyone else firing at the raiders?"

"I believe some others of the town's people were firin' at them. I saw two or three of the town's people fire at them.-I could fire five or six shots a minute with my carbine. I thought these men were Confederate raiders."

The lawyers at the prosecution table scribbled frantically on their note pads. Conger said the raiders fired their pistols as they rode out of town.

"They fired at me several times." He ducked slightly, sweeping his hand past his head, remembering bullets whistling by.

Before he could go on again, Abbott interjected: "Stephen, why did you believe the men were Confederate raiders?"

Speaking as though he had not been interrupted, he said: "And when the people were called to arms, they said these were Confederate raiders."

Abbott let him go on. "It was not a runnin' fight until they got out of town. I saw one house on fire after they passed. It was a store. This was a couple of minutes after they passed it. I did not hear any of the raiders declare what they were."

Abbott let the young man's testimony sink in. "No further questions, your honor," he said, sitting.

"Mister Devlin?" the judge asked.

From his seat, Devlin said, quietly: "No questions."

"In that case, court is adjourned until tomorrow at 10 a.m.," Judge Smith intoned.

The prosecution lawyers filed papers away in their brief cases and quietly left the courtroom. But the prisoners and their lawyers were jubilant, remaining in the court room.

"How did you get him to testify for us, Mister Abbott?" Young asked, his eyes blazing with excitement.

"He is nineteen years old and works for his father. Every young man needs money. We paid him fifty dollars. Simple as that," said Abbott.

"You, sir, are a genius," Young declared, a broad smile on his face. "Do you think his testimony helped us?"

"One never knows how a judge will rule, but I think his testimony bolsters our case that you are not just robbers and murderers."

"I hope you're right," Young said as he and the others were led off to jail again. That night, Young thought about the testimony he had heard that day. Although Stephen Conger's statements seemed to bolster his and his colleagues' spirits, he was not certain he was the witness who would see Young and the others leave as free men again. He slept fitfully, waking in the wee hours, his mind churning. He told himself not to think about something he had no control over, but it took him more than an hour to get back to sleep.

The next morning, Judge Smith announced he would hear arguments on Abbott's motion regarding jurisdiction.

Abbott rose. His argument was the same one he had made before Magistrate Coursol: that the arrests of the Confederates were illegal since the Governor General did not issue a warrant.

"This indicates to us that the government of Canada arrested these men because the United States government asked them to," Abbott turned to look at the government lawyers opposing him. "I contend there is no law in force in this province in which a warrant can be issued, except the law which has passed the British Parliament requiring the authority of the Governor General before the arrests of these men could be made."

Devlin stirred in his seat. Abbot was sure Devlin was concerned Judge Smith might come to the same decision Magistrate Coursol had.

Abbott pressed his argument home. The affairs of the kind the court was considering were regulated entirely by treaties between independent nations. The treaty he referred to was negotiated in 1842 between Daniel Webster for the United States and Lord Ashburton for Great Britain.

"Therefore, my lord, I respectfully claim that you have no authority in this case and I request the warrant be withdrawn and these men freed," Abbott resumed his seat.

"I will take your argument under consideration, Mr. Abbott," the judge said. "This court will recess for one week. I will then deliver my decision. That's all until then."

Abbott turned to his clients and whispered. "Well, at least he didn't immediately rule against us."

"Do you think it will help our case?" asked Young as he and the others stood.

"I don't know the answer to that, Bennett. More important to the case are the documents from Richmond. I'll be in to see you this week if they arrive."

"Let's hope the judge sees our side of the argument. If not, then pray we hear from Richmond," Young said. The guards led the prisoners away.

For the next week, the Rebels whiled away their time in jail receiving adoring visitors, playing cards, and dining sumptuously in the evenings. A week later, they returned to the courtroom to hear Judge Smith's decision.

On the way from their cell, Swager joked with the others, saying he was laying two to one for a favorable ruling. No one took him up on it.

The prisoners sat at the defense table, awaiting Judge Smith's arrival in the courtroom. Within minutes, he emerged from chambers and climbed to the bench as the bailiff ordered everyone to rise. Judge Smith opened a folder, studied it briefly and looked at the assembled lawyers and the accused Rebels.

CHAPTER 21

"IN THE matter at hand," Judge Smith began, "the Provincial Parliament has full power to enact any laws to carry out the provisions of the Ashburton Treaty, as well as to the manner of carrying them into effect. The provisions of the treaty gave jurisdiction to the judges and magistrates of the Province of Canada."

He looked up at the prosecution and defense tables. "Consent to this jurisdiction was given not only by the treaty, but also by the act of the Provincial Parliament in 1843 for carrying the Ashburton Treaty into effect."

He paused and looked around the courtroom, noting all eyes upon him. "Therefore, the defense motion is denied."

Young slumped in his seat. "I thought as much," he muttered.

Swager laughed ruefully. "You could have made a little money had you bet."

Abbott stared at the notes he made during Judge Smith's comments. He stood now and told the court that the prosecution had put a Vermont lawyer in the witness box to prove the raid was an offense against the state of Vermont.

"I contend, your honor, the raid was solely an alleged offense against a state whose jurisdiction is separate and distinct from that of the United States which the Ashburton Treaty has nothing to do with," Abbott stated.

With a nod from Devlin, T. G. Johnson stood and argued that the wording in the treaty referring to "in the jurisdiction of the United

States" meant territorial jurisdiction, not court jurisdiction. "The warrant for the arrest did not allege the offense was committed against the United States, but against the peace of the State of Vermont, one of the United States." He paused for effect. "If the defense arguments are accepted, there could be no extradition of fugitives except for those who have fled from the District of Columbia."

Rising, Stephen Berthune, representing the Canadian government, asked: "Is the State of Vermont within the jurisdiction of the United States? Every witness swears it is." Both men sat down.

Smith again asserted his jurisdiction. "The warrant charging the prisoners with having committed a crime against the laws of Vermont, within the jurisdiction of the United States, is properly stated and is necessarily within my jurisdiction." He looked toward the prosecution table.

"Anything further on this matter, Mister Devlin?"

"No, your honor."

"Very well. Mister Abbott, you may now put on your witnesses."

"Thank you, your honor. I call on Lieutenant Young." The audience stirred. Young strode to the witness box, all eyes on him.

After the preliminaries, Abbott asked him, "Lieutenant Young, are you a commissioned officer in the army of the Confederate States of America?"

"Yes sir, I am," Young replied. He straightened his long frame, gripping the rail of the witness box.

"And do you have proof of that?"

"I do."

"Would you show it to the court?" Young reached inside his jacket and produced his commission, signed by Secretary Seddon.

"Would you hand it to the clerk, please?" The clerk took the document and returned to his seat.

"I enter this document as Defense Paper 'M' in the record," Abbott told the judge.

"Now, Lieutenant Young," he continued, "you were ordered to carry out a raid against a northern United States town in retaliation for Federal crimes in the South. Do you have documentation to that effect?"

"I do."

"May I have it?" Young produced his orders and handed them to the clerk. "I enter this in the record as Defense Paper 'N'," Abbott said. "Now, Lieutenant, do you have a statement you wish the court to hear?"

Young stood straight, his hands at his sides, and spoke firmly in answer to his attorney's question.

"My heart is opposed, as most others, to measures of retaliation, but I have suffered so many hardships and endured so many privations in the cause of liberty and freedom that my heart is steeled against sympathy for the invaders and oppressors of my beloved, my native land."

He paused again and looked around the courtroom. All eyes remained on him.

"Fresh from the scenes of devastated firesides and ruined villages, and listening so lately to the wail of the widow and the cry of the orphan, when I behold the track of Federal troops, can any man wonder that the fire of revenge and retaliation should slumber within my bosom and only need the opportunity to burst into flame?"

The audience murmured and a few shouted, "Yes! Yes!" prompting the judge to rap his gavel.

"Truly," Young continued, "in this war, civilization has been made to shudder and demons to rejoice in the backward march of all that is ennobling and worthy of the creatures made in the image of God and after his own likeness."

He said the cause he fought for was right, and if the court sent him back to Vermont, he knew what his fate would be. He touched his neck with his fingers.

"I can die as a son of the South, and the agony of ten thousand deaths will never cause me to regret what I have done and the part I have borne in the struggle of right against might."

The gallery burst into applause.

Young looked directly at the prosecution. "I can only feel astonishment and disgust at the words and actions of the lawyers for the Province of Canada, who have, in the opinion of all right-thinking people, turned against us, and who have not been true to the Queen's neutrality proclamation that recognized the Confederate States as a belligerent power."

He turned to face the judge. "I am safe as I can be but feel that his Honor before whom I am now brought will give me right, though heavens fall, and his sense of justice is far above government influence and the clamor of the fearful."

Young withdrew a handkerchief from his pocket, wiped his brow and continued: "The flag of the Empire has been the emblem of protection for the oppressed and outcast alien for many a long weary year and it will not fail to give me that impartiality which has made it the hope of the fugitive for ages past."

Young's and the judge's eyes were locked, but the judge showed no emotion. Not a sound emanated from the gallery. Young turned to look at Abbot and nodded, indicating he was finished.

"Thank you, Lieutenant," Abbott said. "I have no further questions." The judge looked toward Devlin, who shook his head.

"I call William Hutchinson," Abbott said when Young returned to his seat.

After being sworn, Hutchinson testified: "I am a citizen of the state of Georgia, owing no allegiance to the United States. Our friends and neighbors and relatives have been plundered and in many instances murdered by the Yankee hordes led by that criminal Sherman." he said.

He recalled Sherman's devastating march through his state, "and it is the bounden duty of every Southern man to protect and avenge them. No civilized people could do more and no patriot of whatever clime could do more." Hutchinson raised both hands, palms up, indicating he had no more to say. Again, Devlin declined cross-examination.

In the witness box, Swager talked about joining Morgan's Raiders and later teaming up with Young in Canada.

"I feel it is my duty to harass and annoy the army of the United States," he began. "To cripple and destroy its shipping and commerce, capture and burn its towns and cities and to otherwise damage, if possible, a government which seeks our destruction." His object, he asserted, was to bring war to the heart of the New England states and to make their people feel some of the horrors in retaliation for the crimes and outrages in the South. Young glowed with pride.

Spurr followed Swager. He had no allegiance to the United States, he said, and what he and the others did at St. Albans they did as soldiers of the Confederacy, doing their duty under the command of Lieutenant Young.

Spurr turned to face Young and continued: "I first met the lieutenant when he was a new private, signed legally as a soldier of the Confederacy then as he continues to be today. He did what he thought was right and righteous for the Confederacy when he planned and carried out the raid upon St. Albans."

The prosecution again declined cross-examination. To murmurs from the crowd, Spurr left the stand and resumed his seat. Young smiled at him and mouthed the words: "Good work."

Abbott addressed the judge again. "I have no further witnesses at this time, your honor. However, I request a delay of thirty days to get further proof from Richmond, Virginia, that Lieutenant Young indeed was commissioned in the Confederate Army and that he was issued orders to carry out the raid against St. Albans."

Devlin began to rise, but thought better of it and sat again.

Abbot informed the court that the Governor General of Canada and President Lincoln had turned down their requests for help. Lincoln, he said, refused to permit a courier to go through Federal lines.

He glanced at the prosecution table. "Even the Canadian government has gone out of its way to bring influence to bear upon this case," he charged. "And it is ready to yield up the prisoners as a peace offering to the United States in order that their fears might be assuaged and the bugbear of future danger averted."

"I object," Devlin declared, rising to his feet.

"What are you objecting to, Mister Devlin?" the judge asked, looking over his glasses. "Not Mister Abbott's description of your government's position in this matter, I trust."

Temporarily flustered, Devlin shook his head. "This attempt on the part of counsel for the defendant is but an effort to defeat the ends of justice. The defense side has been given ample time to secure proof while the case was before Magistrate Coursol and since then."

Devlin paused and turned to look at Abbott. "The raiders should have come fully prepared to show their authority for sacking the town of St. Albans. If such were acts of war and have to be justified on that ground, we have a right to say 'Show us your authority to commit such deeds against your adversary.' " He turned toward the judge. "The petition should not for a moment be entertained.

A delay would simply amount to a denial of justice and the total extinction of the case."

Judge Smith straightened, took off his glasses and announced his decision. "A delay of thirty days is granted the defense as requested. This thirty-day delay will simply give the prisoners the means of saying all they can say in justification of the acts which their opponents have designated as acts of robbery, but which they, themselves, contend were acts of war. Court adjourned."

Devlin and his colleagues slumped in their chairs as pandemonium reigned in the gallery once more. Young slapped Abbott on the back and shouted in his ear: "Good work! We have a chance."

"I hope we do, Bennett," the lawyer replied. The other raiders gathered around the two men.

"Now, boys," Young told them. "We have a long thirty days to wait. Maybe less if we have any luck. We'll just have to keep our spirits up." Young shook Abbott's hand and the prisoners were led out of the courtroom.

Back in their cells again, the mood of the men grew cautiously optimistic.

"I hope we have better luck this time," Swager said.

CHAPTER 22

Two days later Abbott visited the prisoners.

"We are sending four couriers this time," he said. "One of them is Lieutenant Davis. Do you remember him, Bennett? He was to lead one of the squads on the Camp Douglas raid."

"Oh, yes, I remember," Young replied.

"We are also sending a woman, Sarah Slater," Abbott said. "She's sometimes known as Kate Thompson. Sarah's been a reliable courier for the Confederate agents here in Canada and she's gathered intelligence about Northern troop movements for your army."

"But, a woman..." Young said. "What if she is caught? They would go hard on her."

"Don't worry, Bennett. She can take care of herself. Reverend Stephen Owen is the third. He was a chaplain with a Virginia regiment," said Abbott. "A Canadian has volunteered to go to Washington to try to talk with President Lincoln or Secretary Stanton. His name is Solicitor Houghton. He's prominent in Montreal and he's sympathetic to your cause."

"Good luck to them, sir," said Young.

After Abbott left, Young thought about the couriers. He was not sure they could succeed, and he feared for Sarah Slater's life. How can these people possibly get through the Yankee lines? And that Canadian solicitor. I don't think Lincoln will even receive him. He looked around at the others. Their lives were in the balance here. This whole thing has become a fiasco, a dangerous one, and I'm the one to blame for it. He closed his eyes and rested his head against the cell wall.

Finally he pulled out of his slump. This kind of thinking isn't helping us. I've got to stay positive. Five days later, while the prisoners lingered in their cells, Houghton was ushered into President Lincoln's office in the White House.

"Mister President, thank you for taking the time to talk with me. I have been asked by the attorneys in Montreal representing the prisoners who conducted the raid on St. Albans, Vermont, to seek permission from you to pass through the lines. They need proof they were acting under their government's orders."

Lincoln pinched his nose in weariness. Why is my time being wasted like this? he thought. He looked out the door of his office to see more than a dozen people awaiting a chance to ask a favor of him.

He sighed and addressed Houghton. "No, I will not give you a pass. These men are Rebels. They go cutting and slashing around and I don't see that it's any part of my business to help them."

A crestfallen Houghton asked: "I understand, Mister President, but sir would you permit me to ask General Grant to send a dispatch to General Lee to send on to Richmond?"

Lincoln looked at Houghton. "No, I cannot do that."

The President stared into the distance for another moment. He pulled a sheet of paper from his desk and wrote a note to Secretary of State William Seward: "Please see this gentleman from Canada. A. Lincoln." That was as far as he would go.

The next morning, Houghton went to see Seward and asked him the same questions he asked the President. Seward replied angrily: "Those men are bandits who should and will be hanged if they are returned to the United States."

"But, sir..." Houghton began.

"No, Mister Houghton, I will not lift a finger to help them. They killed a man during that raid in Vermont. They are not only bandits, but murderers." The secretary turned his attention to papers on his desk. "Now, if you will excuse me, I have work to do."

"Thank you, Mister Secretary. I apologize for using your time." Houghton left.

Dismayed but still undaunted, he walked four blocks to the British Embassy and talked with Hume Burnley, the British charge d'affaires. He, too, declined to help.

"You must understand, Mister Houghton," said Burnley. "Relations between Great Britain and the United States are strained at the moment, perhaps even more than strained. The Province has welcomed thousands of Confederate citizens and soldiers, much to the dismay of the United States."

He stood and stared out the window behind his desk.

"There is reason to believe the Confederacy is working day and night to draw Britain into the war on its side, or at to least supply the Rebels with credits and arms," he said. "The situation is very delicate. I'm afraid we cannot lend you any assistance. Good day, sir." Burnley dismissed the Canadian.

In his room that night, Houghton made a last-ditch effort. He wrote a note to Seward, again pleading to be allowed through the lines. He delivered it to Seward's office in the morning. Early that evening a reply came by messenger as Houghton was eating dinner in his hotel.

The note read: "The United States can hold no communication or correspondence upon the subject. The prisoners, if they submit themselves to the authority of the United States, need no foreign intervention. So long as they remain under the protection of a foreign government and a demand upon that government for their delivery to the United States is pending, communication concerning them can be received only from that foreign government through the customary channels of international intercourse."

"Submit to the authority of the United States?" Houghton said aloud, causing other diners to turn and look at him. "That would be the end of them."

To make matters worse, Seward ordered Houghton to leave the United States. Dejected, he left Washington the next day.

The first courier sent to the South, Lieutenant Sam Davis, crossed into the United States at Niagara Falls, taking a train to Dayton, Ohio, where he disembarked for an overnight stay. After dinner at his hotel, he bought a newspaper and re-entered the hotel lobby. He did not notice two young men seated in the lobby as they drew their heads close together, whispering.

Davis retrieved his room key from the desk clerk and walked up to his third-floor room. Not long after he settled down to read his paper, there was a knock on the door. Startled, he thought of escape, but there was no way out except through that door. Cautiously, he opened it to see a man in civilian clothes, accompanied by two policemen in uniform.

"Mr. Sam Davis?" the civilian asked.

"Yes. How may I help you?"

"I am Lieutenant Dugan of the Dayton Police. You are under arrest, sir." Davis's face paled.

"How did you find me?" he asked, his voice barely a whisper.

"There will be time for that later. Please come peacefully." At the Dayton Police Station, Davis learned that two men who had seen him in the hotel lobby had been prisoners at the notorious prisoner-of-war camp, Andersonville, in Georgia. Davis had served as a guard there while he recuperated from wounds he'd suffered in battle. The two men had escaped while on a firewood detail outside the deadly, overcrowded prison compound, and they'd found their way home to Ohio. And now, they recognized Davis.

Another of the couriers sent from Canada, Reverend Owen, made it all the way to Richmond, Virginia, aboard a blockade-runner similar to the one that carried Young to Wilmington. Owen learned that Secretary Seddon had already turned over hand-written copies of Young's commission and orders to a woman courier just the day before. He asked Seddon to give him a second copy. Seddon mumbled his displeasure, but complied.

A few days later, Owen slipped back through the Yankee lines and boarded a carriage, riding it to the outskirts of Washington where he rented a small boat to cross the Potomac River. Inside his jacket pocket were the two documents sealed in a waterproof envelope.

Halfway across the river, a shell fired by a Union battery threw up a column of water, tossing him out of the small craft. He surfaced and swam safely to the far shore and hid in the rushes. Soon he heard voices close by—soldiers searching the riverbank for him. Within a few minutes the voices faded, but he lay among the rushes a while longer.

Finally, he made his way to the home of a Confederate sympathizer in Washington. From there, accompanied by two women dressed as nuns, he took a train north disguised as a Catholic priest.

CHAPTER 23

SHORTLY after nine on the morning of February 10th, Abbott entered the cell area at the jail in Montreal, unaware that Owen had succeeded in Richmond and was on his way back to Canada, and that the woman, too, may have made it through.

With all eyes on him, he shook his head and told his clients: "None of the couriers has returned yet. We're not certain if they made it to Richmond at all."

He paused, seeing the dejection on the Rebels' faces.

"But don't despair, we may hear something soon. If we don't hear within a few days, I will ask the judge for more time. I will see you in court soon."

Young sighed and sat with his back to his cell wall. Nothing to do but wait.

In court a few days later, Abbott asked the judge for an extension of time. Attorney Devlin whispered audibly, "I told you.

Judge Smith frowned, but said nothing.

T. G. Johnson rose for the prosecution to reply to Abbott's request.

"If this request is granted, it could be done a hundred times more," he said.

Another prosecution lawyer, Stephen Bethune, stood to reiterate the prosecution's claim that a court in the United States should hear the case. And, he added, even if the prisoners had received the documents, the prosecution had proven their guilt as robbers.

Unwilling to let the prosecution's claims remain unchallenged, Abbott argued that if the United States had the right to try the defendants, then every Confederate general who took refuge in Canada could be extradited on the same charge.

"The prosecution's fight against delays is a part of its strategy to prevent any communication with Richmond," he said.

Judge Smith raised his hand. He had heard enough.

"If the action of the Federal government in preventing access to Richmond should entitle the prisoners to further delay, then the investigation could not proceed until the termination of the war. The defendants' request is denied." He rapped his gavel and adjourned court until the next morning.

Once again the men returned to their cells, fearful they would be sent to the United States where certain death awaited them. Young lay restlessly on his bunk. This could be the end for us, he thought. We've fought so hard. I know our case is right.

The thought of him and his men being turned over to the Americans for trial and most likely hanging kept him awake through the long hours. The next morning, Judge Smith looked toward the prosecution. "Do you have any witnesses?"

"No, your honor, any further testimony would be fruitless," said Devlin. "The guilt of the prisoners was abundantly proved."

"Very well. Mister Abbott?"

Abbott rose. "We have a number of witnesses, your honor, but I wish to state this: We do not deny the fact that the prisoners made an attack upon the town of St. Albans and partially sacked and set it on fire. But the additional facts we wish to prove are these: That they were Confederate soldiers acting under a duly commissioned officer, authorized by their government through its agents; that they owe their allegiance to a nation at war with the Federal states and were acting under orders of the constituted authorities of that nation.

"Suppose these facts be proved, would they not conclusively show that there had been no offense within the meaning of the Ashburton Treaty and therefore that the treaty and the statutes based upon on it did not apply to the case at all?" he asked.

Abbott paused and was about to speak further when the judge interrupted. "The treaty of extradition was intended to meet cases of ordinary crime of the nature specified in it, not to offenses committed against each other by belligerents recognized by Great Britain as being engaged in warfare."

Abbott was taken aback at the judge's comment, but he covered his surprise and calmly replied: "That is correct, your honor."

He turned, raised his eyebrows and smiled at his colleagues, who were now sitting erect, paying rapt attention.

"Your honor, I would like to present my witnesses. I call Joseph Bettersworth."

"Mister Abbott," Judge Smith interrupted. "If I recall, Mister Bettersworth was a witness for the prosecution the last time he was in this courtroom."

"Yes, he was your honor. But he has some evidence to support the accused."

On the stand, Bettersworth testified that he met Young in Chicago during the Democratic Convention. It was there he learned Young was a commissioned officer in the Confederate Army and that he was to lead a raid against towns in the northern frontier.

"Is there anything else you wish to say, Mister Bettersworth?" asked Abbott.

"Yes, he, Lieutenant Young, told me the raid was authorized by Richmond and the arms that were to be used in the raid were stored in Chicago."

Abbott next called Thomas Stone, who served with Morgan. Stone testified he volunteered in Canada to join the raid on St. Albans, but later withdrew. He said he saw Young's orders.

"He showed it to me and I read it before we went to Chicago," said Stone. He said Young told him he was to report to Clay, one of the two Confederate commissioners in Canada, and follow Clay's orders.

Abbott asked the clerk to show exhibits "M" and "N" to the next witness, Charles Withers, an adjutant general with Morgan, who, like most of the prisoners, had escaped from a Yankee prisoner-of war camp. Withers testified he believed the exhibits were genuine. Units such as the one Young headed were considered special secret service, he said. They were sent in groups from three to thirty men inside the Yankee lines to harass and destroy facilities or act as scouts.

When Withers stepped down, Abbott faced the judge: "I call William A. Carroll."

Carroll identified himself as a former brigadier general in the Confederate Army.

"Were you in Richmond at the same time as Lieutenant Young?"

"Yes sir."

"Do you recognize these two exhibits, 'M' and 'N'?" Abbott handed the papers to a clerk to deliver to Carroll.

Carroll looked them over. "Yes, I do."

"Please continue, sir."

"I was at the office of Secretary of War Seddon when he signed the commission and the orders for Lieutenant Young, and I saw them again before the raid against St. Albans."

Next in the witness box, Montrose A. Pallen of Mississippi, a former surgeon general in the Confederate Army, looked at the two documents and confirmed their validity. He also confirmed the validity of a memo Clay sent to Young after the latter had returned from Richmond to recruit his men. Abbott asked him to read the memo aloud.

"Your report of your doings under your instructions of the Sixteenth of June last from the Secretary of War covering the list of twenty Confederate soldiers who were escaped prisoners, collected and enrolled by you, is approved," Doctor Pallen read. "Your suggestion for a raid upon accessible towns in Vermont, commencing with St. Albans, is approved, and you are authorized and required to act in conformity with that the suggestion."

Pallen added: "I did not see Mister Clay write his name to said document, but if I were a cashier in a bank in which Mister Clay had a deposit, and a check was presented to me with that signature, I would pay it."

"Thank you, Doctor Pallen," Abbott said. "That is all."

Judge Smith looked to the prosecutors. They declined to cross-examine Pallen, just as they chose not to question the others.

"I call William A. Cleary," Abbott said.

On the stand, Cleary identified himself as secretary to the two Confederate commissioners in Canada, Thompson and Clay. Cleary verified Clay's signature and said: "I was personally aware that Mister Clay had sanctioned the raid against St. Albans." Cleary was the last witness of the day and Judge Smith adjourned court for four days.

CHAPTER 24

A DAY before Reverend Owen and the two women disguised as nuns arrived in Montreal, there was a knock on the front door of Abbott's home. He opened it to find a pretty young woman on his doorstep. She wore an ankle-length black dress and black hat that partially hid her black hair.

"Mister Abbott?" the young woman asked.

Taken aback, Abbott was speechless for a moment,

"How may I help you miss, or madam?" he asked.

"I'm Kate Thompson, Mister Abbott. At least today I am." She smiled. "Usually, I am Sarah Slater."

Abbott suddenly realized she was one of the couriers who had been sent to Richmond in search of Young's official documents.

"Oh, oh....please come in, Sarah," he said, stepping aside. He looked at her for some signal that she had been successful in Richmond.

"Thank you."

Abbott directed her to his study and asked her to sit. She settled into a chair and smiled.

"I trust you had a safe journey from Richmond and if the smile I see tells me what I think it does, then you have good news," Abbott suggested.

"Yes, the trip was uneventful, well mainly uneventful, but that is all I can tell you. Yes, I have good news." She reached inside a carpetbag and handed him an envelope.

"Some documents for you."

He quickly opened the envelope.

"Yes, yes! Oh, my, yes!" He stood, walked around the desk and took Sarah's hands in his. "You have given us the weapons we need to end this travesty. I cannot thank you enough, and I am sure my clients will thank you, as well."

"I am happy to do whatever I can to help these unfortunate men, Mister Abbott. Now, sir, if you will excuse me, I am very tired and I must get home."

Abbott thanked her again and walked her to the door. He watched as she disappeared into the night. He let out a deep breath. "Yes, indeed. I believe we have what we need."

Rushing to the jail, Abbott was led directly to the cell block holding the Rebels. He waved the two pieces of paper he had received from Sarah Slater.

"Great news, gentlemen!" he said. 'I have Lieutenant Young's official documents."   Young and the others reacted instantly, slapping each other on the back and expressing their surprise.

"I have not yet heard from any of the others," Abbott said. "But I do believe what he have here will suffice."

"How did you manage to get them?" Hutchinson asked. "Who brought them?"

"I think we will let those questions go unanswered, at least for now," Abbott told Hutchinson, who nodded his understanding.

In the meantime, a newspaper war had erupted in Canada. The *Witness,* an anti-Confederate paper, called the prisoners "plain murderers and robbers, plying their trade under the pretense of war." The *Minerve* newspaper responded with editorials defending the raiders, saying their government, not they, should be held responsible.

In Toronto, the *Globe* called for the immediate extradition of the Confederate raiders, while the opposing *Toronto Leader* wrote glowing editorials in their favor. The *Evening Herald* and the *Telegraph* chided the prosecution for jailing Bettersworth with Young and his men in a low-handed attempt to secure damaging evidence against the Rebels.

The day after Sarah Slater handed Abbott the documents, the Reverend Cameron and his two female companions arrived with duplicates.

After hearing the Reverend's story, Abbott told him: "That was a very brave thing you three did. We are grateful to you and thankful, Reverend, that you were not injured or killed in Washington." Seeing the documents the Reverend had given him were the same as the ones delivered by Sarah Slater, he added. "We shall enter these as evidence and ask you to testify. Is that all right? I do not want to compromise our other courier's identity."

Cameron agreed without hesitation.

When court resumed on February 15th, Abbott called Cameron to the stand.

"Did you bring anything of interest with you from Richmond?".

"I did. These two documents." He handed the papers to Abbot who in turn handed them to the clerk. Abbott asked that they be entered as defense exhibits.

"What are those documents?" Devlin asked.

"They are a commission for Lieutenant Bennett H. Young in the Confederate Army and his orders, both signed by Secretary of War Seddon in Richmond," replied Abbott. The gallery stirred, sensing that the defense had scored what might be the winning point. Young hoped the tide had once more turned in his favor.

Devlin rose. "May we have a moment to study those supposed documents, your honor?"

"Certainly, Mister Devlin. Take a few minutes if you need them."

The three prosecution lawyers huddled with the lawyers for the Canadian government. They all read the documents.

Now that his key evidence was entered in the record, Abbott decided to get his witness off the stand.

"Thank, you, Reverend," he said. "That is all I have for this witness, your honor."

The judge looked at Devlin. "No questions, your honor."

"If you have nothing more, Mister Abbott," Judge Smith said. "Mister Devlin?"

The Rebels and their lawyers sat back, confident that whatever the Canadian Government had up its sleeve, it was not enough to overcome the newly introduced documents from Richmond.

Taking an entirely new tack, Devlin tried to show the prisoners had established residence in Canada and thereby violated the neutrality of the province when they conducted the raid. The government then returned to its original claim that the prisoners were simply robbers and killers. Spurr and Tevis robbed Breck inside the bank, prosecution attorney Stephen Bethune asserted, and all the prisoners were equally as guilty because they went to St. Albans for the purpose of robbing the banks and they all fled as a group to Canada.

Nelson Mott, the hotelkeeper in St. Jean-sur-Richelieu, Quebec, testified that Young, Hutchinson, and four others registered there on October 11th. He said the men read newspapers from St. Albans and inquired about the distance from St. Albans to Frelighsburg, Quebec.

When Mott ended his testimony, Judge Smith announced he was not feeling well and adjourned court for the rest of the day. Before leaving the bench, he asked if either side had more witnesses.

"We have no more witnesses," said Devlin. "We rest our case."

Judge Smith looked toward the defense. "No more witnesses, your honor. We also rest our case," said Abbott.

"Very well, gentlemen. Be ready for final arguments tomorrow. If I am not feeling well enough to hold court in the morning, you will be notified in time."

That evening, Abbott, Kerr and LaFlamme huddled and decided that if the judge ruled against the prisoners, they would need legal ammunition to present to an appeals court in Great Britain. They prepared documents to send to Sir Hugh Cairns, the widely known and respected legal authority at Lincoln's Inn in London. Although Sir Hugh's opinions did not guarantee an appeals court would overturn the Canadian court's verdict, having him on their side would bolster their case.

Feeling better, Judge Smith brought the court to order the next morning at nine. He nodded to the prosecution. "You may begin your summations, gentlemen."

Devlin rose, adjusted his sleeves and reiterated the claims his side had made during the trial—that the Rebels were robbers, that the United States did not recognize them as legitimate soldiers, and that the judge did not have the authority to examine the evidence since it was only necessary for the prosecution to prove a prima facie case of robbery within the meaning of the Ashburton Treaty.

"Should the court refuse to extradite these men," Devlin said, nodding toward the defense table, "then the treaty might as well be abandoned as a dead letter and open Canada to criminal refugees of every description. Furthermore, release of the prisoners would give sanction to others to make raids from Canada into the United States." That, he claimed, could precipitate war with Britain. Young smiled at the thought of the United States being involved in another war. That would be something, he thought.

Bethune followed Devlin. He claimed the Rebel documents did not prove that Young was a commissioned officer because the defense failed to provide proof that the Confederate Senate had confirmed the commission. Bethune also claimed no evidence existed that Young had taken an oath. Hence, the raid was illegal.

Turning to the documents, Bethune pointed out differences in the copies that had been entered as evidence. He claimed the copies that Reverend Cameron had just brought from Richmond were written long after the raid and therefore were invalid. He told the court that in the original orders produced by Young in Magistrate Coursol's court, Young was ordered to report to Clay, while the one brought to Canada by Reverend Cameron said Young was to report to Clay and Thompson.

Abbott rose for the defense. He ignored Bethune' assertions that the Confederate Senate had not confirmed Young's commission and that Young had never taken an oath.

Instead, he countered Bethune's claim that more raids might be launched from Canada into the United States if the men were released.

"Refusal to extradite would not involve a judgment upon the act, nor would it decide that the prisoners could return to Canada to engage in future expeditions of this kind," Abbott said. He paused for a drink of water, and continued. "We do not ask you to approve what was done in St. Albans. We ask your Honor neither to approve nor disapprove of the conduct of the prisoners. We ask you to declare that the case does not fall within the Ashburton Treaty. We do not ask that the treaty be disregarded, but that it be only made to apply to the circumstances consistent with its intentions." Devlin and Bethune stirred in their seats, their eyes on the judge.

Abbott asserted that Judge Smith had no legal authorization to decide the case solely on the prosecution's claim that the prisoners were simply robbers, but must consider whether a robbery within the meaning of the Ashburton Treaty had been committed.

"Your lordship, I again state that Lieutenant Young was a duly commissioned Confederate officer and all his men were on active duty at the time of the raid. They were ordered by their government to capture St. Albans and rob the banks as an act of war." He paused for emphasis. When he spoke again, he reminded the judge once more that Britain recognized the Confederacy as a belligerent power.

Without further pause, he described the case of a Confederate officer who had seized a Federal gunboat on Lake Erie and sailed it to Canada. At no time during his hearing in Canada did he identify himself as a Confederate officer. In his finding, the Canadian judge wrote that if the man had proved he was a duly commissioned Confederate officer and his orders had emanated from Richmond, he would not have extradited him. With this, Abbott resumed his seat.

Speaking for the Canadian government, Bethune countered: "Seddon surely did not write such orders, being a sane man." He pointed to the documents lying on the clerk's desk. "They have been fabricated to meet the expediency of the prisoners' position after their capture."

He ran his fingers through his hair and sat down.

Abbott asked the clerk to hand him the documents entered as evidence and he read from them. "Do they not give Mister Young the rank of first lieutenant in the Confederate Army?"

From his chair, Bethune cried: "I say no."

Abbott waved the documents at Bethune. "Who is to judge whether it is not?"

"A jury," Bethune countered, icily.

"In such a case," Abbott countered, "Mister Young would surely be tried by his political enemies who would ignore his status as a belligerent." Bethune harrumphed, but did not counter the argument.

Abbott then turned to another aspect of the case. "Our sovereign has recognized the Confederate States as belligerents. Surely we cannot deny them the right of appointing their own officers. Do we know better than they do whom they appoint? Young was appointed to the rank of first lieutenant and ordered to do what his instructions show and he did so. Is there any better proof of his acceptance of an appointment than the performance of his duties?"

Young nodded and looked at his companions, who nodded back, some of them smiling.

Speaking for the Canadian government, attorney Edward Carter claimed the Queen's proclamation of May 13, 1861, extended no further than a mere recognition of the equality of the two warring powers with respect to their trade with Britain. Should Judge Smith recognize Young's "so-called" commission it would amount to nothing less than recognition of the Confederacy as an independent power. Carter claimed only the British government could do that.

Turning toward Carter, Abbott said: "Learned counsel does not understand there is a difference between an independent state and its recognition as a belligerent nation.

"If we concede to the Southern States their rights as belligerents, we must recognize their commissions when they appear before our courts. If we admit their right to appoint an officer and then declare all commission of their officers to be inadmissible, such would be illogical and a ridiculous mockery."

Judge Smith interjected: "Since the Sovereign of England has recognized the Confederate States as belligerents, the courts are bound to recognize them to the same extent as the Sovereign has recognized them." That comment seemed to brush off Carter's points.

Carter stood again to promote his claim the Rebels lost their belligerent character when they established residence in Canada, where they were subject to British law and had become British citizens.

His voice dripping with sarcasm, Abbott told the judge that Young's crossing into Canada after the St. Albans raid had nothing to do with his becoming a Canadian citizen. "This is neither sustained by the legal authorities nor by the evidence."

Devlin countered that Young crossed into Canada only to carry on hostilities against the United States. Therefore, he could not be considered a political refugee, and so, he asserted, Canada was not obliged to offer asylum to political refugees whose conduct was not above suspicion.

Bethune then claimed the robbery of Samuel Breck inside the St. Albans Bank was a violation of the code of war recognized by many nations and therefore the Rebels were not entitled to the protection of the courts. But Abbott countered that Federal soldiers in the Shenandoah Valley had committed far worse atrocities.

"That is beside the point," said Devlin, jumping to his feet. Young and his fellow prisoners paid rapt attention to this argument.

"If this is beside the question," Abbott argued, his voice rising, "why have my learned friends urged with so much vehemence as an argument for extradition of these men that their acts in the raid in St. Albans were atrocities, prohibited by the laws of war and contrary to the law of nations?"

He turned to look at Devlin and went on: "If these citations of Federal raids upon the South are beside the question, why have my learned friends resorted to such an argument?" Abbott looked at Bethune, who kept his eyes on the papers spread on the table in front of him, his face flushed with anger.

I think Abbott has them on the run Young thought.

Abbott pressed his attack. Sheridan's army had turned the Shenandoah Valley of Virginia into a desert, he said. "If therefore it were necessary to show that the attack on St. Albans was a fair measure of retaliation on the part of the Confederate Government, we could do so without difficulty. If the Confederate States had a right to give orders for such an expedition at all, it is not for us, nor your lordship, to say whether this was a proper occasion to exercise that right. It is for the belligerent nations, themselves, to decide in what way they will carry on hostilities. If each party does what the laws of war do not recognize as lawful, the only remedy is reprisal and retaliation."

Young felt like applauding, but restrained himself growing more pleased in the job Abbott was doing in his and the others' defense, countering the prosecution and going on the offensive.

When Abbott sat down, Judge Smith adjourned court for lunch, but before leaving the bench, he asked how much longer both sides would need to complete their final statements and arguments. They agreed they could finish that afternoon.

Young and the others returned to the jail where they had lunch.

Swager pulled out his pipe and a nearly empty pouch of rough-cut tobacco. As he stuffed some of it into the howl of the pipe, he commented: "I reckon I better run out and get some more 'bacca."

The others laughed.

"Bring back the newspapers while you are out," Young said.

"Anybody want something else?" Swager chuckled. He struck a match and leaned back against the cell wall, sucking on the pipe and blowing blue smoke that billowed toward the ceiling and then slowly drifted down.

"Damn, Charles, you're gonna choke us all to death here. Won't matter what the judge decides, us lying here deader 'n doornails," Hutchinson complained. The four prisoners retreated to their own thoughts of the morning's events.

Shortly after 1:30, the lawyers shuffled papers and awaited the emergence of Judge Smith from his Chambers. At the defense table, Young and Swager talked in whispers.

"I wonder what the Canadians will come up with now," said Swager, his nervousness evident in the way he fidgeted in his seat.

"I don't know. What could they claim they haven't already brought up?" said Young.

"I'm not sure, but you can bet they will have something."

The judge's chamber door opened. "Be upstanding!" the bailiff shouted. Judge Smith took his seat and addressed the assemblage. "Let us proceed."

The prosecution wasted no time. The raid had violated Canada's neutrality, Devlin asserted. Young tried to listen as Devlin built his case once more, but Young tuned him out, weary of the Canadian's arguments, wishing he were home in Kentucky with his family or anywhere other than in this overcrowded courtroom.

When Devlin sat down, Abbot argued that his clients planned the raid in Chicago in July the year before. Even if the raid had been discussed in Canada, Abbot asserted, it would have been a matter between the British and the Confederate governments. It was absurd to assume, as the prosecution had, that Canada should turn the prisoners over to the United States just because they had violated Canada's neutrality.

"If they have committed an unlawful act against Canada, is the United States entitled to have them extradited?" Abbott asked. "If they had violated Canadian neutrality and their government had authorized it, then it would be for Britain to lodge a complaint against the Confederate government." He paused, and looked toward the prosecution. "The United States has nothing to do with a breach of our laws. It is for Britain to enforce the law which prohibits such proceedings."

He took off his glasses and rubbed his eyes, his face tight with fatigue.

"If the United States government has any right at all, it is to remonstrate against Great Britain." He set his glasses back on his nose and, taking a deep breath, pressed home his argument: "Are we to refuse them their belligerent rights because they have offended us in another respect?"

He threw his shoulders back and took a deep breath. "A breach of our laws has no bearing whatever upon the act done at St. Albans. Is there another nation in existence that would stoop so low as to deliver over to foreigners for punishment offenders against its own law?"

The gallery erupted. "No! No!"

"Let them go!"

"Free them!"

The judge glared up at the gallery and rapped his gavel. Young looked around the courtroom and up to the gallery. Several of the onlookers were still on their feet.

Once quiet returned to the courtroom, Carter rose again. To free the prisoners, he said, would be nothing less than an act of war against the United States; it would be the equivalent of taking sides in the struggle of North against South.

"To harbor such persons would be to turn a neutral state into an aggressor," Carter said. He sat down. The judge waited for someone to stand and continue, but no one moved.

"Is that all? Are we finished?"

The prosecution and defense lawyers nodded silently. "Well, then, I will consider my verdict and announce it in five days. Court is adjourned." Smith left the bench.

With that, one of the longest trials in early Canadian history drew to a close.

The lawyers for the defense huddled with Young and his co-defendants. "I never predict what a jury or a judge will do," Abbott cautioned, "but I think we tipped the balance in our favor today."

"I agree," Kerr chimed in. "The judge just did not seem to believe their major points, or at least give them much weight." He gathered his papers together and smiled at Young. "Well, lieutenant, you certainly made some history this past year. How do you feel?"

"Sir, when we were planning the raid, we never figured on anything like this happening," Young said. "Maybe getting shot or strung up, but nothing like this." He shook his head. "I've gained a respect for the law and for you lawyers these many months."

His eyes wandered to the large windows at the side of the courtroom, his thoughts now hundreds of miles away in his beloved Kentucky.

"You may not know it, but I studied for the ministry, just like my brother. But now, I don't know if that is what I want to make my life's work."

He turned to the others and chuckled at the irony of his comments. "Life's work! I may not have much life ahead of me, but whatever the judge rules..." he paused to choke back tears, "I want to thank you all for the way you conducted yourselves. I am truly grateful."

The lawyers packed their briefcases and left the prisoners to be returned to jail. In the corridor leading to their cell, the aroma of something delicious floated in the air. Jailer Payette and his deputies had arrived with yet another perfect hot meal—venison stew with homemade biscuits, prepared and brought to the jail by one of their admirers. As the men settled down to eat, Young chuckled.

"Well, if we are going to meet the hangman, at least we will have our bellies full of this delicious food." The others laughed a bit nervously, but eagerly devoured the meal, washing it down with homemade beer.

"I swear these biscuits are almost as good as my Momma used to make," said Swager. "These ain't risen as high as Momma's, but..."

"I noticed you didn't leave any," said Hutchinson. "Anybody mind if I finish the last of the stew?" He shoveled it onto his plate before anyone could reply.

Young took the last bite of his dinner, set his fork down and leaned back. His thoughts shut out the banter of his fellow prisoners. The specter of swinging from the gallows in a Yankee prison camp had leaped to the fore in his mind often during the long imprisonment in Canada. His emotions, too, had risen and fallen so many times.

Now, he thought once more, maybe we have a chance.

CHAPTER 25

THE prisoners fretted as the days passed. As Young lay on his bunk late into the night, his mood shifted from euphoric to despondent. He had never flinched in combat with Morgan, but the thought of hanging from a rope in a Yankee prison made him shiver. And again, thinking about his documents before Judge Smith, and Abbott's final arguments, his spirits rose.

Finally on the fifth day, March 9th, the deputies arrived to take them back to the court. As Young left the cellblock, he thought: We are soldiers and we did our duty. This was more than just an incident at St. Albans, much more. I hope we get out of it with our necks.

In the courtroom, the Rebels squirmed in their seats while their lawyers talked among themselves. Then the clerk intoned: "Be upstanding."

Everyone stood as Judge Smith swept into the courtroom. There was no indication on his face as to what the verdict would be. Confirming that all were present, he began reading his findings in a monotone. The prisoners looked nervously at each other as the judge quoted prevailing British and Canadian law and pertinent sections of the Ashburton Treaty.

He affirmed that the Confederate Government commissioned Young a first lieutenant; that the raid he led was not a criminal act, but an act of war recognized by international law. He paused.

Young realized the judge was reciting the main defense arguments and hope suddenly felt even more real. He glanced at the prosecution table where the lawyers for the United States and the Canadian government grimly followed the judge's words and scribbled notes.

Judge Smith said that although the raid was an act of war, it was not up to a court in a neutral country to determine whether the acts in St. Albans were in accordance with modern usages of war, but instead up to the United States Government and the Confederate Government. He droned on, pausing every now and then to drink from his water glass, kept full by a bailiff. He affirmed that since Great Britain recognized the Confederate States of America as a belligerent nation, Canada, a colony, also was obliged to recognize it.

"The attack upon St. Albans must therefore be regarded as a hostile expedition, undertaken and carried out under the authority of the so-called Confederate States by one of the officers of their army; that it was, therefore, both a belligerent act of hostility and a political offense against the state now demanding extradition— and that the Ashburton Treaty did not contemplate, nor do the statutes of the province authorize, the extradition of belligerents or political offenders."

At that, the lawyers for the Rebels exhaled simultaneously. Young sat up stiffly in his seat. Yes. It's all right. It has to be.

Swager poked an elbow in his side. "Am I dreaming, Bennett, or are we on our way out of here?"

Young shushed him, but gently, and looked at the opposition's lawyers, who appeared grim.

The judge took another sip from his glass and continued reading. He said the raid was planned in Chicago, so it would not be up to Canada to punish them. He also stated the evidence did not prove the men had become Canadian citizens by virtue of having lived in the country. Even if they had become citizens, that would have had no effect on their extradition to the United States.

Judge Smith paused and looked toward the defense and prosecution tables and then at the gallery, indicating he was nearly finished. The tension in the courtroom was palpable.

His voice steady, the judge announced: "I have come to the conclusion that the prisoners cannot be extradited because

I hold that what they have done does not constitute one of the offenses mentioned in the Ashburton Treaty...and because I have consequently no jurisdiction over them, I am of the opinion, therefore, that the prisoners are entitled to their discharge."

The prisoners leaped to their feet as the gallery exploded in hoots and cheers. Some threw their hats in the air and pounded each other on the back. Some ran down the stairs and outside to inform the huge crowd that had waited patiently in the cold most of the afternoon that one of the longest trials in Canada's history had finally ended after just over three months.

Reporters who covered the hearings from the first days raced out of the court house to their newspapers or for the telegraph office. The Rebels hugged and danced with each other as the realization they were once again free sank in.

Young hugged Swager. "We are on our way out of here, Charles!"

"Yes! Yes! Thank the Lord!" Swager said.

The defense lawyers congratulated each other and shook hands with their opposing attorneys. Abbott told the Rebels to wait before leaving the courtroom. He walked over to Devlin and the other prosecutors to ask what their plans were. Devlin pulled some papers from a briefcase and handed a copy to Abbott. The government of Upper Canada was filing charges, claiming the Rebels had violated Canada's neutrality.

"You arranged this in advance just in case you lost, didn't you?" Abbott said tersely to Devlin. "Well, we shall see." Abbott stuffed his copy of the charge in his briefcase.

When Devlin left, Abbott gathered the four Rebels around him. Again, he was forced to dash their hopes at the moment of triumph.

"I'm afraid you will have to go back to jail, gentlemen." He filled them in on the prosecution's latest move, explaining that Upper Canada had filed the charge in advance in case Judge Smith freed Young and the others.

Young's heart sank lower than it had at any time during either of the two trials, the euphoria of the past few minutes completely erased. His men threatened to escape, but Young talked them out of it, remembering his re-arrest by Constable Ermantinger near the Quebec-New Brunswick border after Coursol's ruling. Instead of leaving as free men, they faced more peril.

Anger growing in his voice, Hutchinson shouted: "This isn't right!"

"Easy Hutch, easy," Young said, grabbing his friend by his shoulder. Hutchinson shrugged Young's hand away. "They want to get us there in Toronto so they can hold another hearing on the same extradition charges. They'll send us back to Vermont and hang us!" he cried out.

Young tried to sooth his friend. "I don't think we have to worry about it, Hutch. Mister Abbott doesn't seem to think they can make that charge stick. Don't forget how hard he and our other lawyers have worked. We'll be all right.

Hutchinson nodded, but it was clear to Young his friend was not convinced. Nor was Young.

CHAPTER 26

YOUNG turned to see a policeman approach him and his friends. Sergeant Robert Dunlop of the Toronto Police addressed him: "I'm sorry, sir, but you will have to come with us. You and your men."

Young saw Hutchinson's anger flare up again and he placed both hands on his friend's chest. "No, Hutch."

"I have a warrant from Upper Canada for your arrest," the policeman said. "You will be taken to Toronto to stand trial." He handed the warrant to Abbott. Two other constables moved closer to the Rebels.

Abbott turned toward Devlin, who was watching. A smile played at the corner of the prosecutor's lips, as though to infer "We haven't finished with your clients yet."

That night, the Rebels and their guards boarded a special train at Bonaventure Station for Toronto. After a sleepless night, they arrived at the lakeshore city early the next morning, March 29th, where other constables met them. They loaded the Rebels into carriages and took them to jail.

This time, there was no friendly sheriff or homemade meals and drink. They appeared in court that afternoon, but Young told the judge they were unable to retain a lawyer.

In the jail, Young had asked for one of the best lawyers in Toronto, John Hillyard Cameron, whom Abbott had recommended, but Cameron was out of the city on business. The judge continued the case until Saturday, April 9th.

A few days later, Henry Barwick, an associate of Cameron's, arrived at the jail.

"Lieutenant Young?" Barwick asked, looking from one Rebel to the next.

"I'm Lieutenant Young. Are you Mister Cameron?" Young asked, rising.

"No, sir. Mister Cameron is unavailable, but he asked me to call on you to see if you would permit me to represent you." The prisoners looked Barwick over. He's young, thought the Rebel leader. Uncomfortable at the intense scrutiny, Barwick tried to assure the men he was capable.

"Sir," he said, "I do have considerable courtroom experience and if you would care to brief me now, I will prepare your case and present it to you well before court begins."

Young looked to the others for their opinion

"He seems to be all right, Bennett," said Swager. Spurr, Hutchinson and Tevis nodded their assent.

"Very well, Mister Barwick. Let's begin." Young and his men described their experiences in the Montreal court and the strategy their lawyers had used so successfully.

"Well, this is quite different from those hearings," said Barwick. "You are facing a different charge, as you know. Violating Canada's neutrality. But I think we can come up with a good defense. Give me a few days to think this out and plan a strategy. As I said, I will consult with you before court." Young and his comrades nodded.

"Good day, gentlemen," Barwick said, and he left.

The morning of April 9th dawned and the prisoners were routed from their bunks, fed and told to get ready for court. Barwick arrived and briefed them on his strategy. The smiles he elicited told him they believed his strategy just might work.

It was to be a day they would always remember, although they did not know it yet.

Not long before, at Petersburg, Virginia, south of Richmond, Robert E. Lee and his dwindling army had slipped away from the Northern forces under General Grant after months of siege. Lee vainly hoped to save his army by moving laterally across Virginia, to slip around General Grant's forces, but the Northern commander cut the outnumbered and nearly destitute Confederates off. Realizing further resistance would only mean more bloodshed,

Lee asked for a meeting with Grant. The two opponents met for several hours and then returned to their troops.

The next day, April 9th, Lee, Grant and their top aides met at the little country town of Appomattox Courthouse. Lee surrendered the remnants of a once-proud and determined Confederate Army. Except for scattered action in Louisiana and a few other states, the war was over.

In Toronto that very day, Young and his men were loaded aboard carriages and driven to a courtroom in the center of the city. They were heavily guarded against threats to kidnap and free them. News of Lee's surrender had not yet reached the public.

The prosecutor rose when the judge asked if he were ready to put his first witness in the box. Godfrey A. Hyams, a Confederate soldier from Arkansas who had escaped from a Yankee prison camp and fled to Canada, testified he had overheard Young tell another man he planned the raid in Canada. But Barwick was ready for this witness.

When it was his turn, Barwick stood, facing Hyams.

"Mister Hyams," Barwick began. "When did you decide to testify for the prosecution?"

Hyams's face fell and he stammered. "Ummm, well, suh, just a few days ago when they asked me."

"And when they asked you, Mister Hyams, was there something they offered you?"

"I don't understand what you mean, suh," replied Hyams, shifting uncomfortably in his seat, eyes darting around the courtroom.

"What I mean, is" said Barwick, his voice growing louder, "were you offered money by the prosecution to switch sides? Did money help you change your mind from testifying for the defendants?"

"I, uh, I...." Hyams stammered.

"Mister Hyams, did you or did you not accept money to testify for the prosecution?" Hyams looked toward the prosecutors' table. Seeing no help there, he turned to look at the judge who waited impassively for his answer. Hyams mumbled something.

"What did you say, Mister Hyams?" Barwick demanded. "The court did not hear your last remark."

"I...yes, they offered me money and I took it." His face flushed, Hyams looked toward his lawyer, who was staring at the ceiling.

"Thank you, Mister Hyams," said Barwick. Turning to the judge, he asked: "Your lordship, in light of the fact that the prosecution has only one witness and paid for his testimony, I move the charge be dismissed."

The judge looked toward the prosecutors. "Does the Crown have any further evidence to present to this court before I announce my decision?"

The prosecutor stood. "Your honor, the Crown requests that if you rule in favor of the defendants, Mister Young be detained while we pursue other avenues."

The judge made a note on a pad, and then spoke: "I hereby order Mister Young to remain in custody so the prosecution has time to pursue whatever course it deems necessary. The others may go."

He addressed the prosecutor. "But you will pursue your inquiries in a timely manner and report your progress to this court."

Stunned, Young turned to Barwick. "What happened?"

"I'm not sure, Bennett," replied Barwick. "But, I shall talk with the prosecution to see what they have in mind." Young's companions turned to their leader.

"We won't leave you, Bennett," said Tevis. The others nodded. Young shook each one by the hand.

"Go. Go while you have the chance. Leave Canada. I'll be all right." Tevis nodded and reluctantly, he and his friends walked out of the courtroom.

"My lord," Barwick said, standing to face the judge. "This man has suffered enough at the hands of Her Majesty's government. Twice our courts have cleared him, and yet he is still held so the government can pursue 'other avenues.' We assert the government has failed to carry the day on the charge. It is time to let him go home in peace."

The judge peered down from the bench. "This court has pronounced its ruling and has no desire to change it. We shall wait to see what the government returns to this court with. I am setting bond at $10,000." Barwick produced the bond that afternoon and Young was released, but he was ordered not to leave Toronto.

Young found a room, and the next day, April 10th, he stopped to pick up a copy of the *Toronto Star*. He saw half a dozen people reading their copies and exclaiming among themselves.

He read the front page, stunned at the headline: "U.S. Civil War Ends."

He slumped onto a nearby bench to read the entire article.

"The war! Over?"

His mind reeled. He read the rest of the article, but didn't want to believe it. The paper must have got it wrong. But he knew it was not wrong.

"All for nothing. All for nothing."

His thoughts returned to his adventures with Morgan. To the battles and skirmishes, the long days and nights in the saddle. The evenings when he'd collapsed on the ground and fallen asleep instantly. He remembered the chaos and defeat at Buffington Island and his later capture with Morgan. His imprisonment, escape to Canada. The two long hearings. The months behind bars.

"The raid against St. Albans," he said half aloud. "It worked. I knew it would. I was meant to lead those men and I did. We did what we set out to do. But it was all in vain."

Shattered, Young walked for blocks, not caring where his legs took him, thinking only of his beloved Confederacy and the sacrifices he and thousands of other Southern men and their families had made. Late that night, he returned to his room and slept fitfully.

A few days later over coffee, Barwick told Young the prosecution did not appear to have any other charge pending against him, but they kept insisting that he be detained in Canada. Young appeared in court several times over the ensuing five months, but without his lawyer, whom he had dismissed. As time passed, he became more despondent. But he was determined to keep fighting.

Early that September, with a handwritten petition asking the court to release him folded in his suit pocket, he again walked into the courtroom where he had been frustrated so many times before. Handing his petition to a clerk, Young awaited the court's answer. It was not long in coming. The court scheduled time for Young to appear the next day.

The following morning, Young returned to the courtroom. The judge took the bench, opened a folder and looked at it, and then looked at Young.

"Mister Young?" he asked looking down at the young man. Young stood. "Since the Crown has come up with no new information on your activities in Canada during the time of the war in your country or thereafter, I think it is time we ended this and let you go. Case dismissed."

The judge rapped his gavel and closed the folder.

Young wanted to shout, to shake everyone's hand in the courtroom. But he controlled his emotions. He'd been here before.

"Thank you, your honor. Thank you." Young sat on a chair in the courtroom for a long time, finally beginning to accept the fact that he was free.

He looked around the empty courtroom.

He was free.

POSTCRIPT

ALTHOUGH Young was freed of all charges he had faced in Canada, he could not return home to Kentucky. The Federal government denied amnesty to him and to many other former Rebels whom the United States claimed had committed illegal acts during the war.

Young remained in Canada and courted Mattie Robinson, the daughter of the Reverend Dr. Stewart Robinson of Louisville, Kentucky, who had ministered to the Confederates early on in their trials in Canada. Young and Mattie Robinson were married in Canada by her father in 1866 and then left for Belfast, Ireland, where Young studied law at Queen's College. He later transferred to Edinburgh University in Scotland.

The couple returned to Canada, where Young studied law under another formerly banished Kentuckian, Judge Joshua Bullitt. In 1868, when Young was given amnesty, he and Mattie returned to Kentucky, settling in Louisville, where Young opened his own law practice. He became one of the most important criminal lawyers in the state.

Young was elected a delegate to the Kentucky Constitutional Convention in 1890. A year before, he had written a highly respected guide to the state's constitution entitled, "The Three Kentucky Constitutions." It was printed just before the 1890 convention, which was called to draft a fourth constitution. Later, he was approached by political leaders to run for governor, but he declined.

Young and another lawyer formed the Louisville Southern Railroad. He pushed for a commission to curb railroads in the state, but it was perceived as an effort to curb the activities of a competitor, the Louisville and Nashville Railroad, the very same railroad he tried to wreck as a member of Morgan's Raiders. The Louisville Southern eventually went bankrupt.

Young also helped develop the Monson Railroad and founded a company to build a railroad bridge over the Ohio River, which greatly expanded commerce in the Louisville region. A rail bridge his company built over the Tyrone River, known as the Young High Bridge, still stands.

Young organized a school for black orphans in Louisville and supported it financially for many years. He also helped found a school for the blind. He was a founding member of the Filson Club Historical Society and the Public Library, both in Louisville. He also was an avid collector of Native American artifacts

A prolific writer, he wrote *The Prehistoric Men of Kentucky*. His most widely known work, *Confederate Wizards of the Saddle*, is still available today. It describes famous Confederate cavalry raiders, including a long chapter on Morgan and his Christmas Raid.

He also published *A History of Jessamine County, The Prehistoric Men of Kentucky, The Battle of the Thames in which Kentuckians Beat the British*, and several children's stories.

Young died in Louisville in the afternoon of Sunday, February 23, 1919.

Since the St. Albans raid, some sources reported the Rebels stole $208,000 in Treasury notes, bank notes, both federal and those issued by the three banks, as well as gold, silver and U.S. dollars.

No one knows if that amount is accurate.

For a well-researched and highly readable account of the raid and where the stolen money may have ended up, read *The St. Albans Raiders*, by Daniel S. Rush and E. Gale Pewitt, available from the Blue and Grey Education Society, 110 Franklin Turnpike, Danville, VA 24540.

SOURCES

YOUNG, Bennett H. *Confederate Wizards of the Saddle. Being Reminiscences and Observations of One Who Rode with Morgan.* Chapple Publishing Co., Boston. 1914.

Andrews, Roland Franklin. *How Unpreparedness Undid St. Albans.* The Outlook. 1910.

Benjamin, L.N. *The St. Albans Raid, an Investigation into the Charges against Lieutenant Bennett H. Young and Command for their acts at St. Albans, Vermont the 19th October, 1863.* John Lovell, Montreal, 1865.

Branch, John, and Edmund H. Royce, Edmund D. Steele, Alice Henderson Chumbley. *St. Albans Raid October 19, 1864.* Franklin-Lamoille Bank, publisher. 1980.

Brown, Dee Alexander. *Morgan's Raiders.* SMITHMARK Publishers, Inc. New York.1959.

Buffington Island Battlefield. Trail of the Great Raid. Buffington Island Battlefield Archeological Project. No date.

Clark, Henry Scott. *The Legionaries, A Story of Morgan's Raid.* The Bowen-Merrill Co., Indianapolis. 1899.

The Confederate Reader. How the South Saw the War, Richard B. Harwell, editor. Dover Publications, New York, 1989.

Dee Brown's Civil War Anthology, Stan Banash, editor. Clear Light Publishers, Santa Fe, New Mexico, 1998.

Duke, Basil W. "A Romance of Morgan's Rough Riders," *Century Magazine,* January 1891.

Duke, Basil W. *The Civil War Reminiscences of General Basil W. Duke, C.S.A.* Cooper Square Press, New York. 2001.

Famous Adventures and Prison Escapes of the Civil War, G.W. Cable, editor. The New York Century Co. 1909.

Horan, James D. *Confederate Agent, a Discovery in History.* Crown Publishers, Inc. New York. 1960.

Johnston, Col. J. Stoddard. *Brigadier General John Hunt Morgan.* Confederate Military History, Vol. 9. (Internet).

Johnston, Col. J. Stoddard. *Brigadier General Basil W. Duke. Confederate Military History. Vol. 9 (Internet)*

Kentucky: A History of the State. Perrin, Battle, Kniffen, Jefferson County, 8th Edition.

Kinchen, Oscar A. *Daredevils of the Confederate Army, the Story of the St. Albans Raiders.* Christopher Publishing House, Boston. 1959.

Kinchen, Oscar A. *General Bennett H. Young Confederate Raider and a Man of Many Adventures.* The Christopher Publishing House, West Hanover, MA. 1981.

Miller, Dr. John W. *Copperhead Activities.* Heidelberg College Archeological Project, The Cincinnati Civil War Roundtable. 1996.

Mosgrove, George Dallas. *Following Morgan's Plume Through Indiana and Ohio.* Southern Historical Society papers, vol. XXXV. Richmond, Va., Jan.-Dec. 1907.

Neace, James Clell and Edgar Porter Harnet. "Civil War Veteran Bennett H. Young Left His Mark on Kentucky," *The Kentucky Explorer Magazine*, 1998.

Rush, Daniel S. MD, and E. Gale Pewitt. *The St. Albans Raiders. An investigation into the identities of the Confederate Soldiers who attacked St. Albans, Vermont on October 19, 1864.* The Blue and Gray Educational Society. McNaughton and Gunn, Saline, Michigan. 2008.

Sass, Herbert Rovenal. *Affair at St. Albans.* The Saturday Evening Post, March 27, 1958.

Stier, William J. *Morgan's Last Battle.* Civil War Times, September 23, 1996.

Trail of the Great Raid, Buffington Island Battlefield. Internet.

Varhola, Michael J. *Everyday Life During the Civil War, a Guide for Writers, Students and Historians.* Writer's Digest Books. 1999.

Wiley, Bell. I. *The Life of Johnny, Reb.* The Bobbs-Merrill Company, Indianapolis. 1943.

Wiley, Bell I. *The Life of Billy Yank.* The Bobbs-Merrill Company, Indianapolis, 1952.

Wilson, Daniel K. *The Case of the St. Albans Raiders, a Thesis in the Field of History for the Degree of Master's of Liberal Arts in Extension Studies. Harvard University. 1988.*

Wilson, Dennis K. *Justice Under Pressure, The St. Albans Raid and its Aftermath.* University Press of America, Lanham, MD, 1992.

Interview with Colin Conger, direct descendant of Captain George Conger who led a posse into Canada after the St. Albans Raid. In Georgia, Vermont.

About the Author

TED TEDFORD is a semi-retired journalist with nearly fifty years experience as a reporter, bureau chief, and editor on five daily newspapers in Connecticut, New Jersey, and Vermont.

Since retiring from daily papers, he has been editor and general manager of a weekly community newspaper and has been a freelance reporter for a twice-monthly paper in his region. He lives in Vermont with his family.

This is his first novel.

Acknowledgments

I WISH to thank a number of people who helped with this book from the beginning to publication: first, my wife, Marie, who prodded and coached and made me realize the right way to write it; my daughter, Paula, for her careful reading and editorial suggestions; my daughter, Pat Goudey O'Brien, whose encouragement, editing and publishing made it a book; my son-in-law Jonathan Draudt for his artfully descriptive book cover; Don Minor, former director of the St. Albans Historical Society and Museum, for allowing me to research museum files and for providing copies of photographs, some of which are in the book; Alex Lehning, current museum director, for similar assistance; the staff of the Filson Historical Society, Louisville, Kentucky, for help with research; Faith Allen of the Jesssamine County Public Library, Jessamine, Kentuck; Daniel S. Rush, MD, co-author of *The St. Albans Raiders*, whose work identifying the men who conducted the raid was of immense help; Colin Conger of Georgia, Vermont, a direct descendant of Captain George Conger who led a posse that chased the raiders toward Canada. Thank you to members of my writing group, Grant Corson, Joseph Nelson, Richard Mindel, Marie Tedford and Mary Elizabeth, for all their encouragement and suggestions. And thank you to Emilie Gruppe Alexander of Jericho, Vermont, who organized my first public reading of a work-in-progress...way back when.

Finally, thank you to Donna Howard at The Eloquent Page bookstore in St. Albans, who allowed me to talk about and sell the book during the 150th Anniversary Commemoration of the Raid in September, 2014.

www.ingramcontent.com/pod-product-compliance
Lightning Source LLC
Chambersburg PA
CBHW031243120726
47905CB00002B/697